TRAIL OF TEARS . . .

"Eduoard . . . did you hear? Women can go along! I'm going with you!" Gale announced excitedly.

He shook his head. "No, my dear. I'm afraid it is not for the best." Finality was in his tone. "It isn't that I don't want you . . . you know that. What about Cassie? We can't leave her alone. It is bitter medicine leaving you to care for her when you feel as you do. But there is no other way."

"Of course there is no other way!" Gale's rage struggled to the surface. "You married that little girl and forced me to share everything I own with her . . . my meals, my clothes, my husband, every minute of my life. And then you go off to the ends of the earth and leave me to nurse her while she has *your* baby!" The pent-up emotions of the past nine months erupted like a volcano. "It should be my baby . . . *mine,* do you hear?"

Then the tears came, a tempest which for so long had been dammed behind a mask of cool aloofness. And with the tears came the warm security of Eduoard's arms. She did not push him away. She had almost forgotten the sheer delight of his strength, and the feel of his lips against hers. It had been so long. . . .

". . . a rich, powerful, and deeply moving novel that brings to life one of the great stories in American history. Every page is touched with romance."
— *Paul Gillette*

SALT LAKE

by
Lucile Bogue

PINNACLE BOOKS   NEW YORK

Although some of the main characters in this book were real people, and some of the events herein depicted did take place, in several instances both the people and the events were fictionally intensified to add to the drama of the story.

SALT LAKE

An original Pinnacle Books edition, published for the first time anywhere.

First printing, August 1982

ISBN: 0-523-41319-X

Cover illustration by Bruce Minney

Printed in the United States of America

PINNACLE BOOKS, INC.
1430 Broadway
New York, New York 10018

To my mother . . .
who used to recount
many of the incidents
that appear in this
book, true stories
of the pioneers

Though deepening trials throng your way,
Press on, press on, ye Saints of God!

—Hymns, the Church of
Jesus Christ of Latter-day
Saints, Number 285

SALT LAKE

One

1845 had saved the hottest day in July to watch the *Fulton City* panting up the vast glaring swell of the Mississippi. The paddle wheel thrashed through the water, straining against the river.

The little steamer, owned and operated by the Latter-day Saints, was making its regular northern journey from New Orleans to Nauvoo, loaded with new converts. Like a horse nearing the home stretch, it surged ahead in an added burst of speed, puffing along the Illinois shore with sparks flying.

Gale smiled into her bridegroom's dark eyes and returned the pressure of his fingers on hers on the railing. They were coming home—to a home she had never seen. Suddenly the years opened before her in rich flowing colors through the life ahead, hers and Edouard's. She imagined peaceful Nauvoo streets, a white house with a wide lawn, shade trees and a picket fence, a fine front parlor where she and Edouard would sit in the evenings, she playing a piano, Edouard singing in his deep voice. The children would be upstairs asleep in their white beds, tucked in snugly after their prayers. She could see herself in a big sunny kitchen, geraniums at the windows, the children squabbling playfully over bits of cookie dough. She smiled again, her gaze drifting along the Illinois landscape.

The other passengers leaned on the railings and watched with approval as the rich farmland flowed by. They had seen much on the journey that had carried them from Boston with their young missionary leader, Brother Simon. He was bringing them, as members of a new faith, to the holy city of Nauvoo.

In their weariness there was but one word which could arouse them. And Edouard Simon spoke that word, quietly. But the word carried from where he and Gale stood at the prow.

"We are almost home," he said. "Nauvoo lies just half an hour up the river.

Home! The word spread like a fire gone wild among the travelers.

"Elder Simon says we are almost home . . ."

"Nauvoo is just half an hour up the river . . ."

"Home . . ."

"Almost home . . ."

Gale's heart gave a leap of joy. She longed to throw her arms around her husband and dance around the deck as all the children were now doing. In her excitement, she shoved back her bonnet and her copper-colored hair blazed out in the sun. But the dignity in Edouard's face quelled her exuberance. After all, he was an Elder of the Church, and she must not shame him before this congregation. She bowed her head in a moment's humility, remembering that at seventeen one was a young lady and must act like one. Her days of romping and running about over her father's New England hills were over. Her father was gone, and she had a strange feeling that the hills of New England were gone too.

She was now a different person, a young matron, settling out West with her new husband. She

2

laughed in sheer joy, her eyes sparkling as bright as her hair. She squeezed Edouard's hand, hard.

"You're a comely one," he whispered, but he didn't smile. He wore his air of responsibility like a cloak, almost like a uniform.

"He is so *good*!" her heart sang. "A real Saint. I must be worthy of him."

Two

The tall awkward boy called Bub, who drove the hack, pulled his horse up before Nauvoo House. It was a huge red brick building extending its neat substantial front along two streets in an L-shape. Gale's eyes shone with curiosity as she surveyed it, standing calm and inviting after the long journey. She loved its atmosphere of peace and security, as she loved the whole city of Nauvoo from the first moment she set foot on the wharf, her hand clasped in Edouard's.

The boy jumped down and lifted their bags out. He turned to Edouard, who was helping Gale down.

"Kin I carry the satchels in for you, Brother Simon?"

"No thanks, Bub. There's not much, and I can manage, thank you. I hope we didn't make you late for lunch, having you drive us all around town this way."

"Oh, lunch doesn't matter." He looked at his dusty boots to avoid staring at Gale, who he thought was the most beautiful creature he had ever seen.

"Thanks for the tour," Edouard slipped a shining half-dollar into the lad's hand.

"Gee . . . thanks!" Bub shuffled his feet uneasily, then jumped into his hack and drove off without a backward glance.

"An odd chap," Edouard mused. "Been an orphan since he was ten. Has done everything for a living, from playing his accordion in a New Orleans wine cellar to being an errand boy on a stylish river steamer. When he learned about Nauvoo, he traveled north and became one of us."

"He seems afraid of his shadow," Gale said.

"Yes, he's a bit timid. From the pillar to post life he's led, I expect. But he's a genius as a musician! Come, Sister Simon, you must be very hungry." He picked up their carpetbags.

"Will everyone call me that, instead of Mrs. Simon or Gale?" she asked concerning the friendly but somewhat formal title.

"Yes." Edouard seemed curt as he hurried into the hotel. For the first time she sensed a strange sternness in him that she could not understand.

She followed meekly at his heels into the coolness of the building. A neat smiling woman came out from a back room to greet them.

"Welcome home, Brother Simon!" she cried. "So you've finished your mission! How was it?"

"Quite successful, thank you. I have brought back many converts."

"So I heard." She smiled, looking at Gale with open curiosity.

"May I present my wife, Gale."

"I'm mighty glad to know you," the woman's voice was hearty.

"Gale, this is Sister Smith. Her husband was Joseph Smith, founder of the Church of Jesus Christ of Latter-day Saints."

"It is an honor." Gale bowed her head.

"Sister Smith, I know it's quite late, but I wonder if we might have a bit of lunch? We haven't eaten since an early breakfast on the riverboat."

"Oh, of course!" She turned and called into the back of the house, "Emma!"

An older woman appeared at the door to the kitchen.

"Emma, isn't there still a bit of dinner hot for Brother Simon and his wife?"

"Brother Simon! Bless my soul! So you've come back! And brought us a convert!" She hurried in and took Edouard's hand, then turned to Gale.

"May I present my wife, Gale. Sister Smith."

The older woman took both Gale's hands in hers. "I'm proud to make your acquaintance, my dear. Your husband is one of the finest young men in the city, and I'm sure you're going to be very happy with us."

"Thank you," Gale spoke uncertainly, "Sister . . . Smith?"

Edouard interrupted. "And we want to ask about a room, too. Have you a vacant one? Brother Eldridge is hunting for a house for us, but we'd like to stay here for a while until we find something."

"Why, yes, I think so," she turned to the younger Sister Smith. "Isn't the upstairs room on the south corner empty?"

"I'm not right sure. Remember that lumberman from up river was in it last night, but I think he left this morning. I'll ask Matilda." She went to the door leading off the large parlor and called, "Matilda!"

A small, dark, sharp-featured woman appeared, a direct contrast to the other two.

"What is it?" She sounded ill-tempered.

"Is the southeast corner room empty?"

"Yes. I just finished changing the sheets."

"Fine! Brother Simon and his wife want a room."

The little woman's harsh features broke into a

7

smile. "A bride! Isn't that a fine bit of news, though!"

Edouard put his hand under Gale's elbow. "Sister Smith, my wife, Gale."

Gale looked from one woman to another, puzzled. "Sister Smith? ... I am happy to know you."

In their room, Sister Matilda Smith set the jug of water on the washstand and went out, closing the door. Gale began pulling the pins from her bright copper-colored hair and letting it fall in a shawl over her shoulders.

"I'm anxious to use some of that appealing hot water. It seems years since I've really washed my face!" She began brushing her hair vigorously.

Edouard began splashing noisily in the washbasin.

"Edouard, how does it happen that there are so many Sister Smiths? Are they old maid sisters?"

His retort was muffled in the splashing water.

"I beg your pardon? Are they sisters?"

"No," he sounded evasive. "They were all married ... once."

"Not to the same man, surely," Gale laughed playfully.

Edouard was a long time in answering. Finally he spoke. "Joseph Smith built this building when he moved here six years ago." Then there was another silence, and when he spoke again, it seemed he had forgotten the question he had started to answer. His words were musing, almost a soliloquy. "A good man. Yes, even a great man, with the love of God and his fellow man in his heart. But because he was so different from the rest of us . . . so close to God . . . *and unshakable in what he believed* . . . *he was murdered.*"

"Murdered!" Gale whirled. "Why murdered?"

"Thousands of people hated him."

8

"But why?"

"Joseph Smith was one of the few men this world has known who was privileged to have direct intercourse with God through revelations from heavenly messengers!" He turned to Gale, a religious fervor blazing in his eyes. "Joseph Smith was God's Prophet!"

"I know. You told us all that back in Boston. But why did they kill him?"

"Because they were too ignorant to understand his teachings . . . because they feared the growing numbers of his followers . . . because they didn't *know* him!"

"Who killed him?" Gale asked, a little afraid of this fiery stranger.

"Forgive me," he spoke softly, recovering his composure. "I sound like a confirmed preacher, don't I?" He went on quietly. "Joseph and his brother Hyrum were murdered last summer by an insane mob over at the jail in Carthage. The whole affair was the result of a personal grudge held by a fellow who printed a newspaper here in town. William Law was his name, a hotheaded man who was jealous of his wife. In his muddled brain he got the idea that Joseph Smith was fond of her, and published a torrent of foul scandal in the *Expositor*. Everyone in town was shocked and angry."

Gale finished pinning up her hair and poured a basin of hot water, listening intently the while.

"And then?"

"The next day Brother Joseph, as Mayor, and the city council ordered the city marshall and members of the Nauvoo Legion down to the printing office and they demolished the type and closed the place as a public nuisance. Perhaps they were too hasty. I don't know. I only know that they thought they were doing what was right."

He took his last clean shirt out of his carpetbag and put it on, buttoning it as he spoke.

"Law was furious and rushed over to Carthage to take out a warrant for Joseph Smith's arrest, along with his brother Hyrum." He shook his head, remembering. "Poor Brother Joseph. The day they took him away to the jail, his face was deadly pale, for he knew the hatred that the people of Illinois had for the Saints."

"Why should they hate the Saints? I don't understand." Gale's face paled, too.

"They say we are a dangerous cult. People always fear something new, something they don't understand."

"What happened then?"

"He wasn't afraid. I had to admire his courage. He would have gone alone if we had let him, but two of the Saints went along to see that he was treated fairly." Edouard sat down heavily on a hard oak chair, his mouth bitter with remembrance.

"And was he?"

"Hardly! They killed him . . . him and Hyrum . . . a mob of two hundred crazy angry men. They never had a chance, trapped like rabbits . . . in the upstairs of that jail. Not a chance. Their friends brought their bodies home the next day, riddled with bullets . . ." He bowed his head shaking off the memory.

"How terrible!" Gale cried, her eyes flashing.

"But the mobs were disappointed, if they believed that murdering our Prophet would bring an end to us. It has only made us stronger. And our new leader is a man of towering strength."

"Who is that?"

10

"Brigham Young. I think he will be a great man."

A sharp knock on the door startled them. Edouard opened it to one of the Smith women.

"Pardon me, but Brother Eldridge is downstairs waiting to see you."

When Edouard and Gale entered the parlor, a tall well-built man sprang from a chair at the far end of the room and came quickly toward them. Unconsciously Gale noticed the lithe grace with which he walked.

"Simon, old man! Welcome home!" His voice was warm as he shook Edouard's hand in both his own. Gale saw a faint tinge of white at the temples, in strange contrast to the youthfulness of his face and the steely blue of his eyes. He turned an engaging smile upon her. "And you've brought home a perfectly enchanting wife! Congratulations!"

His eyes devoured her as he took her hand in his. His hand felt soft and smooth, like a woman's. Gale had an impulse to pull away, but she restrained herself. He bowed slightly, still holding her hand.

"Sister Simon, your husband is a very fortunate man."

She shrank closer to Edouard, feeling embarrassed by his bold scrutiny. But when he turned to speak to her husband, she recovered her poise, watching the play of warmth and intelligence in the animation of his handsome face.

"Rather too . . . daring," she thought. "But fascinating."

"I've located a vacant house for you," he was telling Edouard, "but I'm not sure it's what you'll want. It's a little two-room log cabin down on the riverbank, sort of a tumbledown affair, one of the first cabins built when Daniel Wells settled here and called the place Commerce. The owners have a new home they've built over in the east end of town and are offering this one for sale. Not much for looks, but it's clean."

Edouard turned to Gale in his usual deliberate fashion. "What do you think? Shall we look it over?"

"You'd be wise not to delay," Eldridge interposed, "if you're at all interested. With new converts pouring into town by the score, houses are snapped up the minute they're vacant."

Gale felt composed now, and quite matronly.

"I agree, Brother Eldridge. Edouard, let's hurry over the minute we've had lunch."

Edouard agreed and left the room to see if lunch could be served immediately. Left alone the two strangers stood looking at one another. Again Gale's poise left her, and she wondered what she could say to this man who, by turns, made her feel either extraordinarily sophisticated or extraordinarily shy and frightened. She wondered what he was really like and what he had done to arouse this confusion in her.

"I hope you will enjoy being a Saint," he smiled.

"Yes," she whispered uncertainly, "I . . . I hope so."

Three

The young Simons were at breakfast in their new home, Gale proudly pouring hot mint tea, Edouard eating hot biscuits and maple syrup in vast contentment. The windows were open to the warm July morning, and new white curtains fluttered in the early breeze from the river. When Isaac Eldridge had said the cabin was "on the riverbank," he had been quite literal.

The little house sat on the immense shining curve of the Mississippi as it encircled the city. Freshly whitewashed inside and out, it had a thorny bush of yellow roses at the front door. An ancient gnarled willow with half of its tangled roots left bare by the high water of many springtimes guarded the rear. The backyard was a brief patch of matted grass which dropped off abruptly to the river three or four feet below.

"Oh, I love it!" Gale had exclaimed when they first saw it, and sank down to sit in the shade of the willow. A great lumber raft came floating by, and Gale could hear the rollicking song of the men who rode it.

"I love it here!" she cried again after Eldridge left. She kissed Edouard excitedly. "I couldn't be happier if I were in a palace!"

The house was furnished only with crude makeshift stools and a rough table, a bed on the floor and Gale's trunk, for her family furniture, coming by the slow freighter that sailed from Boston, through New Orleans and up the Mississippi, had not yet arrived. But the house was bright and clean, and the floor boards were scrubbed until they were the color of a honeycomb.

Gale gulped her mint tea and jumped from her stool to throw her arms around her husband. "Oh, my darling! I'm afraid I don't deserve anyone as wonderful as you!"

He pulled her down on his knee, caressing her hair. "You're a silly girl," he smiled.

"Do you think this will last?"

"What will last?"

"This happiness. It . . . it seems so strange . . . and beautiful. As though we were in another world. I can hardly believe that I am really a Saint . . . and out West in Illinois!"

"It is all real enough," he said morosely, staring out the window. "Maybe too real."

Gale sat beneath the willow, her needle flying over an apron she was making. She was startled by a cheerful "Yoo-hoo!" at the corner of the house, and a crisp starched woman appeared, carrying a plate covered with a napkin. A woman of forty or so, she was shining with cleanliness from the hem of her dress to her blond hair and broad Teutonic face.

"Ach!" she laughed, speaking with heavy accent. "Vot a picture you make! There in der shade, mit der river like a looking glass behind you! I knock on der door, but I hear nobody inside, so I come around to see if I find somebody. I bring you blitz kuchen, fresh out of my oven. Mit nuts baked all over der top. You like, I think."

Gale jumped to her feet and took the cake.

"Oh, how nice! Of course we'll like it!"

"I vant to see Brother Simon's vife for so long time, efer since ve hear of such a beautiful bride. But you know, mit der kids and der vash and der bake and der cleaning house all der time, iss no time left to visit."

"Won't you come in the house and have a seat? You must be ready for a rest."

"Ach, no! I am in der house every day, but never do I come into der yard to look by der river." She eased her ample form down on the grass. "This morning I say to Jock, he iss my husband, I say, 'This day I see Brother Simon's vife, if ve do not eat!' So I leave Cassie, my oldest girl vot iss fifteen, to vatch der kids and der rising bread. She iss no help, no good at all around der house, und I hope she does not let der bread run over on der floor."

Gale laughed at the other's hearty good humor.

"I hope not!"

"Ve live by der river too, yust up der street two yumps or three, but never it seems ve haf time to sit und vatch der riverboats, like you." She clucked admiringly. "You know how to live und be happy, I think."

Gale flushed.

"Yes, I am very happy, Sister . . ."

The other threw apologetic hands in the air.

"Ach! No manners I got, like a dumb ox! Here I come to visit, und never say who I am! I am Sister Meier. Jock, my husband, works in der carpenter shop mit your man Edouard. Brother Simon iss a fine man, and Jock iss glad to have him back from his mission in der East. Jock says your man iss one of der great men in der church, even so young."

Pride swelled in Gale, but she answered modestly.

"Thank you, Sister Meier." She wanted to exclaim, "Of course he is! So noble and good!"

The older woman spoke gently. "I hope you can love your man as much ven he gets der second und third vifes."

Gale stared at her, not understanding.

"Second . . . and third . . . wives? What . . . do you mean?"

Sister Meier's motherly face showed surprise.

"You don't know about der Saints und vot they call der plural vifes?"

"Plural wives?" Her disbelief floundered for words. "You mean . . . you don't mean . . . ?"

"Gott und Himmel! I vas a clumsy fool! I think you already know, or I say nottings. Ach! I could bite der tongue in my head! It iss not yet said aloud to der vorld. Only a chosen few . . ."

Gale stared at the river, and plucked bits of grass, speaking under her breath. "That explains it . . . all the Smith women . . . and Edouard unwilling to answer my questions."

The bottom had fallen out of the summer afternoon.

"Oh, no!" she thought miserably, "not Edouard! He wouldn't ever bring home another wife . . . never in a million years! Oh, please God . . . not Edouard!"

"Don't let your heart vorry, child," Sister Meier patted Gale's limp hand and made a comfortable little clucking noise. "It iss not so bad like you think. It hurts at der commence, yes. But you get over it, and soon it iss a pretty nice thing, some ways."

Gale turned horrified eyes to her.

"Nice!" she whispered. "How can you say such a thing?"

"I know. Ven last summer my Jock bring home

16

Sophie to court for a vife, und she vas slim and tventy like I ain't, I vas so mad . . . I almost bust!" She breathed hard, remembering. "At first I think I die. Then I think I ain't der one to die . . . I do no wrong. It should be Jock, and that Sophie! So I tell Jock she haf to leave my house or I throw scalding vater in her face . . . und him too! But he vas yust sitting there and don't be moving. Und he tells me about der . . . der celestial vifes, und how God told Joseph Smith in a revelation that der Saints dey should live as der prophets in the Old Testament with several vifes. I thought it sounded fishy." She laughed shortly.

"Yes," Gale murmured, "it does." But she didn't hear herself speak.

"But Jock he says Brother Joseph Smith has Nauvoo House full of vifes und all der leaders in der church have many, und he too must obey God's vill. Und who am I to say? I am yust a voman. So I say notting und I let Sophie stay. Und in der vinter Jock a little house in der backyard he builds for her. Now I get used to it. Jock sleep in der backyard every odder veek und I get a good night's sleep. Iss not so bad."

Gale's face was frozen.

"Do you mean . . . every Saint has more than one wife?"

"Ach, no! It is yust a few leaders now. Und dey pretend to keep it secret, and vait for a while to tell der vorld. But der secret is one yoke. Everyone in Nauvoo, dey know it. A man cannot haf a house of many women und not haf der news escape. It yust ain't natural."

Gale looked stricken. Her words were scarcely audible.

"Edouard told us . . . in Boston . . . the Saints

17

are honest . . . chaste . . . virtuous . . . Chaste! He can't have known!"

Sister Meier got heavily to her feet.

"Forgive me, please. I am being so sorry it vas me to make you sad. You think I do it deliberate, maybe. I am a dummy."

Gale arose, trying to smile. But her lips were too stiff.

"It's all right. I would have discovered it myself, sooner or later. The Saints! *Saints!*" She laughed . . . a harsh laugh.

At sundown Edouard came home to find her slumped against the willow, the unfinished apron crumpled in her lap. She turned a mask to his call.

"Gale . . . what has happened?" He dropped to his knees beside her. She smelled the pungence of pine shavings on him.

"Nothing. Nothing at all."

She pulled her fingers from his caress and turned her face to the river. Nonplussed, he stared at her. Suddenly the grim line of her mouth broke, and she flung herself into his arms, sobbing.

"Oh, Edouard . . . it isn't true . . . is it?"

"What, my dear?" He held her tenderly.

"About . . . all . . . about all . . . the wives!"

"Who has been talking to you?" He was angry.

"Oh, it doesn't matter. Is it true?"

"It does matter. Who has told you?"

"Then it is true! What she said is true . . . after all! I've been praying . . . praying it was a lie . . . or a nightmare, ever since she left."

Edouard shook her gently. "Who has been gossiping to you?"

She jerked away from him.

"What difference does it make? Sister Meier

18

wasn't gossiping. You can't expect women to live like that . . . and not have it known! Why didn't you tell me? Before you brought me here? Why didn't you tell me that I was to become one of a . . . a harem? Perhaps I am not the first! Perhaps you have other wives you have not told me about!"

"Gale! Gale!" His words were soft, as though to a hysterical child. He took her gently but firmly in his arms. "Hush. You don't realize what you are saying." He stroked her hair and the slender curve at the back of her neck. Gradually her stormy weeping subsided, and he spoke in a low caressing tone.

"In a revelation, God told Joseph Smith of the doctrine of celestial marriage. In the next world we are to live as we do in this, with the same wives and families, living on through eternity until we finally attain the glory of Godhood. We are to become the fathers of vast generations," he continued, "and thus walk in the footsteps of our Father in Heaven."

"Do you really believe that?" Her scorn seared him.

"Of course. It was a holy revelation."

"And you too intend to pave your way to heaven with a houseful of . . . females?" Disgust curled her lip.

Suddenly he dropped his head in her lap, the action of a contrite child.

"Oh, darling . . . it's you I love . . . now and for eternity!"

She stared at the head in her lap, as though it were some unfamiliar animal.

"I had thought so . . . once."

"I love you, Gale! Can't you understand? The church doesn't *force* us to take more than one wife."

He raised his head and her heart leaped at the love she saw in his dark eyes.

19

"If I want my happiness now, in this world, alone, with you . . . that's my own business!"

A faint hope flickered in her.

"Edouard . . . can you promise me . . . that there will be no other wife . . . for you?"

He crushed her body in a fierce embrace.

"I promise you that I will always love you more than life itself! More than heaven!"

A calm enveloped her and began to bloom in a faint smile on her full lips.

"I knew all that couldn't mean you."

She ran her fingers lightly over the crispness of his hair, and her eyes turned to the green twilight across the river. The ache eased.

Four

Gale's family furniture had just arrived and she was rushing about, wrapped in an apron, her hair covered by a dustcap. She was tearing the coverings from the oak table and chairs, breaking the crates from the walnut highboy and the lovely old desk where her father used to sit. She must hurry because she wanted to see the astonishment spread over Edouard's face when he came home and found their home settled in glowing hospitality, roses on the polished table, painted china in the cupboard, a rug on the floor, the bed resplendent with the silk pieced quilt her grandmother had made. When he left that morning, there were only the makeshift stools and table.

She paused a moment in the center of the floor, wondering whether the mirror would look better between the south windows, or over the trunk at the end of the room.

A quiet knock at the open door startled her. A small girl stood there, looking in shyly. Gale's first impression was of her paleness . . . her pale gold hair, her pale blue eyes, and clear, porcelainlike skin. "But she's pretty, in spite of being so pale," Gale thought as she invited her into the cabin. The girl handed her a plate covered with a napkin.

"I'm Cassie Meier," she said in a small timid

voice, her wide gaze wandering about the cluttered room. "Mamma just finished making these crullers for you."

As she spoke, Gale saw that she was older than she first appeared, perhaps fourteen or fifteen, but tiny and fragile, like a flower stunted by growing in a dark place. The hair hanging loose around her shoulders made her look even smaller.

"You don't look at all like your mother!" Gale exclaimed.

"I know," she seemed to apologize.

Gale lifted the napkin and looked beneath.

"Oh, how delicious! Won't you have one?"

"No, thank you," she murmured, staring at Gale fixedly.

"Well, I will! M–m–m! Luscious! Please do! I feel like a pig eating alone."

Cassie took a cruller, still staring at Gale, who turned away from the staring gaze and began munching her cake.

"I can't decide where to hang this mirror. What do you think? Between the windows, or on that wall there?"

Cassie was silent a long time. At last she spoke in a very small voice.

"On that wall. You have the river to look at from the windows."

"Of course! Why didn't I think of that?"

The girl watched silently as Gale drove a heavy nail and hung up the mirror. Gale turned to find the other's gaze still on her.

"Do you mind if I go ahead with my unpacking? I want to surprise my husband when he gets home from work. He'll be here about six-thirty."

"I know. He comes home with Papa."

After two busy hours, Gale began to feel uncomfortable under the other's watchful eyes. The girl was quite silent.

"Don't you suppose your mother wonders what has happened to you?"

"She knows I'm here."

"Doesn't she need you to help her?"

"No," she answered simply. "I'm no help."

"Won't she be expecting you for lunch?"

"No. I'm not hungry."

Gale stifled a sigh and went on with her work. Late in the afternoon, after Gale had created order from chaos, she stood back to survey the cozy gleaming house. Cassie suddenly spoke.

"I'm going home. You have to get cleaned up before Brother Edouard comes home."

"Yes, indeed!" Gale wiped the perspiration and grime from her forehead.

And Cassie was gone, as suddenly as she had come, and as silently.

"Whew!" Gale said, laughing with relief. "What a strange girl! I hope she doesn't call often!"

Two days later, Cassie again appeared, her hair shining in the early sun. The shadow of a smile flitted across her face as Gale called a cheery greeting from her perch on a chair, where she stood to arrange her fancy china on the top shelf.

"Hello there! Come in!"

"Mamma sent me to ask if you knew about the picnic and dance they are having out at the Bowery on Wednesday night."

Gale jumped lightly from the chair.

"Why, no. Edouard hasn't mentioned it."

"Mamma said to tell you everyone always goes. It's to make money to finish building the Temple."

"I see."

"Mamma says you and Brother Edouard are welcome to ride out with us, if you want to. We always go in the big wagon. Mamma and Papa and Sophie ride on the seat and us kids ride on the hay in back, but Mamma said they could fix a board for another seat for you if you want to go. It's fun." Her pale cheeks flushed slightly from the daring length of her speech. She stopped, breathless.

Gale laughed. "It sounds like fun. How far is it?"

"Six miles, I think. We have to start early. Everybody gets off work early on the nights we go to the Bowery."

"What is the Bowery?"

"Oh, sort of a big hall, more like a barn, I guess. That's where they dance. But we eat outdoors. There's trees all around and it's awful nice. There's big swings down by the creek, and lots of long tables. Everybody brings supper in baskets, and they fry chicken, and we spread it out on the tables and take our plates and go around and eat anything we want. Oh yes, and Mamma said to tell you she'd lend you a basket to carry your supper in, if you don't have one." Again she stopped, overwhelmed by her own volubility.

Gale's face brightened with anticipation.

"Oh, I think it sounds like great fun! I'm sure Edouard will want to go."

"Mamma said for you not to wear your best dress because it will get dirty." The girl was losing her shyness under the stress of delivering the numerous messages, and her soft voice was almost gay. "The seats are just logs, and besides the dancing raises a fearful dust. So you'd better wear a wash dress."

"I'll wear a kitchen dress," Gale laughed.

"Oh, no!" Cassie was shocked. "You must wear something pretty."

24

Gale became thoughtful.

"Something pretty? The only pretty one I have is the white one I had when I left the seminary. And that's my best one, the one I got married in. All my summer dresses got faded or stained or torn while I was working for the Muldoons."

"Muldoons?" Cassie's eyes widened. "Did you work for Muldoons, the people that came from Boston?"

"Yes." Gale shuddered, remembering those dreadful days, working as the kitchen scullion for Mary Muldoon, and trying to avoid the grog-laden advances of her husband, Pat Muldoon. It had been the only position available after she had been expelled from the seminary for slipping away to attend Edouard's missionary meeting.

"You don't look like . . . like you'd work for Muldoons."

"Well, I did for a while."

"Mamma says Brother Muldoon doesn't belong in Nauvoo. And Sophie says—" She cut herself off short, flushing. "Well, I must go home now. Goodbye." And she was gone like a shadow.

Gale sat happily beside Edouard on the bouncing board seat of the Meiers' wagon. She rode with her head high, feeling extremely gay in the new dress which she and Sophie had just finished making. Other wagons and carriages rattled on ahead, and more followed behind. A fine dust lifted from the horses' feet and settled over stout Jock Meier and his two wives, over Gale and Edouard, and over numerous children and food baskets which were scattered about in the rear of the wagon bed.

Her dimity dress was sprigged with tiny yellow

25

roses, and she wore a new straw bonnet with a cluster of yellow rosebuds on the crown.

"Edouard, I'm so happy," she whispered.

"You're really quite stunning, you know," he whispered back. "I can categorically state that you are the most attractive young lady in Nauvoo."

"Hush," she chuckled. "Husbands needn't pay such fancy compliments to their wives."

"They do, if they have an amazingly beautiful wife."

"I'll bet Jock Meier doesn't," she murmured, "and Sophie is beautiful, with all that black hair." But suddenly she stopped, sensing unsafe ground.

She had stubbornly refused to think about their horrible conversation about plural marriage. She forced herself to think only of her own happiness and of the security of Edouard's love. And she was *not* going to think of the disagreeable subject tonight!

She was young, and beautiful, and deeply in love—and this was to be her first dance! Nothing would spoil it! Under the strict upbringing of her Puritan father, there had been no parties or dances. It was glorious to be seventeen, and married to the handsomest man in the state of Illinois!

"Edouard!" she cried suddenly in panic. "I don't know how to dance! I've never tried!"

"Don't worry. You'll soon learn. All the Saints dance, from children to grandparents."

A small riot erupted in the rear of the wagon, as the three Meier boys tussled madly to see who would be the first to leap over the tailgate.

"Emil! Pete! John!" Sister Meier bellowed above the din.

Even the warring culprits heard and raised shamed eyes to their mother's stern gaze.

26

"Down you sit, quick! You want you should fall out und break der necks?"

"But Mamma," they called above the rattle of the wheels, "we're almost there! We could jump out easy, Mamma, and we could beat you all there. It's just a little ways, Mamma, over in those trees there!"

"You're not tellin' me vere der Bowery iss! Sit!" she shouted over the Simons' heads. "Und don't try no monkeyshiners till ve is stopping! You hear?"

At this stentorian request, the children settled down meekly to await their arrival at the picnic grounds. Gale thought she could now understand why Cassie was so subdued. And she couldn't help wondering how Jock Meier had ever had the audacity to bring home another wife.

Five

Brother Meier had some difficulty finding an empty place at the hitching rack among the long line of carts and carriages, hayrack and surreys, while the children chafed under the delay. Finally Meier stopped to tether the team to a bush at the edge of the grove, and the children were gone like a flash, tumbling from the wagon helter-skelter, making a beeline for the children playing under the trees. The boys and little Ella were far in the lead, with Cassie lagging behind, pulling baby Willie by the hand.

The twilight was already bright with bonfires, and the aroma of frying chicken was sweet in the air. Gale jumped lightly from the wagon into Edouard's arms, her full skirts swirling about her.

"Now you young folks go on," Sister Meier said, climbing down heavily over the wagon wheel. Jock Meier, in order to avoid showing partiality, alighted hastily by way of the wagon tongue, and was busy at the horses' heads.

"Run along," Sister Meier motioned Sophie along with the Simons, "und haf fun mit der peoples. Me und Jock vill bring der baskets."

Sophie's black eyes flashed in a willful young face.

"I'll go with my husband, thank you!" she flared.

29

Gale and Edouard, embarrassed, hurried off toward the picnic area. A tall lithe figure came striding toward them, silhouetted against the glow of the fires. A vaguely pleasing memory stirred in Gale's mind. She was startled to recognize Isaac Eldridge, handsome in shining boots, fawn-colored trousers and satin waistcoat.

"That outfit will be ruined before the evening is over," Gale said. "Cassie said not to wear our best."

"He always dresses a bit like a successful river gambler," said Edouard.

"Brother Edouard! And the lovely bride!" He grasped a hand of each. Gale wondered if he were squeezing her husband's hand as warmly as he was her own. But then she flushed in embarrassment at the thought.

"We hoped you would be here," he went on. "I mentioned you to Grace on our way out from town. Say, by the way, are there others still coming? Everyone is anxious to begin eating, so I came out to see."

"Yes," said Edouard, "There are still several rigs behind us."

"The children are teasing to eat," Eldridge spoke laughingly, turning and coming back to the tables with them. "We won't wait for the late arrivals."

"Is Brother Young here yet?" Edouard asked.

"Of course. Isn't he always the first one everywhere?"

Edouard frowned. "Then perhaps we had better let him make the decision," he said quietly.

At the fires Edouard and Gale embarked on a round of introductions. The confusing rush of flickering shadows on new faces was interrupted by Eldridge.

"Here is Brother Simon now. Brother Young, allow me to present the bride, Sister Simon."

Gale bent her head slightly in proper response to the introduction, and then raised her eyes to the heavy powerful man before her. She knew that out of the jumble of new faces, here was one she would never forget. Not yet middle-aged, there was something stately and imposing about the way he stood, his feet set firmly on the ground, as though heaven and earth could not budge him until he willed it. His heavy head was set with self-assurance on his wide shoulders, and the gaze she met from his deep set eyes was intently cold and gray.

'He's stern,' Gale thought, noting the thin hard line of his lips. Edouard's right. He'll be a great leader.

An unexpected transformation changed his face into one of gentle kindliness, with smiles crinkling at the corners of his eyes. "We hope you'll like us and our city," he spoke with open simplicity.

"I do already." Her answer was spontaneous.

"Well, what about beginning the supper?" Eldridge moved adroitly into the conversation.

Brigham's eyes were cold again when he turned to the man beside him. "Tell them they may start as soon as I ask the blessing."

A little later Gale stood at the edge of the milling throng, a plate of supper in each hand as she waited for Edouard to join her. The familiar figure of a woman broke from the crowd and bore down upon her, her red face fairly bursting with suppressed excitement. It was Mary Muldoon, her lashless eyes almost popping. She came close.

"Here ye are at last!" she hissed in a whisper. "I've hunted this place over for ye! I'm wantin' to

31

know if ye know what a hell-hole that husband o'
yours got us into when he led us to Nauvoo!"

"What do you mean?"

"Ye don't know? Ye mean to stand there and tell
me ye've lived in the place a month and don't know
that the whole city is a nest of concubines, paradin'
around under the fancy name o' religion? Why, girl,
he must be pullin' the wool over your eyes as slick
as he did the rest o' us when he brought us here!"

"Must you spoil the party? Let's forget it
tonight."

"Then ye do know!"

"I want to be happy tonight, and dance, and forget all the ugly things in the world!"

"That holier-than-thou husband o' yers likely has
a string o' wives already, or is plannin' on a new
one! Why else would ye be snifflin' like that?"

"Sister Muldoon, I won't listen to such talk about
my husband!"

"Don't fret, my pet. Yer not the only frog in the
stew."

"If some of the Saints are bad, it's not his fault!
He is good . . . and fine . . . and noble! A million
times better than . . ."

"I know. I'm scared stiff about Pat, too. I think
he knew what a gaggle o' prostitutes he was gettin'
into when he came West; I'm bettin' me best bonnet
on it! And I was fool enough to think I was gettin'
him outa the grog shops. Grog shops! Huh! I'd give
me right eye for a good honest grog shop right now,
in place o' all these bawds paradin' around under
the name o' religion."

Edouard appeared, and Sister Muldoon whirled
on her heel and stamped off.

"What happened?" he asked, amusement mingled
with surprise.

32

"Oh, nothing much." She forced lightness into her voice, keeping her telltale tears beneath the brim of her bonnet. "Just another of her rages. You know how she is."

She handed Edouard his plate and blinked the tears back.

The music stopped as Edouard led Gale, panting and laughing, to a window in search of the freshness of night air. All the windows were open, and the candles, stuck on spokes in the logs around the room, sent up wavering flames in the heated air, and dropped hot wax on anyone thoughtless enough to stand beneath them. Dust floated up from the floor, suspending the merrymakers at the opposite end of the room in a golden haze. The long hall echoed with laughter.

"Wife, you have deceived me!" Edouard said with mock severity.

"How?" She had never felt so buoyantly alive.

"You have been dancing all your life. You no doubt danced in the New England woods . . . with the witches."

She laughed, delighted with his unusual air of playfulness. He never joked, seldom laughed. He always seemed to be above such things. She squeezed his arm, and her eyes skimmed the crowded room jubilantly.

"Goodness gracious, there is Barret Nickols and his wife! I'd never expect to see them at a dance—that woebegone schoolmaster!"

"All the Saints dance, as I told you. It's a way of keeping up our spirits."

"Look! There's Addie Voak! Our Boston friends all seem to be here. I wonder if she's alone."

33

"No, I saw her earlier with the Jenkinses. I think she must be boarding with them."

The band struck up a gay Viennese waltz. Gale's foot tapped the rough boards, and her eyes followed the dancers as they began to swirl out into the center of the floor.

"Sister Meier is dancing with her husband!" she exclaimed.

"She is a fine dancer," said Edouard.

"Yes, but . . . but . . ." she stammered. She was thinking, '. . . but Sophie will be angry.' Instead she said, ". . . but she is so heavy. I should think dancing would not be easy for her."

"Not at all. She's as light on her feet as a girl."

"Poor little Cassie huddled there in a corner like a lost robin. I suppose the other children have gone to bed in the wagon."

Edouard bowed ceremoniously, extending his arm to Gale in invitation.

"Madame, may I have the honor of this dance?"

"Darling, why don't you ask Cassie?"

"Cassie! Good heavens! She's a child!"

"She's fourteen or so, and besides, she looks so starved for fun."

"I prefer my wife, thank you."

"Look at her. She looks as though she were about to cry. Please, dear."

"And leave you standing here alone?" He was shocked.

"I'll be all right. I'll sit down as soon as there is a space on the benches. Please."

"Well . . ." He started off unwillingly.

She stood watching the astonished pleasure of Cassie's face. Suddenly she felt a heavy hand on her own arm and turned to meet the breath of Pat Muldoon, heavy with liquor.

34

"Yer gonna dance with me now, ain'tcha?" She wasn't sure whether he was swaying, or whether it was her own fright that made things waver.

"Oh, no . . . that is . . . I'm out of breath. I'm resting." Terrified, she couldn't meet the gaze that slid down from her face over her neck and bodice.

"Come on, Sister!" He had her arm in his hot fingers, propelling her on to the dance floor.

They were stopped by a hand on Muldoon's shoulder and he whirled to meet the cool smile of Isaac Eldridge.

"Pardon me, but isn't this the dance that Brother Simon arranged for me?"

"Oh yes, thank you!" Gale pulled away from Pat's clutch and put her hand on Eldridge's sleeve. Grateful for her deliverance, she smiled up at him graciously.

"What the . . ." Pat blocked their path. "Ye told me ye was restin'." His face twisted in anger.

Eldridge plucked a bit of straw from Muldoon's jacket and smiled.

"You wouldn't call a lady a liar now, would you, stranger?"

"Stranger be damned!" Pat exploded, striking the other's hand away. "I'm a Saint, same as you!"

"I beg your pardon," Eldridge was still smiling. "Saints don't drink. Forgive me."

"Miss Fancy Pants here don't need to put on airs!" Pat blustered. "She used to carry out my slops, back in Boston."

"Hm! She knows you, then!" Eldridge's smile flashed cool and white. "Perhaps that is why she chooses to dance this one with me."

The music stopped abruptly. People began shouting. Everyone made a wild surge toward the

35

door. The three had been too intent on their own conflict to notice the crowd that had gathered around little Emil Meier. He was sobbing out an incoherent story. Women screamed in hysteria. The men pushed grim-faced toward the door that was already jammed. Bodies smashed against Gale, knocking the breath from her. Somewhere nearby a woman fell, shrieking, and was trampled beneath rushing feet.

"The mobs! The mobs!" they were shouting.

Eldridge pulled Gale from the panic-crazed crowd and forced their way to the side of the room, where he thrust her unceremoniously against the wall. She caught her breath, feeling bruised and exhausted.

"Stay here until the crowd clears out a little," he ordered as he turned to go. "You'll be killed if you don't."

"What's it all about?" she cried.

"The mobs, come to terrorize us again! And the wagons are full of sleeping children!" He was gone in the throng, his mouth grim. Many more level-headed men were crawling through the windows and dropping to the ground outside.

Gale saw Mrs. Nickols, biting her knuckles and moaning, "Oh Lord, save my babies! Save my little girls!" And crawling through the window, Barrett Nickols was repeating, "I know nothing good would come of this frivolous entertainment. I knew it! I knew it!"

Cassie was standing terrified on a bench on the opposite side of the room. But Gale could not find Edouard's dark head in the insane crowd.

Through the cracks in the logs she could hear the angry shouts of men at the edge of the grove, and the squeal of frightened horses. Her heart pounded

36

in an agony of terror. Edouard was out there! Oh, God, let nothing happen to Edouard, she prayed. She thought she heard a distant shot, but in the tumult she could not be sure.

Six

Mid-morning sunshine lay serene on the great curve of the Mississippi. The city was humming quietly with its weekday industry. Here and there a clean laundry fluttered on the lines, blacksmith shops were ringing with the steady rhythm of the anvils, the odor of baking bread floated from the kitchen doors, grocery shops and meat markets were busy with morning customers, and boys and girls shouted along the riverbanks as they sailed leaf boats and paper ships.

Pale and shaken from the episode of the evening before, Gale sat at the kitchen window endeavoring to mend the rips in her yellow print dress. She worked fitfully, for her fingers were unsteady and her nerves ragged. She would sew with intense speed for a moment, then the dress would fall into her lap and her eyes would rest unseeing on the river, as images of the Bowery flashed through her weary mind.

At last she jumped up, and flung the dress into a chair. "How can they stand it? How can they go on calmly as though nothing had happened? I can't just sit here! I'll go mad here alone!"

She pulled off her apron and tied a bonnet over her hair. She hurried up the street to where the Meier home sat in stolid German cleanliness. There was no sign of life at the front of the house, so she went around to the kitchen door.

"Goot morning!" Sister Meier called cheerily. "Come in, child. I vas seeing you from out der pantry vindow." She appeared with her hands and arms white with flour, dough clinging in little lumps to her big hands. She apologized, "I am being late in mixing up der bread this morning on account little Ella her head hurt her so much. But she iss sleeping now, und I haf time. The boys I send down to der river und also Cassie to vatch that Villie do not yump in der vater."

"Ella? Was she really hurt last night?"

"*Ja*. She vas cracked on her head some. Ven der horses start to run away, she stood up and yumped from out der vagon like I always tell them not to. But she iss not hurt bad, thank Gott!"

Compassion and wonder filled Gale's eyes, and a kind of shame too, in the face of the older woman's calm courage.

"How can you be so . . . so undisturbed?"

"Ve are only thanking Gott it vas no vorse. In Missouri der mobs dey shoot us, und beat us to death, und put on der tar und feathers, und rape der mothers und girls und even grandmothers, und chase us out in der bushes to starve und freeze, und set fire to der houses und haystacks, und shoot our cows und horses."

"But how can you *bear* it? Your child, or even all your children, might have been killed!"

"Last night vas notting. Only . . ." She swallowed hard to gain control of her emotions. "Only . . . ve vas hoping in Illinois ve vould find peace."

"But why all this horror?" Gale's eyes were almost black. "Who does all these terrible things to you . . . to us? And why?"

40

"Vell . . . in Missouri it vas der outlaws . . . der cutthroats, Jock calls them. Dey vas afraid of us . . . afraid of honest folk . . . afraid ve vas so many ve could vin der elections und run der state. Dey told der lies on us . . . und pretty soon everybody hate us . . . so dey chase clean out of der state all der Saints. But . . ." She shrugged and threw her big hands wide. "In Illinois . . . I don't know. Ven ve first come, dey treat us nice . . . make us at home . . . tell us dey happy ve come. Den all in a sudden . . . boof . . . like dot . . . dey make us trouble same like der mobs back in Missouri."

"But why, Sister Meier? I can't understand it."

"I think . . . but I not say for sure . . ." she lowered her voice, "I think it iss on the account der plural vifes . . . I think dat gives der Saints a bad name. I ask Jock iss it not so . . . but he gets red in der face like a turkey und he say it iss no one's business but us, und besides, nobody knows about it. But I tell Jock women cannot be treated like dis und keep der secret!"

As though she had said too much, she turned abruptly and thrust her hands into the great pile of dough swelling in yeasty fragrance on the table. The kitchen was silent for a long time, except for the soft thud of the woman's hands in the bread, and the dying hum of the teakettle over the fire.

"You don't think it is right . . . do you . . . these wives?"

"Dat I cannot say." She was gruff. "Ve are only vomen. This religion, I am thinking, iss for der men."

There was another silence while the older woman rounded off the dough and put it in a deep pan to rise, punctuating the end of her task with a resounding whack. She turned to Gale, sitting dejectedly on

41

the stool, staring with blind miserable eyes at the floor.

"Cheer up!" Her great laugh boomed through the kitchen. "You vas like Cassie. You look like a flower vat is not vatered for von veek!"

Gale tried to smile. She shook her head, as though to shake the tears from her lashes.

"It's silly . . . I know, when Edouard and I are so happy together. But I had thought, and hoped . . . that Nauvoo would be perfect . . . that the Saints were fine, and good. It seemed beautiful and peaceful . . . on the surface. But underneath . . . there is so much . . . Oh, I don't know . . . I am so mixed up!"

"I know." She put a hand on Gale's shoulder and shook her gently. "It iss hard for us. But it don't help none to fret."

Gale straightened her shoulders and retied the bonnet strings with a firm twitch.

"I'm sorry. Here I am moping about . . . I should be rejoicing. Edouard is the best husband in the world! I'm going home and bake him a cake."

"*Ja.* Brother Simon iss von fine man."

Gale smiled, her natural high spirits returning.

"Thanks for talking with me. Seeing you so calm in spite of everything . . . well, it makes me feel a lot better. I'm sorry I bothered you."

"It vas not a bother, child. Come some more again."

"Good-bye." Impulsively she kissed the woman's rosy cheek, and rushed out the door.

Gale found it easy to forget the affair of the Bowery and the troublesome subject of plural wives in the days that followed. Her life with Edouard was idyllic, filled with the joy that is known by two peo-

42

ple who are welded for life by a chain of deep love. There were serious moments when Edouard read from the Book of Mormon in the evenings, his voice rolling on in majestic eloquence, or when she knelt to join him in prayer in the mornings before they dressed. There were gay moments too, when she amused him with her imitations of Sister Muldoon's endless monologues, or of Tillie Tavenner's indolent nasal twang as she whined about her abundant brood, or of Barret Nickols pacing about the room with shoulders bent, hands clasped behind him, prophesying a morbid future in hollow tones.

Sometimes when a careless phrase was dropped by a neighbor, she realized the strife and terror that held sway outside the city. But the Saints seldom mentioned such things, seeming to hope that by ignoring the ugly facts they would cease to exist.

There was an increase in social events, for every known method of raising funds was used in order to rush the completion of the Temple on the hill. It was very nearly finished, and they hoped to be able to utilize it by the first of the new year. It was a splendid building of glittering white sandstone, rising against the blue of the sky as a tribute to the faith of the Saints.

And so there were pie socials, dances, band concerts, and dinners served in Nauvoo House. The leaders were even planning a big barbecue and picnic at the Bowery to celebrate the exceptionally fine crops the Saints had grown on the rich rolling Illinois prairie that lay about Nauvoo. It was to be a Harvest Festival, held in late September.

Fortunately Gale was one of those rare people who absorb a kind of joy from the very act of living, much as a plant absorbs moisture from earth that is apparently dry. She found joy in seeing the drooping

43

branches of the willow against the river, green shining leaves in the morning sun, black silhouettes against the evening sky. There was joy for her in watching the puffy August clouds, in listening to the cool lapping of the river beneath the bank behind the house, in watching a bee hunting among the dried berries of the rosebush for blossoms.

Cassie's visits had become almost a daily occurrence. Gale was becoming accustomed to her strange silences, broken by sudden bursts of volubility. Gale tried to curb her own impatience with the other's immaturity.

"Guess what!" Cassie burst in early one morning.

"I can't guess," Gale answered, stacking the dishes on the breakfast table. "What?"

"We are going to have two new babies in our family in February!"

Gale was startled.

"Two . . . babies?"

"Yes. Mamma and Sophie are both expecting!"

"Oh. How . . . how . . . nice." Gale couldn't think of anything that seemed appropriate to say.

"Please, Sister Simon, let me wash the dishes for you! I'll wash them good."

"No thanks, Cassie. It won't take me long when I get started. You can dry if you like."

"Please! I'd love to wash. You have such pretty dishes, and it's fun to wash *pretty* dishes. Ours are old and cracked."

"I expect your mother would like to have you at home right now doing her dishes, even though they are cracked. She'll need help more than ever from now on. You can be a big help to her, Cassie."

"No, she says I'm just in her way."

Gale chuckled inwardly, agreeing with Sister Meier.

44

"Maybe you could help Sophie, then," she spoke aloud. "Didn't you tell me yesterday she wasn't well?"

"Oh, she's all right. Mamma says she just babies herself to get Papa's sympathy. Mamma says she won't stay in bed when she gets four or five kids to look after. And besides . . . I don't like Sophie." Her lips drew down in a pout.

"Really? I think she's pretty."

"You wouldn't if she was married to *your* husband!"

Gale flushed. "Oh . . . I don't know . . ."

"Mamma acts like it's all right. She pretends Sophie is just one of the family . . . but she dislikes her, anyway."

"Oh, no! Your mother isn't the spiteful kind. She couldn't dislike anyone."

"We both dislike Sophie. Mamma can't help it if she is old and fat and has lots of babies . . . and Sophie is young and pretty and has lots of nice clothes. She won't be able to put on so many airs now, she'll soon be as fat as Mamma."

"I must make the bed now," murmured Gale, walking out of the room and its bitter revelations. But Cassie followed her into the bedroom.

"I forgot to tell you," continued her chatter. "I went to a wedding yesterday."

"You did?"

"Mamma said you probably knew them. They came from Boston."

"Boston?" Gale's interest was aroused. "Who in the world would I know who is getting married? Was it Addie Voak?"

"That big tall woman who looks like a man, sort of?"

"Yes. Was it Addie?"

45

"No, it wasn't her. Guess again."

"Oh, Cassie! I can't guess." She was impatient. "Tell me."

"It was funny how we happened to go. Mamma and I were going past the chapel and we saw people going in, so we knew it must be a funeral or a wedding, in the middle of the week like that. So Mamma says, let's go in and rest our feet and see what is going on. It was the first wedding I ever saw. Only it wasn't much of a wedding. No flowers or pretty dresses or anything."

"Cassie! Stop prattling and tell me who it was!"

"Gee, I guess I can't remember their names."

"Tell me what they look like."

"Well, the man was real old . . . and had a wooden leg, and he had white whiskers under his chin and—"

"Cliff Sutler!"

"Yes, that's it!"

"Good heavens! Who in the world did he marry?"

"The woman was old, too . . . but not nearly as old as he was. And sort of stiff looking. She wore an old black dress . . . awful old-fashioned. There were two women that looked almost alike, and it was the youngest and happiest one that got married."

"Two sisters? Surely not . . . not the Wilbe girls!"

"Oh, they weren't girls! They were real old."

"I know, but everyone called them the Wilbe girls back in Boston. They were spinsters, the last of a very fine old Boston family. Extremely refined and well-educated."

"Yes, those were the ones. They are old maids, all right!"

Unbelievable! Cliff Sutler, the crippled, weatherbeaten man of the sea who had not known a woman's love for half a century! And the Wilbe girls, reared in the cloistered seclusion of a Boston mansion!

"Which one did he marry?"

"The nicest one."

"Well," Gale laughed, "I thought they were about the same. Was it Deborah, or Agnes?"

"Let's see . . ." Cassie's brow furrowed in concentration. "After the wedding, the bride put her arms around the other one and says, 'Aggie, you don't mind, do you?' But the one called Aggie just looked down her nose and didn't say nothing, so the married one says, 'Aggie, what would Father say?' And Aggie says, sort of hard like, 'You've done it. Now make the best of it.' "

Gale laughed at the picture the girl painted of this unlikely wedding. She put the embroidered pillow shams over the pillows and Cassie walked out.

"I'm going to wash your dishes now," she announced over her shoulder.

"No, Cassie, please don't!" Gale called after her. "I have some good cups in the pan I want to be especially careful of."

At that moment there was a deafening crash from the kitchen. Gale rushed in to find Cassie standing stunned in the center of the room, an empty dishpan at her feet, and fragments of china dotting the spreading circle of water on the floor. The ragged strand of Gale's patience broke.

"Go home!" Her voice was shaking with anger.

That was all she said, but it was enough. Cassie turned and fled.

Seven

"Gale, would you like to walk up the hill and look at the Temple?" It was a warm dusk in September and the Simons had just finished their supper.

"Oh, yes!" Delight sparkled in her dark eyes. "But I thought only the workmen could enter."

"The Apostles passed that ordinance in order to preserve the sanctity of the Temple, but I don't think they would object to your going in after hours, since it isn't quite complete yet. Jock and I have been working on cabinet fittings and I have the keys with me. Shall we go?"

"Oh, I'd love to!"

Their walk carried them across town and up the street that climbed the gentle slope of the hill. Above them the cool white spires of the Temple shone against the deepening sky and caught the last of the western light.

A tall gangling figure in uniform lumbered toward them out of the dusk, a musket swinging awkwardly from his hand. They recognized Bub Leary, the youth who had driven their hack the day they arrived.

"Good evening, Bub."

"Oh, hullo Brother Simon!" Gale liked his drawling Louisiana accent.

"Are you enrolled in the Legion?"

"Yessuh. I bin in sence last spring, when the mobs began molestin' folks round hyah."

"Do you like being a soldier?" Gale said to make polite conversation.

"I don't know rightly. We ain't done nothin' yet."

Edouard chuckled at the disappointment in Bub's voice. "Do you want to declare war?" Edouard asked.

"Yessuh, I think I'd like to." He became suddenly self-conscious and began polishing the butt of his gun. "Reckon I'd best be on my way. Colonel won't like it if I'm late."

"Are you going to drill?" Gale asked.

"No ma'am. I'm on guard duty at the edge of town."

"Guard duty?"

"Yes ma'am. We got guards posted all around town."

"Why?" Alarm rang in her voice. "Is there . . . danger?"

"Well . . . we jest want to keep the mobs from comin' in and pilferin'." The gentle drawl in his words was reassuring. "Ain't nothin', really."

They left him and walked up the hill, but Gale's heart was beating harder than it had been. As they reached the top of the hill in full view of the Temple they stopped involuntarily, drinking in the sudden beauty of the white shrine. Behind it, the blue of the sky was deepening to black, spiked by early stars. The light from the west seemed to light a phosphorescence within the limestone itself, giving it an unearthly glow. Across the front of the building column after column of white stone marched in perfect rhythm.

Edouard unlocked the great doors and they swung open with a wild echo. Inside the blackness

50

was intense. He searched for a flare while the great emptiness echoed his breathing, his footsteps, the rustle of his clothing. His steps faded out and he was gone. She stood very still, feeling that her slightest breath would be magnified a thousand times and broadcast to a listening God.

A torch flashed at the far end of the great room and he came toward her, his steps ringing to the ceiling. The tall pointed windows caught the reflected light of the torch. Gale's heart swelled and her throat was tight. Here was history, beauty, eternity in the making! She was seeing the birth of a great faith and its shrine, a cathedral that would be the tangible emblem of the new religion down through the centuries! She turned a little away as he approached, so that he would not see the tears running down her cheeks.

"We are trying to finish it by the end of the year, but there is still so much to be done," his voice echoed.

"So . . . beautiful!" Her whisper echoed the length of the room.

"I want you to see the baptismal font in the basement. We've had goldsmiths from Philadelphia working on it for a month now. Come."

Downstairs the flare picked out the shadows of seats rising in four tiers down two sides of the room. At each end of the room was a space prominently empty, awaiting the altars.

As Edouard led the circle of light further into the room, the baptismal font raised out of the darkness in a blaze of gold. Gale caught her breath. The great tank was paneled with religious paintings, rich in purples and blues and reds. It was supported by twelve oxen, beautifully carved and overlaid with

51

gold. The light from the torch glittered in little points of flame from the tips of the carved horns.

"Oh, Edouard . . . it's magnificent! I had no idea! Why didn't you tell me? I had no idea there was anything this gorgeous in Nauvoo . . . !"

They stood in silence, looking, and the only sound was their breathing and the tiny crackle of the flame. When he spoke there was pride in his voice.

"Our people have done well. Nearly a million dollars this Temple is costing, and every penny comes from the thin purses of the Saints. If that isn't faith, surely there is no such thing on earth."

Gale found it hard to go to sleep. Edouard breathed heavily at her side, deep in slumber. His arm was flung across her breast, his fingers cradled in her warm hand. A late moon had risen, lighting the room and the world outside with a soft radiance. The river lapped tenderly at the roots of the willow.

A strange sound aroused her. Her eyes opened and she wondered if she had dreamed it. Again came the sound, the rustling of bodies, moving swiftly. There was the grating of a boat against the riverbank behind the house, and then feet in the grass. Her heart jerked and stopped, then pounded in her throat with violence. She lay frozen. Memory of the mobs roared over her. Burnings . . . floggings . . . tar and feathers . . . murder . . . rape!

"Edouard! Edouard!" But it was only her mind screaming at him, for no sound would come from her lips. She lay, a terrible stone, unable to move. Then came discreetly subdued pounding on the door, bursting like a bombshell through the silent house. She sprang up, her fingers digging into his shoulder, jerking him awake.

"Edouard! It's the mobs . . . from the river!

They're at the door!" she whispered. "But they won't get us! I'll kill myself first!" Cold madness was in her words.

The pounding began again, sharper, more insistent. Then came the thin wail of a tiny baby. A baby! Thoughts struggled up through the terror, trying to rearrange themselves to make sense. A baby! Mobs wouldn't be coming to the door with a baby.

Edouard stood close to her in his nightshirt, his eyes still blind with sleep. Instinctively he put his arm around her shaking shoulders.

A man's voice, low and intense, came through the door.

"For heaven's sake, let us in! Can you hear me? Let us in, before they get us! I'm Olaf Pederson . . . from up river. Let us in!"

In an instant Edouard was at the door and Gale was pulling a wrapper over her gown. A family stood framed in the square of moonlight. Pederson was in the center of the group, a blond giant whose nightshirt came barely to his knees. On his shoulder he carried a small child, and with his other arm he endeavored to support the fainting form of a young woman, whose head dangled on her breast like a broken flower. An older woman carried the bundle of a baby. Several small children cowered against the legs of their elders. All shivered in their nightclothes, their bare toes curled tight against the chill.

They crowded into the kitchen. Edouard hung blankets over the window before he lighted a candle. The children sobbed quietly, but their hysteria began to mount as Edouard had trouble with the candle.

"Oh Lord save us, she's fainted!" cried the older woman as the young mother slid into a lifeless heap on the floor. The children wailed aloud.

"Listen to me!" Edouard stifled the hubbub,

53

speaking directly to the children. "Do you want them to find you? Can you be quiet?" After that there was only an occasional quiet sob or a sniffle.

He turned swiftly to Pederson. "Your boat. Where is it?"

Pederson lifted impatient eyes from where he knelt on the floor.

"What do I care about my boat? Can't you see Hulda is dying? Can't you help me with her?"

"Where is your boat?" Edouard repeated sternly. "Did you leave it fastened to the bank? Do you want to leave it there as an invitation to the mobs?"

The other got slowly to his feet. "I guess you're right. I tied it to the willow. We'd better haul it up on the bank if we can handle it."

"No! We'll cut it loose and let it float down the current."

"Cut it loose!" The man was angry. "That is my boat! It cost me good money! I need it!"

"You need your life more! You're not safe, even here in the city! We have no time to lose!" He slipped out the door, a knife in his hand. A moment later he was back, his face grim. "It's done."

The baby began to cry again, and the older woman bounced it to hush it as she bent over to peer at the white face on the floor.

"If this doesn't finish her, nothing will." There was no softness in her voice. "This baby a day old, and its mother running out in the night without clothes."

"She almost died when the baby was born," Pederson spoke with stiff lips.

"She'll not live to see snow fall," Sister spoke with an air of clipped finality.

"Take her in to our bed," Gale's voice was soft and firm. "Watch . . . you're letting her head drop.

Now you men go in the kitchen and keep the children warm."

Dawn was creeping in around the blankets at the windows when Gale and Sister Pederson came quietly into the kitchen, closing the bedroom door. Gale's lips formed the word, "Asleep," and managed an encouraging smile for the anxious husband.

"I don't rightly know how we're going to thank you for everything you've done tonight," the Swede paced about the room with bare feet. He had donned a pair of his host's trousers and a shirt, both much too small for his gigantic frame, but Edouard's shoes had proved adequate.

"It's no more than you'd have done for us, or any of the Saints in a like situation." Edouard sat with folded arms, his eyes absently staring at a knothole in the floor. He raised his head. "After breakfast we'll go down to the Relief Society and get each of you an outfit of clothes. Do you suppose you'll find anything back home?"

"Home!" The man's snort was bitter. "There isn't any home now. We looked back and saw the whole place in flames. Fire was shooting out of the kitchen and bedroom windows . . . and the stack of grain . . . the one I just finished putting up last night, was going up like a bonfire. The barn too . . . we could hear the horses and the cows bellowing for a mile!"

Everyone was transfixed by a blood-curdling scream from the bedroom, a scream which rose and fell in hysteria.

"Oo-o-o-oh . . . don't let them get my baby!" The cry died in a moan.

They rushed to the young woman's bed. She was sitting up, rocking from side to side, her head rolling. Pederson stood with clenched fists, his face gray.

"The bedeviled mobbers! I'll kill every one of them, if I have to do it with my bare hands!"

Edouard put a firm hand on his shoulder.

"It would do no good. Even if you could find who it was . . . and you probably couldn't . . . they would have a real weapon against you then . . . a legal weapon in the hands of the law. You'd hang for it, as surely as you stand there. And then where would your children be? Alone and unprotected, at a time they need you most. No, Brother . . . forget it."

"Forget it? And Hulda dying?" Rage blazed in his eyes.

"Not forget it, perhaps. But we must turn our eyes to the future, and not torment ourselves with the horrors of the past."

"This isn't past, Brother! This is now!"

"I know, but we must keep our eyes ahead. That is our only hope."

"What future is there for a man lashed from all sides . . . no place to turn . . . no place of safety . . . everything he owns in the world gone up in smoke!"

"There is still our faith, and that's a great deal." Edouard spoke quietly. "God will show us the way."

Hulda Peterson died just as the sun was tipping the spires of the Temple, lighting them like a torch . . . a beacon.

Eight

Even the cheerful stoicism of the Saints began to fail. At last they came to realize that the threats of the people of Illinois were in deadly earnest. Depredations in lower Hancock County were becoming daily occurences, and stories of terrorism were spreading through the city with the arrival of refugees. Work in the city was slowing down as more and more volunteered to take their wagons out into the stricken countryside to collect the frightened Saints and their few belongings that they had managed to retain as they fled from the mobs to hide in willow thickets and brush piles. Day by day they poured into the city, hungry and dirty and haunted with a fear nearing madness.

Some wore stale blood-crusted bandages about their bullet wounds, others were weird scarecrows of black tar, their eyeballs rolling white in their sockets, their hair a matted mass, makeshift garments plastered to their bodies. Others rode into the city, standing up in the backs of the wagons because the lash strokes across their buttocks would not allow them to sit. Some were naked from the waist up because they could not bear a shirt on their mangled backs, where the flesh lay in raw furrows with fresh blood oozing up in the wounds.

Many women and girls rode with their heads bent

in shame and their teeth biting their lips to hold back their sobs, for in their burning eyes was the intimate knowledge of carnal violence. Their hands were clenched white and they rode tense to avoid the jolting of the wagons.

Children arrived, many of them separated from parents, peering into the faces of strangers for someone they might know. Their faces were dirty, with tear-trails down their cheeks. Their bellies were empty and they suffered from colds and exposure.

The reserves of the Nauvoo Legion were called to the colors, and the officers began drilling their men full-time. The guard about the city was doubled, and the parade grounds in the north end of town echoed to the sharp call of military commands.

Edouard came home early from work one day to tell Gale that he had been called. As Gale hurried about the kitchen, making sandwiches of cold roast beef, and pouring a cup of river-cooled buttermilk, a worried frown creased her brow. Edouard seemed almost gay, and it was this strange gaiety that worried her. It was worse than the silent grimness that he had worn since the night with the Pedersons three weeks ago.

"Your lunch is ready."

He sat at the table and began to eat in haste. She watched him with uneasiness gnawing her. Her fingers plucked at her collar. Finally she summoned the courage to speak.

"Does this mean . . . we are going to fight?"

"I don't know," he shook his head, "but four thousand armed men who are well-trained should be of some use."

Her head hummed with unasked questions, but she found it hard to find the right words. She had fallen into the habit of not speaking of things she did not want to believe were true. She refilled his cup with buttermilk.

But she had to ask it. "Do you *want* to fight?"

"We've been turning the other cheek. It hasn't worked."

"You seem almost happy."

"At last we are acting like men!"

"When do you get your uniform?"

"I don't get one. They ran out of uniforms long ago. But I can shoot without one." He pressed a hard kiss on her lips and hurried away, his eyes bright.

After she had cleared the table and washed the dishes, she caught up a bonnet and went up the street to the Meiers', always a substantial haven of peace and pulsing life. She found Sister Meier in the kitchen, her knitting needles clicking through a drift of white yarn. Cassie lay on the floor in a patch of late afternoon sunshine, playing with a fluffy gray kitten, trying to protect it from the attentions of two-year-old Willie, who was poking at the cat partly for his own amusement, and partly to attract his sister's attention.

They all looked up with welcoming smiles when Gale came to the door. Cassie sat up, looking almost pretty with the sun on her hair. The affair of the broken dishes had been patched up, and she was once more Gale's adoring follower.

"Come in, come in!" called Sister Meier. "Take off der bonnet und ve vill have a cup of herb tea und a cruller. Cassie child, fetch Sister Gale a cup from out der cupboard, und fill us up a plate mit crullers from der crock. Now vatch vat you do, und don't be spilling sugar on der floor!" Uneasily she watched the girl's disorganized preparations. "*Ja*,

59

ja. Dot plate is right. It does not make der difference as long as it holds der crullers!"

Willie, left with the kitten at his disposal, seized it by the tail and set out for the pantry amid wild meowing. Cassie was on him instantly, her gray eyes flashing. She snatched the cat and gave Willie a resounding whack on the head. Crooning, she held the kitten under her chin, while the small boy shrieked in rage.

Sister Meier never missed a stitch, but shook her head.

"It don't help to talk, times like this. Der kids get mad und get over it quick. Cassie, drop der cat und fetch der tea. Step, now!"

"Are you making something for the baby?" Gale looked at the soft wool in the woman's lap.

"*Ja*. Iss a shawl for cold vinter. I begin early, but I have so much things to make. Villie there, he vas a holy fright. He vear out everything, he not lay still von minute. So I must start over again, like dis iss der first."

Gale caressed the soft wool. Her eyes showed her longing. The other saw it and laughed.

"Don't fret, child. In von year, you vill be knitting a shawl also. Der first baby it iss hard to get sometimes, but after dot, dey come easy."

When Gale got up to go, she had pushed the thought of the refugees, the mobs, and the Legion to the back of her mind.

"Maybe I'll unravel Edouard's sock," she laughed, "and bring the yarn over tomorrow so you can teach me that stitch. Good-bye."

As she left, she paused to thrust her head in the door of Sophie's little cottage. The young wife appeared, a glass of milk in one hand and a piece of

60

cake in the other. She wore a rather mussed wrapper, and her face was pale and puffy.

"I'm eating early, because I'm alone tonight." Her voice carried mingled apology and resentment. "Jock is staying with his *hausfrau*." The German word sounded sour on her tongue.

"How are you feeling?" Gale asked cheerfully.

Sophie made a grimace. "Not very good. Take my advice and never have a baby."

"Oh, Sophie, don't say that! You'll love it! You know you will!"

"Forget it," Sophie said, as she shrugged and laughed. "Come on in and eat supper with me. I hate to eat alone."

"Thanks, but I don't know when Edouard will be back, and I want to have something waiting for him on the fire."

"Love!" Sophie spoke, laughing again, more with envy than with scorn. "It must be nice to marry for love instead of a home. You're lucky."

"I must hurry home before my fire goes out. Come down and see me some afternoon."

"Yeah," Sophie said, "some night when my husband is out with his wife."

Edouard returned late, and they sat in the kitchen. He was talkative, his face flushed with excitement.

"We're going to fight for our lives now! With our people being driven from their homes every day, we have all the grounds necessary for military resistance. And our army, with guns in their hands . . . Well, I'm afraid Brigham Young had better give the orders to march . . . or nothing in the world will stop us!"

Her stomach lurched. She was frightened by his unwonted anger.

"But what can you do? Who would you fight?"

"Young says we *can't* fight . . . can't go out and declare war against the state of Illinois. He knows Governor Ford is against us and as soon as we present armed resistance, he'll call out the state militia. That's why Young is trying to hold our men back, stalling for time, trying to find some solution. It's bound to come to a show-down soon, for we can't go on like this!"

"Will you have to go away?"

"The sole purpose of the Nauvoo Legion at the moment is to prevent mobs from marching into the city."

Gale shuddered.

"Let's not talk any more about mobs . . . and fighting . . . and war. Let's go to bed." She began pulling the pins from her hair, letting it fall over her shoulders.

"The candle is burning out," he spoke tonelessly, watching the flame cut away the wax.

They were startled by swift running feet at the front of the house, and a wild pounding and jerking at the door. Edouard sprang to his feet. "Who's there?"

The door handle shook violently, and the answer came, almost unintelligible. "It's me . . . it's me . . . oh, let me in quick!"

Gale jumped up. "It's Cassie! Let her in! Something must have happened . . . !"

He opened the door, and the girl outside almost fell into his arms. Her face was ghastly with fear. He slammed and bolted the door behind her, and they led her to a chair. She was almost naked, her flimsy nightgown ripped from her back and hanging from her neck in shreds.

Gale snatched a quilt from the bed and wrapped it around her. The girl crouched in the chair, her sobs coming in convulsive gasps. Her hair was wild about her face.

"Now, now . . ." Gale knelt and took the child's hands, her voice gentle, "Cassie . . . Cassie . . . you're all right now. You're safe . . . you're all right."

Again the girl lost control in wild sobbing. Edouard caught her by the shoulder. He shook her, tenderly at first, then roughly.

"Cassie, be quiet!"

She pulled away and stared up at him in horror, as though she had never seen him before. But her hysteria was silenced, and there was only the sound of her small quivering breaths, like those of a trapped animal. Looking into her wide empty eyes, they couldn't be sure if she was sane or not.

"Cassie, see if you can tell us what happened." Edouard's voice was deep and calm. "We have to know."

She stared at him for a long blank interval. At last her story came, in broken fragments.

"Mamma . . . they pushed her . . . I saw her, trying to swim . . . and oh . . . she's gone. She doesn't know how to swim . . ."

"Who pushed her, Cassie?" he insisted.

"The men. They came to get Papa. We were in bed . . . I was asleep . . . and Mamma woke me up and told me to hide, quick . . . and then they were coming in . . . and swearing terrible . . . saying they would teach the Saints a lesson." She stopped and shivered. "They saw me climbing out the win-

63

dow. They said, 'There goes a girl. Don't let her get away.' "

"Did they hurt you, Cassie?" Gale asked tenderly.

Again the words were broken into sobs, as she shook her head, "No." The candle, devoured, flickered and went out.

"Poor Mamma . . . she's afraid of the water . . ."

Edouard was at the door, unbolting it.

"I have to go, Gale, to see if I can help. I have the gun. Lock the door behind me. And don't light a candle."

"Oh no! Don't go!" Gale cried, but he was already gone. She bolted the door.

Cassie was weeping quietly. Gale led her into the bedroom and tucked her under the covers. Sitting on the side of the bed, she held her hand gently. Then she noticed a bright glow at the north window, and knew the Meiers' house must be on fire. She put her hands over Cassie's eyelids and began stroking them gently.

"Go to sleep, Cassie," she said, but her own heart was pounding as though it would strangle her. Don't let anything happen to Edouard, she prayed.

She heard distant shouts, and running feet, and doors slamming, and she knew neighbors must be helping to fight the flames. To mask the sounds from Cassie's ears, she began talking softly, aimlessly . . . of her own childhood, of Boston, of the Muldoons, of the trip west.

It was almost morning when Edouard returned and called softly at the door. Cassie was sleeping fitfully, moaning and crying aloud. Gale let him in and they closed the bedroom door. He got a fresh candle from the cupboard and lighted it. His face was black with soot, the tips of his lashes and brows burned off. She threw her arms around him, caressing his blackened face. "Thank God, you're safe!"

"Yes, *I'm* all right!" There was such violence in him that she shrank back. "I am fine! The Saints are fine! The world is fine!" He fell exhausted in a chair. His rage was more than he could express. "What is all this driving us to?"

She stroked his singed hair. She felt her childhood slipping from her, with its fear of the adult world and its shrinking from responsibility. Soothing Edouard's hopelessness, she felt womanhood surging up within her. 'I must be strong,' she thought. 'He is terribly afraid, like a little boy, afraid of the future. But I must be a woman, and keep us going. I can't risk looking ahead. I must look only at tonight and keep us going. I must be strong for both of us.'

"How are things at the Meiers'?" she asked. "Was there anything you could do?"

"No. Nothing." She left him sitting in the chair, his head sunk in his hands, and went to stir up the coals in the fireplace. He went on, "When I got there, the whole place was in flames. I yelled to rouse the neighbors and then went in to see if anyone was there . . . afraid someone might be caught in the fire." He stopped.

She brought a cloth and warm water and began sponging his face. He flinched, and as she washed the soot away, she uncovered an angry burn across his cheek.

"Did you find anyone?"

"Yes. Yes. I found Jock . . . in the kitchen . . . his throat cut like . . . like a butchered hog . . . and blood . . . blood . . ." He stopped again, and was silent a long time, unconscious of Gale's ministrations. "I tried to pull him out . . . but something caved in . . . some burning timber . . . knocked me

65

out . . . and after I came to, they wouldn't let me go back in. Poor Jock . . . only this morning . . . we were working on the altar . . . and he told me a joke . . . something about a river pilot . . . he laughed, thought it was very funny. Jock. Poor Jock. No, Jock, I guess you're not so bad off at that. You no longer have to worry about what we are all going to do!"

At another time she would have been frightened by the strangeness in his tone, by the wildness in his eyes, but now she only patted his face dry, and put grease on the burn.

"What about Sister Meier, and Sophie, and the children? Where are they?"

He brought his eyes to focus on her, surprised that anyone should be talking sensibly. She smiled at him. He began to relax, and when he answered her, his voice was almost normal.

"Sister Meier . . . I guess Cassie was right, about her being in the river. We couldn't find a trace of her."

"And Sophie?"

"She's all right. They didn't even touch her door . . . didn't think anyone lived there, I guess. She didn't even wake up until we started throwing water on the house. I think she fainted when they told her, but there were so many women there then, I don't know."

"And the children. Did they harm the children?"

"No, Sister Meier had told them to hide . . . and hide they did . . . in the bushes and willows. When they saw we were the neighbors, they began coming out, one by one. Even little Willie had kept as quiet as a mouse, even though his legs were terribly scratched by rose thorns."

"Poor baby. Only this afternoon . . . he was teasing Cassie's kitten. Where are the children?"

"Neighbors took them in. They were cold . . ." They sat in silence a long while.

Cassie's moaning from the next room aroused them.

"Mamma!" she cried.

"I must go to her." Gale rose.

"Stay with her. Bring me a quilt and I'll lie here by the fire!"

"Mamma!" Cassie screamed. "Mamma!"

Gale went to her bed. From that night on, Gale was to know what it meant to be a Saint, and a woman.

Nine

On October first Edouard, Isaac Eldridge, Brigham
Young, Wilson Woodruff, and other leaders of the
church, set out on horseback for Carthage, where
the citizens of Illinois had called a meeting. Since
Jock's death, Edouard had been given more and
more responsibility in the decisions of the church,
despite his youth.

With mingled pride and fear Gale stood on the
street corner among the crowd with Cassie at her
side and watched them ride away. He looked so
young among the time-stiffened men who rode with
him. Brigham Young rode well, his shoulders broad
enough to conceal his great bulk. Isaac Eldridge was
the only man among them who still retained the
grace of youth. He sat easily in his saddle and was,
as usual, handsome in gleaming boots and broadcloth riding coat. Gale would have thought him as
young as Edouard, had it not been for his graying
hair and the hard lines appearing in his face.

But her pride soon strangled and died in an en-
gulfing sense of disaster. She remembered those
others, Joseph Smith, Hyrum Smith, John Taylor,
and Willard Richards, who had ridden to Carthage a
year ago. They had been carried home, two of them
corpses, the others bleeding. Oh, God, why do You

let them do these things to us? Please God, let Edouard come home safe!

Her hand reached for Cassie, who was standing close beside her, and the two of them pushed their way out of the crowd that had gathered to see the men off. The Saints knew that the situation could not continue, and they were sending their leaders off with prayer for a solution.

Gale swallowed her tears to conceal them from the noisy crowd. A hand plucked her sleeve, and a voice croaked in her ear.

"Howdy, Miz Gale!"

She turned and recognized the weatherbeaten face of Cliff Sutler, fringed with its white chin-whiskers and bushy brows. He was beaming like a boy, his blue eyes twinkling.

"How be ye, Miz Gale? I ain't seen ye since the *Fulton City* docked way last July!"

"Oh, Mr. Sutler! Good morning!"

"I jest now seen yer husband ridin' off with the big moguls. I bet yer nigh to bustin' with pride."

Gale was glad that he didn't wait for an answer. It gave her time to regain her composure and blink the tears from her eyes.

"Here, here! Ye ain't met my wife yet, have ye?" He turned to the thin, black-clad Deborah, standing behind him. "Miz Simon, I'd be pleased to make you acquainted with my new wife, Debby!"

Gale startled herself by laughing. Cliff, blooming with the pride of a young bridegroom, pulled the flushed middle-aged woman from behind him. Gale thought she didn't look as thin as she used to, and seemed almost happy.

"Congratulations, Sister Sutler!" Gale kissed her withered cheek.

Debby seemed flustered, and turned to draw her

elder sister from the throng at Cliff's back. Nudging her husband, she gave him a meaning look and then dropped her eyes to the ground. Agnes stood, stiff and faded and remote. Cliff cast a cautious look around him, then hobbled a step nearer and spoke in Gale's ear in an undertone.

"This here is Aggie, my second wife!"

Gale was stunned, staring from one to another.

"I know I ain't supposed to let it out, but I guess Debby wants me to tell you, seein's yer from Boston too, and an old friend." He gave a short laugh. "A year ago I didn't put much stock in marryin' one woman, leave alone two! But seein's it's the custom hereabouts, it jest seemed to work out that way. I couldn't seem to he'p myself, and it did seem best for the girls, alone like they was."

Gale stared from one sister to the other. Debby tried to stifle her happiness, for this was the first time in her forty-odd years that she had ever held any advantage over Aggie, and the privilege did not rest comfortably on her. Agnes was openly resentful, but apparently not resentful enough to refuse an offer of marriage.

"I'm glad." Gale seized a hand of each. "Glad for all of you! Women need menfolk out here."

"Thank you, Sister Simon," Agnes spoke with her usual dignity. "We shall be pleased to have you call on us for tea some afternoon from two until five. We are living, temporarily, in the back rooms of the big brown house just three blocks west of the porcelain factory. It's the big house on the corner."

"Thank you," Gale bowed with ceremony. "I shall be delighted."

She recalled Cassie, standing mutely at her side. She put her arm around the child's shoulders and drew her close.

71

"This is Cassie Meier, a neighbor who is staying with us for a while. She's the first one to tell me of your wedding. Remember, Cassie?"

The girl nodded slightly, her face expressionless.

"Well, girls," he said, tucking his wives' hands beneath his elbows, "It looks like the show is over. Wouldn't be surprised but what we'd better lift anchor and set sail for home. What say ye, mateys?"

"Sutler!" Agnes frowned, but seemed somehow pleased. "Do you have to address us in such rough language?"

"Yep. Them's the words I know, and I'm too old to start learnin' highfalutin' talk now. Well, let's set our sterns to the wind and make fer port. Glad to of seen ye, Miz Gale, and yer little friend." He stared curiously into Cassie's unresponsive face. "Bring her along when ye come over to gab, iffen she's a friend of yours. And come over anytime. I don't know why Aggie said we're home from two till five. We're home all the time, day and night, lessen I take a walk down to the wharf fer a look around, or the girls go out fer a spell of shoppin'."

Gale watched them go, an odd trio, Cliff and his two wives. Cliff, from the waterfront, and the ladies from the mansion on the hill.

Late that night Gale heard a step on the path. She ran to the door and drew the bolt. For a brief instant she thought, "What if it's someone else?" But she knew.

"Oh my darling!" She threw her arms around him. "You're back! Thank God . . . you're safe!"

He pushed past her and went to the blazing fire on the hearth. The night was bitterly cold, and he held out his hands to the heat. His face was haggard. She helped him off with his coat, talking softly.

"I knew you'd be cold when you got home, so I kept up a big fire. Isn't it nice?"

He did not speak.

"Your coat is wet. Is it raining?"

He turned his hands to the blaze but did not speak.

"It's so cold, is it beginning to snow?"

Silence. Cassie, huddled in a corner near the fire, stirred and whimpered in her sleep. He turned to her for a moment, then back to the fire.

"Edouard!" She put a soft hand on his sleeve.

He looked at her, a strange look of defeat in his face. Cassie uttered a sleeping cry. "Why isn't she in bed?"

"I tried to get her to go, but she's afraid."

He turned back to the fireplace.

"Dearest . . ." she whispered, "how was it?"

When he finally spoke it was with an effort.

"We are leaving Nauvoo."

She stared at him. "Leaving Nauvoo? You and I?"

"You and I . . . and all the other Saints. We're all leaving . . . as soon as possible."

"All of us . . . leaving? Where are we going?"

Edouard shrugged. "I don't know."

"But . . . how can we? We can't just pack up and move out of our homes, with no place to go. Why . . . winter is amost here!"

"We can . . . because we have to."

"So!" There was a flash of anger in her words. "That's what your meeting led to! Brigham Young sits by and agrees to have this people herded out into the winter without a roof to cover our heads . . . thousands of us!"

73

"Brigham Young can't do anything about it. It has gone beyond human power to stop, now." A sigh escaped him.

She was instantly contrite, and pulling a rocking chair close to the fire, she motioned him toward it.

"Your supper is hot. I'll fix your plate, and you can eat while you're getting warm." She lifted the lid from the iron pot, and the aroma of beef stew rose in the air. "Who tells us we must leave?"

"Senator Stephen Douglas seemed to be the spokesman of the meeting today. But he was backed by General Harding, Commander of the State Militia, and Attorney General McDougal, and Major Warren. But it wasn't just these men who told us what to do. They had a petition signed by thousands of citizens of Illinois, which said we'd have to promise to leave the state immediately. General Harding tried to be decent about it, and said he'd keep his troops on duty from now on, but that he couldn't hope to protect us very long from the growing mobs unless we'd promise to leave right away. We told them we couldn't . . . with winter coming on . . . and no preparations made for such a move. We tried to tell them how it would be . . . thousands of people wandering about without homes or food. But it was no use. They had this petition . . . and said we'd have to agree to it, or they couldn't answer for the consequences. They were all polite enough."

"Do we leave . . . everything?" Her voice was unsteady.

"We can't take much. We can try to sell what we can't take . . . but we won't have much luck, I'm afraid. Those who want to drive us out like cattle won't be generous enough to pay us for what they can take anyway after we leave."

"What a ghastly thing to ask people to do!"

She looked around the room, at the firelight gleaming on the dark wood of her father's desk, at the polished table with its bowl of fall apples. She saw them as she had seen them as a child, in the high dim rooms of the old home back in New England. She saw her father writing at the desk, and bending his gray head in grace at the head of the table. She looked at the mirror, and remembered it reflecting her mother's face.

"Why can't we barricade the city? Surely . . . with four thousand soldiers . . . they could protect us!"

"We can't do that without making war against the government. Anyway, we couldn't last long. We'd run out of food and ammunition in no time . . . and then we'd be cornered like rats. No, it's better to get out . . . and make a home somewhere in the wilderness, than to be exterminated."

The fire popped, and he ate half-heartedly. Gale sat at his feet watching him. "When do we leave?" she asked.

"We're not sure, but just as soon as we can get enough horses, oxen, wagons together. We were talking tonight about what each family needs to start the journey. Young thinks we should have a wagon, three yoke of oxen, two cows, two beef cattle, three sheep, besides a thousand pounds of flour, twenty pounds of sugar, a rifle and ammunition. Then we'll need farming implements and seed."

"But where could we get it?"

"It's impossible, of course."

"How could we pay for it?"

"All that would be ideal, if we are setting out to build up a new land. But Young is a bit of an idealist. I don't see how it is possible."

75

She took his plate and refilled his cup. The fire was bright on her hair, but her eyes were somber.

"Brigham said something tonight about heading West, maybe for Oregon . . . or California. No one seems to know just how far it is, or what kind of a country it would be when we get there. But we must find a place outside the United States, some place we can call our own. Some place where we can have the freedom to worship in our own way!"

Gale looked up suddenly, fresh pain in her eyes.

"Edouard! The Temple!"

"What about it?"

"We'll have to leave it to those . . . those beasts! And it's not yet finished . . ."

"I know. We spoke of that on the ride home. But we're going to start performing ordinances in it anyway, as soon as we can get it into rough shape. Brother Young wants everyone to receive their blessings and ordinances before we set out. You'll want to, of course."

Gale nodded. Cassie's gray kitten, the only remnant of her old life, arose meowing from its pillow near the fire and arched its back in a long stretch. It jumped into Cassie's lap, and she awoke with a cry. She stared at it, then at Gale and Edouard. The fear subsided and she sank back, her eyes closed.

"We'd better go to bed." Edouard arose. "Tomorrow will be a difficult day. From now on there will be hard work for all of us."

"I'll make Cassie's bed here close to the fire. It's turned so cold!"

"We'll have to get used to the cold." His words were grim. "Good night, Cassie."

Ten

News of the edict to leave Nauvoo burst like a bomb over the troubled city. The Saints had expected almost anything as a result of the meeting in Carthage, anything but this. Leave their homes? Leave Nauvoo, leave Illinois? Set out into the wilderness, everyone, women and babies, the sick and the old, set out in the middle of winter, heading for God only knows where? The leaders must be crazy! We *can't* do it! We *won't* do it! We'll stay and fight first! We'll not be kicked out of our homes! We'll show them we'll not be herded around like damned cattle! Let them try to make us leave Nauvoo!

And then came the bitter realization that it was not the decision of the leaders alone. It was a terrible something, greater than leaders, or men, or governments. It had driven them from Ohio, and from Missouri, and was now to drive them from Illinois. It was mob hysteria—fear of the unknown —fear of a strange religion threatening the blind security of the familiar.

This was not unique in history, they reminded themselves. The world had seen it at work in Rome with early Christians being thrown into pits with lions—in Spain during the Inquisition when Protestants were tormented and dismembered—in Salem at the time of the witch hunts when innocent women were hanged or burned. It could make fiends of Christians and send them terrorizing and murdering and torturing their victims.

The helpless Saints watched the refugees flocking into Nauvoo and knew that their leaders were right. It was the only thing left to do. There was the little girl who died of nervous shock, shortly after they had brought her into the city from a distant settlement which had been raided. And there was the fellow named Daniel Banning, who was tossing about on his face at the Jenkinses' home, moaning in delirium, his back a mass of infection, a result of the mob's lashes. Yes, things cannot go on like this. We'll have to get out. It's a terrible thing to ask of us, but it must be done.

Overnight the city became a vast humming workhouse. The people organized themselves into companies—hundreds, fifties, and tens—with commanders, and each had its wagon shop, wheelwrights, carpenters, and cabinetmakers. Perhaps the busiest of all were the blacksmiths, whose anvils could be heard ringing day and night, for theirs was the task of forming thousands of iron parts needed for the wagons, making shoes for the animals, and shoeing both horses and oxen.

Those of the men who were not engaged in building wagons were sent out through the countryside to buy up cattle, sheep and horses, and to endeavor to sell or trade property belonging to the Saints.

"You Mormons get out of the country, and do it pretty sudden," one farmer greeted a buyer from Nauvoo, "or we'll give you a taste of the bullwhip! Get clean out of the state, every one of you! But how you go is your own business, and I'd burn in hell before I'll help you! Now get off my place . . . before I blow your backside full of buckshot!"

Fortunately not all the people of Illinois were so hostile, for many of them saw a distinct advantage in exchanging an old team of oxen and a rattletrap wagon for a fine home in the city. But few of them were generous, and the Saints fell far short of the requirements that Brigham Young had asked of them.

Edouard, whose judgment was trusted, was one of those who traveled about the state for a radius of a hundred miles, obtaining animals and trading off farms and city homes. Gale saw little of him. She packed him a lunch and watched him set out in the chill of October dawns, driving the little sorrel mare and buggy which Bub Leary had donated to the cause.

Bub, with rig waiting, often rapped at the Simons' door before the pink had faded from the eastern sky behind the Temple. But Edouard was always ready, with his heavy coat over a chair by the door, and his lunch wrapped in newspaper on top of it.

"Sal's hitched outside for you, Brother Simon," Bub would say, standing awkwardly on the step.

Gale dreaded his voice at the door, for it meant another dangerous day among the Gentiles, and a lonely one for her with the silent Cassie.

One Saturday Bub was a little late, and Edouard stood at the door, watching down the street. Gale put the newspaper wrappings around a hot mince pie, hoping it would still be warm for lunch. Cassie sat at the breakfast table, her pale face a mask. Gale went to the door to stand with Edouard. The air was frosty and she shivered.

"Oh look!" she breathed, as her eyes caught sight of the Temple, its spires sharp as crystal against the dawn.

His arm tightened about her shoulders, and she felt him shiver too. "A thing of loveliness and beauty," his voice was unsteady. "Next year at this time . . . it will be . . . in ashes."

He's afraid, she thought. I mustn't let him be afraid. He's courageous when there's real danger, but it's times like this when he needs me, when he lets fear get at him.

"Let's not think of that. Let's live just in today." She said laughingly. "You used to be the one lecturing me. And now I lecture you!" She kissed him. "Today is going to be a beautiful day! I almost wish I were going with you."

Edouard turned to her eagerly. "Would you? Why don't you?"

"Oh, I couldn't possibly. I have all these apples to finish drying today, and there are a million other things I must do before we leave. I can't spare a moment. There are extra quilts to make for a bed for Cassie, and winter clothing for all of us. And Mr. Grout is expecting the sailcloth in next week, and then I'll have to start working on the tent and the wagon cover. Oh, I really couldn't spare a day, darling . . . although I'd love to!"

A sudden inspiration came to her. "Take Cassie with you! She needs something to bring her out of the doldrums. She hasn't spoken a word for two weeks. But even at that she would be company for you."

"I don't want company." He was annoyed. "I want you."

"I'm really getting worried about her," she whispered. "She eats nothing. She doesn't seem to be trying to forget. I know it's terrible what she's been through . . . but she isn't getting any better. Maybe . . . if you were to take her out in the buggy . . .

80

get her interested in seeing the country . . . anything. I'm really afraid for her."

"Very well. But tell her to hurry. Here comes Bub."

Not even the flurry of hustling her into her wraps shook the apathy from the girl. Gale followed them to the buggy and tucked a robe around her knees, while Bub stood at the horse's head, his eyes riveted to Cassie's white face, smaller than ever under Gale's black bonnet.

"Get in, Bub," Edouard was impatient.

"Thank y'all, but I'll just hop on the back and ride down to Main Street."

Gale watched them ride off into the grayness of the morning. Edouard's face was grim, Cassie's was frightened.

The next day was Sunday. Everyone who was worthy was to receive their endowment in the Temple before leaving Nauvoo. A gray sky pressed low over the city, chilling the wind that tore at the last of the withered leaves and ballooning the skirts of the women as they climbed the hill to the service.

Gale walked between Edouard and Cassie, breathing deeply of the cold air. She felt alive and free with her body released from firm stays which she had worn since her days at Lockwood Hall, where Miss Adams had issued the stern decree that every girl must wear this undergarment if she hoped to be called a lady. She wished she might never have to wear them again. But wishing was vain, for the only excuses a lady had were old age, pregnancy, and baptism by immersion.

No word was spoken, although Cassie's lethargy seemed to have been broken. Yesterday's outing had done its work, for she was now observing with inter-

81

est the crowds who climbed to the Temple. There were shadows beneath her eyes, which made them appear excessively large in her thin face, but today there was a flush in her cheeks and a tilt to her lips that made her almost pretty.

"Now, Gale," Edouard spoke abruptly as they entered the Temple, "I hate to leave you now, but I can't leave the ceremony upstairs. They need me to administer ordinances. Let Cassie hold your cloak, then wrap up well as soon as you come out and go home as fast as you can! It's a bitter day for baptism, so hurry so you won't catch cold. You're not afraid, are you?"

"Afraid? No, I hadn't thought of being afraid."

"I wish I had time to go with you."

An icy wetness brushed her hand, and she jerked away. A woman and her little girl rushed past them toward the exit, the girl crying. Both were dripping, the mother's face dead-white. Looking after them, Gale felt her first tremor of fear.

"Good morning, old man!" Isaac Eldridge was beside them. "Good morning, fair lady! Say, Edouard, aren't you supposed to be upstairs? Brigham has been asking where you were. They are in a terrific rush and need help badly."

"Yes . . ." Edouard looked uncertain. "Gale is to be baptized for the dead, and I thought I should take a few minutes to go down with her."

"Go on upstairs and don't worry. I'm helping down here, so she'll be all right."

"Thank you!" Edouard pressed his friend's hand gratefully and turned back to Gale. "Good luck, dear heart," he whispered.

Downstairs, Gale and Cassie stood in the crowd that moved toward the baptismal font. Eldridge was lost in the throng. One by one the congregation

82

climbed the short flight of steps and were immersed in the cold water, to emerge dripping at the other side. The stone walls echoed the soft splashing of the water and the involuntary gasping of Saints as they were submerged. A dark streaming trail led from the tank and up the stairs as they hurried toward home and dry clothing. There was the plop of wet shoes on cold stone and the constant dripping of water. Gale shivered and drew her cloak tighter around her.

Gale saw a slender black-clad figure forcing her way back through the crowd and recognized Deborah Wilbe Sutler. She seemed wildly intent, searching the faces. When she saw Gale relief shown in her eyes.

"Oh, Sister Simon! You must stop her! You can make her listen, perhaps. Oh, Sister Simon, we can't allow her to do it! It will kill her!"

"Who, Agnes?"

"Yes, yes . . . Oh, do come! Maybe she'll listen to an outsider. In her condition, it will kill her . . . and at her age!"

She fastened her thin hand on Gale's wrist and pulled her through the jostling crowd. Gale wondered at her frantic anxiety. Many older people were emerging from the tank, surviving as well as the younger ones. At the moment a white-haired grandmother emerged from the font, smiling triumphantly.

"Don't worry," Gale told Deborah, her voice soothing. "It won't hurt her any more than these others."

"But you don't understand!" She took a deep breath and whispered close to Gale's ear. "She's . . . expecting!"

Gale couldn't have been more astonished if the stones had opened beneath her feet.

"Not . . . Agnes Wilbe! You must be mistaken. Why, she's too old."

"That's what we thought. But the doctor says it often occurs at this age. She's forty-seven." Her face flushed painfully at the thought of discussing these delicate matters, and worse yet, in public!

Above the crowd Agnes Wilbe Sutler's head and shoulders appeared as she climbed the steps. She stood a moment, looking down into the water, her hand clutching the hand of the elder who was assisting. Her lips were set in grim determination and her eyes blazed with religious zeal. Nothing about her bony figure suggested the secret she carried within her.

"Aggie!" Deborah's voice tried to stop her, but it was too late.

The startled Saints turned toward the cry, so few saw the woman close her eyes and enter the water, closely followed by a little old man with a peg leg. The two of them, dripping, hurried up the stairs toward home, Deborah following.

Gale stood transfixed. Agnes Wilbe, pregnant! Her old body carrying the seed of some future generation! Agnes, a mother! And Cliff Sutler, his hair snowy, his face seamed by the salt of sixty years, a father! What kind of child could possibly come of this strange union?

She was startled back to reality by the discovery that it was her turn to be baptized. She looked around for Cassie, who was nowhere to be seen. She hesitated, searching the sea of faces for Cassie's. Was she lost? Would she have the good sense to go on home? she wondered.

"Aren't you ready?" The Elder asked.

"I can't find Cassie. She was to hold my cloak."

"I'll take it." Isaac Eldridge spoke at the far end of the tank. His long arm reached over and caught it from her. Her breath caught in her throat as the water came up around her legs, her chin, and then she was climbing out the other side, shivering, having performed the sacred ordinance.

She closed her eyes a moment to steady herself. With shaking hands she pushed the hair back from her pale face.

"Are you all right?" Eldridge helped her down and wrapped her cloak around her.

"I should feel holy . . . and uplifted," she tried to smile.

"And you don't?"

"No. I'm just cold . . . and a little dizzy."

"Are you going to be alright?" He put an anxious arm around her.

"Yes, I think so." She shook the water from her lashes.

"But you're so terribly pale."

"Am I? If you see Cassie will you tell her to come on home, please?"

"You're going home alone?"

"Of course." She was surprised at the genuine concern in his face. Heavens, do I look that bad? Maybe I *am* sick!

"I'm going to take you home. I have my buggy hitched out behind the Temple."

"Oh, no! They need you here. I'm quite all right. The walk will warm me up."

"Not on a day like this, it won't!" He turned and spoke in low tones to Elder Richards, who stood beside the baptismal font. Then his firm hand was at her back and they were moving swiftly up the stairs. With the hand of a skilled horseman he lost no time

85

in backing out from among the other vehicles, and they started down the hill at a brisk clip.

"Feeling better now?"

"I'm . . . fine." She was trying to control her chattering teeth.

"You're not faint or anything?"

"No . . . not now."

They rode in a silence broken only by the brisk clip-clop of the horse's feet, and by the chattering of her teeth, At the cottage he helped her down and into the house with tender care. A flush of embarrassment rose to her cheeks. He led her to a chair near the hearth and gently but firmly seated her.

"Now sit here and keep the robe around you until I can get a fire going. The house is cold, and if you don't want a good case of lung fever, you'd better do as I tell you."

She jumped up and threw the robe on the floor.

"Brother Eldridge, I appreciate all this," she was more than a little exasperated, ". . . but this is silly, and absolutely unnecessary! I'm perfectly all right. Now if you'll please go back to the Temple . . . !"

Calmly he built the fire and did not respond until he saw the flames licking up the chimney. Then, he turned to her, and her resistance seemed childish.

"I'm going back to the Temple," he spoke coolly. "But not until I'm sure you're alright. Now just draw up your chair close to the fire until the room gets warm."

She sat, but the resentment burned within her. She glared at the fire, while Eldridge leaned gracefully against the mantel. She was startled by his laugh and looked up to find his mocking eyes on her.

"What's so funny?"

"You, my dear Sister Simon! You! The image of

a drowned rat!" He laughed again, taunting. "Pretty women don't like to look like drowned rats, do they?"

Wrath bubbled up in her. She hated him, from the top of his handsome head to the soles of his handsome boots.

"Brother Eldridge, you can do more good at the Temple than you possibly can here!" Her voice quivered with rage. "Thank you for your kindness. I think your hat and gloves are on the chair by the door."

" 'Gale,' I think your name is?" There was a devilish twinkle in his eye. "Your parents were rather prophetic when they christened you, weren't they?"

"And don't forget your lap robe here on the floor. I'm sorry it's wet." But she wasn't sorry.

He collected his belongings and walked leisurely to the door. He made an extravagant bow, still looking amused.

"I think it's safe to leave you now. You seem to be much revived. Your color is good. In fact, I've never seen your face quite so red. Well, good-bye, dear. Perhaps I can do Brother Edouard another favor some day."

He went out, closing the door softly behind him.

One evening in November Gale sat by the fire, knitting. Cassie had gone that morning with Edouard, as she often did. It was nearly eight o'clock as Gale sat waiting for them, now and then lifting the lid of the heavy iron pot to peer inside. She was not alone, for Bub Leary had fallen into the habit of dropping in every evening to wait for Edouard, and to pick up his little mare. If anyone noticed the dull flush that rose in his face whenever Cassie entered the room, no one mentioned it. She sat silent, evening after evening, his long slender fingers drumming rhythmic patterns on his bony knees.

Both raised their heads, alert to approaching footsteps in the snow. Cassie and Edouard came in, shaking drifts of white from their shoulders. Cassie's face was rosy and fresh from the cold, and her eyes were bright.

"Guess what!" she began immediately, scarcely noticing Bub in her excitement. "Sophie's married!"

"Married!" Gale was silent a moment, her mind turning over in quick succession the thoughts of the young woman's brief widowhood, the sudden decision she had made to take Jock Meier's small children and raise them as her own, and now this marriage, with Jock's baby to be born in another man's home.

"Well, I'm glad," she said. "It's hard for a woman, alone . . . and with a family. It was a mighty generous thing for her to do, taking all those children."

"I guess so," Cassie admitted grudgingly. "I don't know why she did it. She sure didn't like the kids when Mama was here."

"Who did she marry? Anyone we know?"

"Isaac Eldridge."

"Isaac . . . Eldridge!" Just the name angered her. "But he's married!" Then she was embarrassed at her own stupidity.

"Does that make any difference?" Disdain was in the look that Cassie turned on Gale.

"We met Isaac down near Burl's Saw Mill," Edouard interposed, "and he rode back into town with us. He'd been down there to see about lumber for our company."

"Say, did you know," Cassie interrupted, "he's the captain of our company? We're company

88

eighteen, he said. I think Brother Simon would have been a lot better, don't you?"

"Well, I'm to be the captain of one of his fifties," Edouard said. "That's something."

"He and Sophie were married last week," Cassie continued. "You'd think she'd at least have told me, wouldn't you? Her and the kids have moved over across town into Eldridge's house, and they never even said a word to me about it! Now she's probably spending her time primping for Old Fancy Britches!"

"Cassie, can't you try to like Sophie?" Her voice was sharp.

"I can try," Cassie pouted, "but I don't think I ever will."

Gale laid her knitting aside and arose to serve their supper. Edouard stood with his back to the fire, warming himself. When he spoke he startled Bub, who was staring fascinated at the fair-haired girl who still stood in the center of the room. "Bub, it's a mighty cold night!"

The boy started from his revery. "Yes suh, yes suh. Mighty cold, suh. Well, I reckon I'd best be moseyin' on. Good night, folks."

He went swiftly into the night, forcing his hat down over his shock of hair.

Eleven

Christmas Day was white. It was snowing when they awoke in the morning and had not ceased all day, falling in great flakes. Gale was reminded of the wonderful crystal ball her Aunt Elspeth had when she was a child, a ball which held a little man and a house and some trees with snowflakes settling over the scene when one shook it.

Gale's heart skipped with joy all through the day, a joy which Christmas Day always fired in her. For a moment, remembering, she felt a pang of loneliness for the little New England village, with the church bells bringing back a clear echo from across the valley.

But then, looking at Edouard sitting at the kitchen window with his razor and shaving mug and mirror, the loneliness evaporated and she knew only the deepness of her love. She bent and kissed the back of his neck, then laughed at the concern in his mirrored face.

"Don't fret, love. I won't make you cut your throat! I'm just happy because it's Christmas . . . and it's snowing . . . and I love my husband very much! So there!" She kissed him again, and then whirled away to the work that this day held.

And now it was nearly over, their first Christmas

together. With her chin in her hand, she gazed into the fire, contentedly weary. A log broke and sent up a covey of sparks. The snow continued to fall, piling a great white drift in the corner of each window.

She looked up from her place on the floor to find Edouard and Cassie standing before her, hand in hand. And before she could wonder at Cassie's bent head, or at the strangeness in Edouard's face, he spoke.

"Gale dear," he spoke unsteadily, "Cassie and I . . . want to be married."

An eternity passed, how long, Gale didn't know. At last the gray numbness subsided and her eyes came to focus on the two figures standing before her. Edouard was speaking.

"What?" She realized that it was her own voice uttering the thick stupid word. "What?"

He spoke again, so low that her ringing ears could scarcely catch the words. His eyes met hers with a queer pleading.

"Cassie and I want to be married."

There it was . . . the end of the world . . . the whole universe crashing in around her. She groped for reality. Did he say . . . married? Why . . . he's married . . . to me. He's mine . . . all his love . . . all his kindness . . . all his gentle nobility . . . that dark dear head . . . his arms. No, Edouard, you've forgotten . . . you're already married . . . to me! It was only a dream that Edouard was different . . . that he loved me. She shuddered at the thought of their nights together.

He spoke again . . . and still she could not answer. She raised her head like an old woman, a woman sick and broken. She tried to listen . . . to understand his words.

"Gale! Gale darling . . . don't look so . . . so

frightened. It isn't as though I've stopped loving you. I love you, darling . . . with all my heart. It's only that . . . that I love Cassie, too."

I must say something . . . something . . . anything. I've been sitting here for months and months, and never have I said a word. I must say something. I am turning to icy stone. Can I move my tongue . . . my lips? Am I able to speak?

Her eyes came to rest upon Cassie, standing beside him, the top of her bent head not as high as his shoulder.

"You . . . you can't mean Cassie! Why . . . she's just a little girl!"

"She's fifteen," he said quietly. "She'll be sixteen in the spring. You were only seventeen when we were married."

And then suddenly all the fear within her, all the sickness and despair burst into uncontrolled fury. There he stood, shameless, with his hand holding Cassie's. And Cassie, her eyes shifting uneasily beneath her lowered lashes. Cassie, the homeless child she had taken generously into her home.

She sprang to her feet and before she quite realized what she was doing, she struck the girl a blow across the face with her open hand. A blow which would have knocked Cassie down if Edouard had not caught her. Cassie's hands flew to a face blanched with terror, and Edouard gathered her shaking shoulders into the protection of his arms. The look that he sent over the girl's fair head was dark with misery.

"You shouldn't have done that, Gale. It isn't worthy of you."

She backed against the masonry of the fireplace, with her nails tearing at the stones behind her. Her eyes glittered in the strange mask of her face.

"Worthy!" Her voice was a scream. "Worthy! Who are you to be telling me what is worthy!" Disgust twisted her colorless lips. "Why did I ever let myself believe in your lovely story of a religion that searched after 'all that is good and true and beautiful'? 'Good'! The slime in the river bottom is cleaner than the Saints! All this time, ever since I came here, I've tried not to see . . . not to believe what I saw and heard! I've put my faith in you . . . and blinded myself to everything else! And now. . . ."

The fury left her as suddenly as it had come. She closed her eyes to shut out the sight of the two before her, and her head sank back against the mantel.

Cassie began to sob against Edouard's shoulder. Gale pulled herself erect and walked past them to the door, with the uncertain steps of a sleepwalker. As she went out into the night, heavy snowflakes fell into the square of light cut by the open door. It closed behind her, and she was alone . . . more alone than she had been in all her life.

Snow-covered trees loomed faintly through the dark. Wet snow settled on her shoulders and hair, and the drifts dragged at her skirts. She was soon numb, but she was not conscious of it. In her sick mind one thought pounded . . . Edouard is gone . . . gone to Cassie.

The sickness spread down through the weary length of her body as she staggered through the heavy wet snowbanks, fleeing, fleeing. She lost all sense of time and place, and even her identity was some vague thing which she groped at moments to remember. But always burned deep in her memory, was the vivid picture of Edouard with Cassie in his arms. Edouard who meant more than life itself. His name rang like a heavy bell . . . Edouard . . . Edouard . . . Edouard.

She stumbled and lay where she fell. The snow was soft, and almost warm. The bell rang. Edouard . . . Edouard . . .

He lifted her and brushed the hair back from her face. For a long time he walked, with her head swinging limp in the crook of his arm. He rested, and started on again, past rows and rows of houses.

She knew dimly that it was Edouard, and that he was taking her home. But now it didn't matter. She knew only that she was tired . . . and that his arms were strong.

Twelve

Oddly enough, it was Edouard who was ill the next morning, his eyes closed and his face drawn with fever. Gale dressed, moving through the routine of her work in a state of hypnosis. Last night's ordeal weighed upon her with a weariness so acute that she was past thinking. She was conscious only that Edouard lay deathly ill.

After the fire was blazing in the fireplace, Cassie got up and dressed. Rebellion was stamped on her face as she pointedly ignored Gale's existence, but Gale didn't know. She moved about in a stupor.

Gale's hands performed the tasks that some inner sense told her were necessary. She bathed Edouard's hot face with cool cloths, and heated turpentine and lard to rub on his chest to ease his labored breathing. She smoothed his pillow while he tossed in delirium, and poured broth between his teeth when he lay quiet. She devoted herself wholly to his care, partly because she still loved him deeply, and partly because she realized that her flight into the storm was responsible for his illness. She was unconscious of her own needs, and paused for neither food nor rest during that long terrible day.

Only once did she arouse herself enough to speak. Cassie started into the bedroom where Edouard lay moaning. Gale spoke dully. "What do you want?"

"I'm going in to talk to him."

Gale shook her head wearily, blocking the way.

"I am too, and you can't stop me!" Cassie shrilled. "You're trying to keep me from him just because you're jealous! I'm going in!"

"Not today."

Cassie tried to push past, but Gale shoved her back into the kitchen and closed the door.

"If he dies you'll have yourself to thank!" Cassie shouted through the planking.

Edouard moaned and for a moment Gale was afraid that he had heard. But she saw that her caution had been unnecessary. He was unconscious of the brief conflict.

Shortly after midnight Gale went into the kitchen and shook Cassie awake. The girl shrugged away her hand and snuggled deeper into her featherbed on the floor. To Cassie's amazement she found herself suddenly and forcibly standing in the middle of the floor, with Gale's hands hard on her shoulders. Their breathing made white puffs of chill in the light of the candle. Cassie shivered, more from fear than cold.

"Dress as fast as you can!" Gale's words were imperative. "Run to Dr. Fletcher and tell him to come right away. Tell him Edouard has lung fever . . . he's spitting blood, and he can't breathe! Run!"

Then she was gone, leaving Cassie to dress as best she could in the thin moonlight that filtered through the frosted windows. The girl sobbed and hunted in vain for a handkerchief as she buttoned her cloak around her neck. She was still sobbing when she returned with the doctor, and her gloveless hands were blue with cold. Dr. Fletcher, a gruff old man, wore a coonskin cap and had an icicle on the end of his nose. He made straight for the fireplace, beating his hands across his chest with vigor. He went into the bedroom.

"Well?" he growled.

Gale turned from the bed. Her knotted hands beneath her chin spelled her anxiety. "I did everything I knew. He's been sick since morning, but he's getting worse."

The doctor, his sharp eyes watching as she spoke, thought he'd never seen such a miserable face. "What's the matter? You sick too?"

"No. I'm alright."

He answered the plea in her eyes. "Yes . . . we'll bring him around. Don't worry. Sick since morning, you say? Had he been well yesterday? A cold or anything?"

"No . . . but he went out in the storm last night . . . and got wet." She choked on the words.

He eyed her quizzically, then turned to Edouard. Opening his bag, he began his examination. At the foot of the bed Cassie was weeping, her face buried in a worn shirt of Edouard's. After a time the doctor straightened and put his things back into his bag. When he turned to face Gale, he shook his head.

"It's bad, my dear . . . worse than I thought at first. But we can't know how it will turn out for several days. This thing has to work itself up to a crisis . . . a turning point. We'll do the best we can for him until then."

She didn't move, and only her eyes on Edouard's yellowed face showed that she heard. Dr. Fletcher watched her a moment in silence and then barked, "Sit down!"

She obeyed, her eyes still on the figure in the bed.

"You're sick too, or I'll eat my plugged hat. You need rest and food. When did you eat last?"

"Mm . . . yesterday . . . I think."

"Yesterday! You mean Christmas Day?"

"Yes."

"Tarnation! Do you want to kill yourself? He tossed an impatient head in the direction of Cassie. "Who is she?"

Gale turned to look at the girl at the foot of the bed, who was still sniffling miserably. Gale tried to find the right words.

"A . . . a friend. She's staying with us for a while."

"Humph!" he snorted in ill humor. "So that's it, huh? Why can't she cook you a good meal, and then look after this fellow a while so you can get some sleep?"

"Please . . ." Gale looked at him imploringly. "I'd rather stay with him myself."

He grinned with one side of his mouth. "Very well. But after you've eaten, you lie down here on the bed beside him and take a nap. You'll wake if he needs you. Now do as I say . . . understand?"

She nodded. He turned to Cassie. "Stop blubbering! Bad thing in a sickroom. Now get out in the kitchen. If you don't know how to cook, it's time you were learning."

When he spoke to Gale he was almost gentle. "I'm going home now to fix a bag of onions in a poultice for this man . . . and when I get back, I expect to find you alseep. Understand?"

She nodded, but he was not sure that she heard, for she was still staring at Edouard.

Two weeks later, Gale sat at the window, knitting a gray wool sock. Winter sunshine made a reflection on her hair and warmed the paleness of her face. Across the room Edouard lay quiet in the bed,

100

watching her with thoughtful eyes. She avoided his gaze as she had for days, dreading what she knew was inevitable.

"Please ask Cassie to come in."

It was true then. Since the night when Cassie had gone for the doctor, she had not attempted to enter the sickroom. As the long days and nights wore on, Gale had almost convinced herself that the whole thing had been a terrible nightmare, and that as soon as he recovered life would go on as before. But now she knew it was all true. Slowly she laid aside her knitting and got to her feet. She would call Cassie. And then she would go away . . . if her legs would carry her.

Behind her, Edouard plucked the thought from her. "Don't go, my dear. I want to talk to both of you."

Words came from her lips, but they were not her words or her voice. She listened to them, wondering at their quietness. "Cassie, come in. Edouard wants to talk to you."

Cassie entered with suspicious promptness, flinging a look of triumph at Gale as she passed. She ran to the bed and bent to kiss Edouard. Gale watched them with eyes which belonged to some aloof stranger. She saw the quick flood of color come into Cassie's face, and for the first time since she had known her, she realized that the girl was lovely. Her hair, soft and loose, with the pale gold of winter sun, brushed Edouard's face. When she straightened her eyes smiled into his. "I'm glad you're better," she said.

Gale knew then that the girl loved him with a love as sincere as her own. But in the knowledge there was no pity, only hatred. Wildly she wondered why God didn't strike them both dead. Then, with a

101

pang, she realized that He had come near doing that very thing . . . to Edouard. And she was glad he had been spared. It was better to share Edouard with another than to face the starkness of life without him.

"Please come and sit here," he motioned Gale to the other side of the bed.

For a moment she was about to refuse. Then she saw the thin yellow skin stretched across the bones of his high forehead, and she remembered the long nights she had watched him, afraid that he was dying. She swallowed the lump in her throat and sat on the bed. While he talked she clasped her icy hands in her lap and stared at the cracks in the floor. With the stubbornness born of pain she tried not to listen, but she couldn't help herself. One night many months ago, she had vowed not to listen to a young missionary who was speaking to a motley group in a dusty warehouse on the waterfront of Boston. But she had listened. And now she again found herself listening to the deep thrill of his voice.

"We will be married as soon as I am strong enough to go to the Temple. It will be easier for Cassie if we're married before we leave Nauvoo. A young girl without a family has no business in a wagon train. There'll be none of the privacy that a single girl requires. And another thing . . . there may be some ruffians among us who would make life a torment for marriageable young women. We try to discourage riffraff, but they are to be found in any group, and so the best plan is to see that there are no single women . . . or at least, as few as possible."

Without realizing it Gale had raised her eyes and was watching him. He made it sound so reasonable . . . and sensible. There was almost a holiness

102

about him, in the depth of his eyes as he looked from one to the other. For the first time in two weeks the weight was slipping from her, and she felt almost at peace. There was a strange power in Edouard's voice. She tried to hate herself for being a puppet in his hands, but she was helpless. In spite of herself, she could see a certain logic in the plan. She stared at Cassie across his head. She saw a lonely child sitting on the edge of the bed, clinging to his hand.

"I'm sorry, Cassie," she said quietly.

The softness left Cassie's mouth, and her eyes narrowed. "You needn't be so high and mighty, Gale Simon!" she flared. "Edouard is marrying me because he loves me! *Loves* me, do you hear? No matter what he says, we love each other!"

She flung herself upon Edouard and pressed a long kiss to his lips. He raised weak hands to check her, but as they touched her soft hair, they lingered. Jealousy flooded back over Gale, more intense than ever. She saw only a brazen woman with her lips clinging to Edouard's. Wrath almost strangled her. She stood up and closed her eyes, fighting for calmness. She bent over Cassie and raised her firmly to her feet. "Wait until he is stronger. Go to the kitchen now."

The girl fell back a few steps and met Gale's level gaze. Then she whirled and left the room. Gale didn't care how much she hurt Cassie, but she must pretend tranquility for Edouard's sake. She must, to keep him alive! As she stared blindly out the window, she twisted a scrap of yarn she still held in her fingers. She turned to find Edouard watching her.

He smiled wanly and whispered, "Thank you, my dear."

Had he seen . . . and understood? She dropped

to her knees at the side of the bed and buried her face in the covers. For the first time since Christmas, she wept. His thin fingers stroked her hair and she grew quiet. There was only the ticking of the gilt clock on the desk, and the crash of floating ice cakes in the river.

Thirteen

Edouard and Cassie were married the following week in the Temple. During the ceremony Gale sat at the cabin window, sewing the heavy canvas that was to be their wagon cover. There was violence in the awl she was using to punch the holes for her needle, but her eyes were dry. More than once the awl slipped and sank into the flesh of her fingers, but she scarcely felt it as she hastened blindly on. The blood made tiny crimson blotches on the canvas, stains that were to follow her halfway across the continent in the months ahead.

As Edouard was unable to walk so far, he had sent Cassie the day before to ask Isaac Eldridge to call for them in his buggy. When Eldridge entered the cabin, the little room seemed suddenly to come to life with vibrant vitality. Gale noticed irritably that his boots were as highly polished as ever, and that the melting snow on them made them look like Japanese lacquer. He was taller than Edouard and now, as he strode across to seize his hand, his own strength seemed to tower over Edouard and make him appear small and frail. Gale hated him for it.

"Simon, old fellow, how are you feeling? I didn't know you'd been sick until the little girl told me. Lung fever, she said. You've been a mighty sick man! Why didn't you let me know?"

"I wasn't able to send messages to anyone," he smiled a little. "For a while I didn't know what was going on."

"But Sister Gale could have." He turned to Gale. "Surely you know that you were welcome to anything in my power. Why didn't you let me know? Haven't you had any help?"

"Thank you. We managed very well."

"You don't look well, Sister Simon. Those hollows under your eyes . . . you look positively ill!"

She bent her head over the canvas. Edouard, watching her, rose unsteadily to his feet.

"Shall we be getting along? I don't like to keep Brother Young waiting." As he tried to struggle into his greatcoat, Gale pushed the canvas from her lap and went to help him.

"Brother Young?" Eldridge cocked an eyebrow. "You're meeting him at the Temple?"

Edouard was ill at ease. "Didn't Cassie tell you?"

"Only that you wanted a ride to the Temple this afternoon. That's all."

Cassie, putting on her cloak, grew uncomfortably red. She bent her head over the buttons.

"Cassie and I are getting married this afternoon."

There was a painful silence. Gale wished that Eldridge would stop watching her so intently. She hurried back to her canvas. She hadn't intended to, but she cast a defensive glance at Eldridge. There was a slow intimate smile in his eyes, but his words were cool and matter-of-fact. He bowed ever so slightly.

"Leave your tent making and come with us. We'll make it a real occasion! There'll be room in the buggy if we put a box on the floor for the little girl."

"I'm not 'the little girl'!" Cassie snapped. "I'm being married, you know!"

"Oh?" Eldridge grinned mockingly, but when he turned to Gale his tone was soft. "Forgive me. And don't worry about Edouard. I'll see that he doesn't get chilled or tired."

As the three of them filed out into the January afternoon, Gale wondered wearily how the man could one moment be so insolent, and the next so tender.

She worked through the dreary afternoon, trying not to think, trying to concentrate on the holes she punched in the canvas, and on the coarse linen thread which persisted in becoming tangled in knots. She tried not to think of Edouard standing for a ceremony with Cassie on his arm, just as he had stood with her last June. She tried not to think that from today on, their hours together, the hours of unhappiness, of misunderstanding, or of passion, all would be shared with the petulant Cassie. She jabbed the awl violently through the canvas and jerked her hand away bleeding.

Outside the cabin, the wind caught up thin spirals of snow and twisted it about the black trunks of the trees. Overhead the clouds crowded in over the city, black and low. The wind coming down the river whipped up droves of white-capped waves that dashed between the ice blocks like frightened mice. Edouard and Cassie's wedding day.

During the ensuing weeks, the city hummed with the hectic energy that everyone threw into the final preparations for departure. In spite of births, deaths, and sickness, the work went on without interruption. The men worked from bitter dawn until long after dark, worked on their wagons, on the harness, the wheels, their guns, and they poured lead for bullets. The women dried apples and pumpkin and beans and corn, and packed their supplies of meal and flour.

Many a dreary day the women sorted and resorted the belongings that they were to take with them and those they were to leave behind. Everlastingly the men repeated, "Cut down that pile of stuff! We can't tote more than we can get in the wagon!"

"I can't leave *that* . . . or that either," the women repeated. "Why, that's my mother's rose bowl! It's been in the family forever! And *that,* I have to take *that*! It's the cradle all our young 'uns was rocked in, and me and all our family besides. Grampa carved it from a maple tree from his lot back in Vermont. We can't leave it for the Gentiles! Of course all our children are grown now, past sleeping in it, at any rate. But we can't leave it to the Gentiles!"

"Well, burn it then!" was the impatient answer. "All I know is, we haven't room in the wagon for all this junk! We have to carry food, enough to last us for a year or more, and grain for the stock, and seed, and a plow, all our clothes, and living paraphernalia for the whole family for the rest of our lives. So make up your mind! Don't take anything we can do without!"

And so, little by little, piece by piece, they made up their minds, and the women's hearts ached as they took one last look at the gilt-framed picture of the baby in her christening gown, and then laid it in the flames of the fireplace where it would be safe forever from the hands of marauding mobs. In place of the cherished picture, and rose bowl, and cradle, and dresser, and love seat, they packed woolen blankets, and heavy shoes, and bolts of muslin, and big iron pots in which they could cook stews and boil the clothes, and sunbonnets for next summer, and the churn, and the spinning wheel, and the carding frames, and a keg for water, and featherbeds, and the dishes . . . they couldn't leave the best china, even if they had to do without food! After all they had to eat their vittles off something, didn't they? And they would all be careful of them at meals, and then when they got to their new home, wherever that would be, they'd have the dishes.

The morning after the wedding the three of them sat at an almost untasted breakfast. Cassie spoke to Edouard, ignoring Gale. "I think I'll go over to visit Sophie today." She sounded like a little girl playing grown-up. "Is that alright? No telling when I'll see her again."

She wants to boast of her conquest, Gale thought bitterly. When has she ever gone to visit the despised Sophie? She wants to escape the possibility that she might have to share in the housework or the preparations.

Cassie was self-consciously adult this morning, trying to see herself as a married woman, although she was as much a virgin as she had been yesterday. She had tried to do her hair in a knot on top of her head, but the attempt was a failure due to her inexperience and the softness of her hair. But she had discarded her ribbon and wore a comb.

They were all uneasy, even Edouard, whose disquiet was marked by jerky movements of his hands. But when he answered Cassie, his voice was as usual.

"Run along to Sophie's and enjoy yourself. I think perhaps Gale can manage without you today."

After Cassie had gone, Edouard put on his coat and hat and came to Gale where she stood stacking the dishes on the table. He took her shoulders and turned her to face him. She kept her head down, but he raised her chin with a firm hand.

"Dear heart, you are magnificent." He bent and pressed a kiss on her lips. "Thank you . . . for everything."

After he left, she took her dishes from the shelves and began packing them in the chest that Edouard had made for her early in the summer. It was a lovely chest, strong and beautifully built, for he was an expert craftsman. She paused a moment in her work to caress the satin smoothness of the lid. It was cedar, and polished until she could see the white reflection of her hand in it. The hinges and bands were of copper, to match her hair, he had said when he brought it home to her.

She was still packing plates between the folds of her linen sheets and pillow cases when she heard the quick thud of horse's hoofs in the snow outside. With apprehension she ran to the door. Bub Leary stood there, twisting his rabbit-skin cap in his hands, his shaggy hair shading a kind of wildness in his eyes.

"It's Edouard!" Gale cried. "Tell me! What's happened to him?"

"Kin I come in?"

"Is he . . . sick?" Fear paralyzed her, but she managed to stand aside for him to enter.

"Sick? Not as I know of. Ain't he here?"

Relief swept over her, leaving her weak.

"No, he's down at the City Hall."

Bub looked about the room, searching.

"Ain't . . . ain't . . . what I mean is . . . are you all by yourself?"

110

"Yes. Cassie went over to spend the day with her brothers and sisters."

Bub swallowed hard, his eyes on the floor, and twisted the cap until a fine shower of rabbit hair fell from his fingers. Finally he burst out.

"Say, it ain't true, is it?"

"What, Bub?"

"That Brother Simon and Cassie . . . well, that they was married yesterday?" The words came out miserably.

"Yes." Gale bit her lip.

"Not Cassie!" he whispered. His eyes brimmed with boyish tears. "I've loved her for so long! I can't rightly remember when I didn't love her. I only been waitin' for her to get old enough."

She could only nod in answer. Watching him, she knew that her own grief was no greater than his. He sank to his knees and burst into sobs, his face buried in his arms on the seat of the chair. She put a hand on his heaving shoulder. There was something terrible about hearing a man cry, it sounded like his soul was tearing out of him. At last his sobbing ceased, but he did not raise his head. He slumped against the chair, and snow melted on the shoulders of his worn coat.

"I could kill him," Bub said quietly, but with deadly vehemence. His hands knotted on the chair, and Gale watched them double into fists.

"No, Bub! No!" Gale sank to her knees beside him, her hand on his arm. "He had to do it, Bub. He . . . he . . . did it only for Cassie's sake. Don't hold it against him. He did it to . . . to protect her on the trip. A wagon train is no place for a young girl, alone."

"I wanted to be like him . . . once!" The words turned sour in his mouth.

111

"Bub . . ." Gale hesitated, "did he know you cared for Cassie like this?" She must know. The answer meant everything. If he had married Cassie when he knew Bub loved her, and that she needed no protection . . . "Did he, Bub?"

Bub raised his head slowly and looked at her. Then he shook his head.

"Nope. I don't reckon he did. I never let on to nobody. I was waitin' till I could care for her proper before I said a word."

"If you had only come sooner . . . yesterday, or the day before . . . you would have saved us both from this. Now it's too late."

The little clock ticked away the minutes. They heard voices approaching in the street, and both started up. The voices went past, but Gale got to her feet.

"Bub . . . there is only one thing for you to do. That is . . . never let her know. Never let anyone know. It's too late now. Telling her about it wouldn't help you or her or . . . any of us. It would only add to all our miseries. Let's keep it a secret between us."

He stared at her.

"I never stopped to think how you'd be feelin' about this! I was only thinkin' of myself. Why . . . you must feel terrible! Holy mackerel . . . and me bustin' in here like this!"

She smiled a little. "It's a secret then, Bub?"

He got awkwardly to his feet and bowed solemnly. "Yes'm. And I crave to beg your pardon. You must think I'm a shore enough baby."

Gale shook her head. "Not a baby. A man."

He backed toward the door, torturing his cap. He

112

bowed again. "Good day, ma'am. And if you ever need a friend, I'll be there. I'm sorry, ma'am . . . about everything. Good day." He backed out the door, stumbling a little on the threshold.

Fourteen

February 4, 1846, was the day of the Saints' first crossing into Iowa, the unknown land which stretched bleak and desolate across the wide Mississippi. Gale, her packing complete except for the few necessities which she had kept out for their immediate needs, sat at the kitchen window knitting. Her fingers moved with mechanical briskness, but her eyes were on the river.

The vast stretch of water had today burst into frenetic activity. Every river craft from miles around had been called into service to carry the Saints and their baggage across the river. Among the cakes of ice lurched log rafts that carried animals and wagons.

At the other window sat Cassie, her hands idle, her eyes somber. Little had changed. She still slept alone on the featherbed on the kitchen floor. Her face was sullen. She spoke only when necessary, and then with abrupt rudeness.

Fortunately for Edouard he was gone from morning until night and thus avoided the painful days of enforced companionship which the two women had to endure. As he regained his strength it was necessary for him to assist in the evacuation of ten thousand Saints from the doomed city. During the bustling days among the wagons and cattle and arguing men, he could gain the composure that would carry him through another evening and morning as the balance wheel between his taut wives.

February fourth dragged its long hours through the cabin just as all other days. But today they could watch the river with half-hearted interest, a welcome change from staring at the floorboards, at their hands, their shoes, anywhere but at each other. Thus passed the rest of the week.

The evening of February ninth saw the snow, which had been pelting the city fitfully for the past month, suddenly begin to fall in earnest. Within half an hour, fence posts and rosebushes had lost their identity beneath a deepening swathe of whiteness. By morning the Saints who still remained in Nauvoo looked out on a strange world where nothing looked quite familiar. Across the river, the luckless Saints who had departed found themselves stranded in a world of drifts as deep as their horses' bellies. Some had gone ahead to the camp at Sugar Creek where there was wood for fires, and the shelter of the hills to break the force of the wind. All activity came to a standstill under the smother of heavy snow. The Saints in Nauvoo clung anxiously to their firesides and dreaded the exodus more than ever. They shivered, looking across the river, but behind them was the shadow of the mob and so they must leave.

Next morning they awoke to the blaze of sunshine on fresh snow. Edouard uncovered the coals on the hearth and fanned fresh wood into flame. Cassie opened an eye for a moment, then snuggled deeper into her featherbed. The kitten on her feet stirred, then curled itself again into a fluffy ball.

Something was missing. It was Gale who first noticed the strange silence. Then Edouard dropped his

116

boots and hurried to the window. She ran to the window to peer out with him.

The river lay, a motionless expanse of gleaming lumps of ice. During the night it had frozen solid. Each ice cake was abruptly halted in its journey, welded into a slippery bridge from shore to shore.

Edouard clutched her arm, his eyes flashing.

"It's come! The big freeze! We've been praying for this. A bridge! A bridge to carry us all across . . . our stock . . . our wagons . . . everything! Now the crossing will go twice as fast!"

After he left, Gale slipped on her heavy cloak and hood and changed into thick boots. She went out into the snow to dig a shoot from the yellow rosebush in the front yard to take with them to their new home. It was difficult. The snow was solid. She cut and chopped with the axe until she uprooted a section of the bush, then wrapped it in heavy sacking. The sunshine and exercise helped restore her spirits.

Stamping the snow from her feet, she went in the house. Cassie lay face down on the bed, sobbing violently. Anger flared in Gale. Then a vivid memory flashed through her mind of another girl, lying face down on a bed, a lonely girl sobbing with the passion of seventeen years. It was a day last May in Lockwood Hall, when she had been expelled for attending Edouard's missionary meeting in the village schoolhouse.

With sudden impulse she took Cassie in her arms, and with her head cradled on her shoulder, she rocked gently back and forth. There were no words, only the rocking. She found herself thinking what a tiny body it was, too small to be carrying the burdens of an adult. Cassie's sobbing quieted and she

117

let Gale hold her for a time. Suddenly she jerked away.

"Why don't you leave me alone? There's no need to pretend you're sorry. I like it better when you hate me!"

"I don't hate you, Cassie." And saying it, she discovered it was true. "It's just jealousy, I guess."

"There's nothing to be jealous of! He doesn't love me. And for heaven's sake, don't feel sorry for me! That why he married me. I thought at first he really loved me, but now I see it. Everybody pities me . . . and I hate being pitied! No one cares if I live or die, really! I wish I *could* die!"

"Oh no, Cassie! Never say that!" In her own misery she hadn't stopped to think that Cassie might be suffering as much as she was. Poor child!

That night Edouard sensed a subtle change in the air. Perhaps Gale was less remote, Cassie a bit less morose. Or perhaps it was only the warmth of the fire on the hearth, more appreciated because it was to be for the last time.

"We will be crossing at dawn tomorrow," he announced, warming his back at the fire. "Are you ready?"

118

Fifteen

By the time the eastern sky had brightened from lilac to rose, the Simons' wagon was loaded and the oxen were shifting about in the crunching snow. Cassie sat on the high wagon seat. She was wrapped in quilts, with her kitten snuggled in her lap beneath her cloak. Edouard was in the wagon rearranging the last of their possessions beneath the arch of the wagon top.

Gale stood alone in the cabin, staring about her at the emptiness and remembering the home it had been, the happiness it had known. She heard Edouard's voice calling, and walked out without another look behind. She wouldn't let them see she had been crying.

Above the city rose the Temple, stark against the dawn. Gale took one final look. What would the Gentiles do to it? Cassie, snuggled in her corner of the seat, was intent only on keeping warm. For a moment Gale's eyes met Edouard's, the barrier dropping away as a look of understanding passed between them. Hurriedly Gale turned away. She climbed into place, and Edouard urged the frightened oxen out on the glare of ice.

The lead ox slipped and crashed on his side. For a moment Gale thought his neck was broken, for he lay still with the heavy hickory yoke pulling at his throat. The other three animals lunged in fright. But he was soon on his feet, shaking his head, and the wagon creaked forward, the axles screaming against the cold. The crossing was slow, the team slipping and stumbling over lumps of ice. Before they reached the far bank, one or another of the oxen went down with a jangle of chains and the bawling of teammates.

"Stop! Stop!" Cassie wailed in terror, clutching at Edouard's arm. "I want to get out! I'm going to walk!"

He drove on with caution, ignoring the gadfly at his elbow.

"Let me out, I say!" she shrieked at him.

His hands were tense on the jerk line tied to the horn of the lead ox, although his face was calm.

"Oh, Edouard!" the girl screamed. "Hurry before the ice breaks through!"

Gale rode silently at his other side, her eyes wide and dark. The team clambered up the opposite bank and began to wallow through deep frozen drifts, belly-deep and churned to glittering powder by the wagons that had gone on ahead. At the top of each hill Edouard stopped to allow the winded animals to puff a bit, steam rising from their nostrils and snow-clotted sides. At each stop, Gale looked back at the city and the Temple, now touched with the gold of sunrise.

Other wagons dotted the white wastes ahead, and still others came plodding behind. All day they rode, but even in the glare of noon there was no warmth in the sun, only a blinding brilliance and the bitter cold. When the hot stones they carried at their feet began to cool, they had to kick their feet against the wagon bed to keep them from freezing.

"Don't let your feet get numb," Edouard warned.

120

"Frostbite can be a serious danger out here on the trail."

They pounded their hands together, and their faces got red and stiff. At last, as darkness was settling into the hollows between the hills, the sight of the camp at Sugar Creek burst upon them. Among the naked trees the camp fires burned bright holes in the dusk. Even the oxen seemed eager to reach the camp as they speeded their pace down the last slope.

A sentry met them, his bewhiskered face peering at them over the wagon wheel.

"Which company do you belong to?"

"Company eighteen, Isaac Eldridge, captain."

"No!" he ejaculated. "You don't say! That's my own company, the outfit with all the Boston fellers in it." He peered closer. "You must be . . . yep, you're Brother Simon, cap'n of the fifty. You don't know me, I reckon. Ain't been in Nauvoo long. Name's Jenkins, Ad Jenkins. Got a wife and a passel o' kids down the creek a spell. You'll run into 'em, else they'll run into you, 'fore you're on the road long. Reckon you're anxious to pitch camp."

"Yes, the ladies are very cold and we'd like to get settled before it gets too dark."

"Yep. Yep. Can't blame you none. You'll find company eighteen down the creek a mile and a half. You can't miss it. There's a whopper of a big oak tree smack in the middle of the trail, and there you turn left till you hit the creek. And there you be! 'Home'!" He laughed at his jest.

When they reached the glowing fires of company eighteen, Isaac strode out to greet them.

"Brother Edouard! I thought you'd never get here, man! Have any trouble?"

121

"Not in particular. Have you been on the trail to-day?"

"No, we've been here a week. If we don't all freeze and our stock starve, we'll be able to rejoice! Your women must be perishing. Come, come! Pull your wagon in here beside mine."

Edouard climbed down stiffly from the high seat, while Eldridge lifted Gale down as lightly as though she were a child. She staggered a bit, for her legs were stiff and as unmanageable as two sticks. He put an arm around her to steady her.

"Cold?" Just one word, spoken low and close to her ear, but it made her angry. She pulled away and leaned against the wagon wheel. Her voice sounded too high in her own ears.

"No. Not cold at all, really. Just stiff from riding."

Cassie's impatient voice cut in.

"Well, are you going to leave me up here all night? One rushes to Gale and the other to the oxen ... and you leave me just sitting!"

"Oh, Cassie, my *child*!" Eldridge rushed to her assistance with mock apology. "Allow me!" He lifted her down with the swooping movement used in playing with a small child. He guided both unsteady girls to the fire where the hot fragrance of stew was rising from the pot which Grace Eldridge was stirring. It was the first time Gale remembered seeing her, and she guessed who she was only because she seemed at home over Isaac's fire. She looked tired, and too old to be Isaac's wife. Gale saw that once she must have been quite beautiful, and despite her gray hair, she was probably no older than her husband.

"Grace, the Simons have just now arrived, and

122

are chilled to the bone. Can you manage some supper for them?"

She looked straight at each of the newcomers. Gale found a look of reserve.

"Yes, of course, there's always plenty." She was expressionless as she turned to stir the pot.

"I wonder where Sophie and the kids are," Cassie whispered, close to Gale's ear.

"Sophie is resting in the wagon," Grace Eldridge said, as though in answer. "The children are playing around camp somewhere."

Cassie subsided into the depths of her cloak. The men returned to the fire after caring for the cattle, and soon the Meier children came straggling in, one after another, their faces red with the cold and their eyes hungrily on the cooking pot.

"Kitty! Kitty!" squealed little Willie, trying to take the cat from Cassie's arms. Frightened, the animal leaped out into the darkness with one wild lunge.

"Willie! You little devil!" She struck him sharply across the head, then burst into tears. "Now the cat is gone and I'll never see him again!" Willie joined her in wailing.

"Supper ready, Grace?" called Eldridge over the ruckus.

But she was already ladling out the thick steaming stew and handing the bowls to the boys. Comparative quiet settled as everyone gathered around the fire to eat.

"Isn't Sophie going to eat with us?" he asked.

Sister Eldridge shrugged and went on ladling stew. He went to the flap of the wagon and climbed in. After a few moments he reappeared and helped Sophie down with great tenderness. For a second Gale stared, astonished. She would not have recognized the heavy bloated woman as the stylish

123

black-haired girl she had known last summer in Nauvoo. She hadn't known that producing a baby could do this to a girl. Intent on her own affairs during recent months, she had forgotten that Jock Meier's child was soon due to arrive. She hadn't seen Sophie since the day of Jock's death.

Her gaze shifted to Eldridge, who was helping Sophie to a seat on a log near the fire. There was a courtly gentleness in his action. Gale shook her head, baffled. There was something fine in a man who was this generous. And yet . . .

She went to sit beside Sophie, who was obviously miserable and self-conscious. After a brief blessing from Isaac, they began their supper, the children devouring with gusto their plates of meat and potatoes, fragrant with onion, and their great chunks of Dutch oven cornbread. As they ate, Gale realized that all the children in the family were the Meier clan. Not one was an Eldridge. Orphans all, yet content in the circle of the Eldridge firelight.

"Well, men," Isaac spoke lightly to the children when they had finished their meal, "it's time to climb into your blankets. Mother, do they have a hot rock?"

Grace pulled large stones from the edge of the fire and wrapped them in heavy burlap, handing one to each child. Eldridge helped them up the wagon tongue, one by one, and into the wagon.

"Good night, crew!" he called, giving each a friendly slap on the bottom as they climbed into the wagon.

The next day Gale learned a great deal about surviving in the open in winter. Breakfast was very late and the three Simons were at a nervous pitch after their first uncomfortable night in the woods. Gale

124

and Edouard slept on a featherbed spread thinly over kegs and boxes in the wagon, while Cassie spent the night in the small tent by the fire.

However the noise and bustle and shouting from one camp fire to another began to lift Gale's spirits. With perverse good humor, the Saints actually seemed to be delighting in the experience. It was like a great good-natured picnic. She was surprised to find herself singing as she washed the dishes on an upturned log near the fire. By noon she had learned where to stand to keep the smoke from her eyes, and how to place the kettle to keep the contents cooking without burning.

Edouard smiling, brought out the little hand mirror and held it up before her face.

"Have you seen the chimney sweep?" he asked.

She had to laugh. Her face was black with soot, and her hood was askew and adorned with feathers from last night's featherbed. And as she laughed, the day seemed brighter. It wasn't going to be as bad as she feared.

During the afternoon, she wandered among the wagons of company eighteen, greeting old friends. The sentry, Ad Jenkins, had been right when he designated it as "the outfit with all the Boston fellers in it." They were all there, every one of Edouard's converts, all but Cliff Sutler and the Wilbe sisters, who had refused to budge until after the birth of Aggie's baby.

Gale found Sister Muldoon, red and perspiring, her sandy hair straggling from beneath her bonnet, as she bent over a pot on the fire, swishing and pounding the clothes she was boiling.

"Hello!" called Gale.

"Hello, yourself!" the woman muttered, a storm brewing in the grimness of her thin lips. "Oh, it's

125

ye!" she raised her head impatiently. She motioned Gale to a log by the fire. "Sit down, can't ye? How they expect a woman to do a civil washin' on a frostbitten picnic like this is beyond me!" Without stopping for breath she launched into one of her nonstop monologues. "And Pat, the lout, goin' off right after breakfast with a bunch o' fellers to some settlement who knows where, and leavin' me to chop holes in the ice and fetch water from the crick! When he comes back (if he ever does, gone off with a good-for-nothin' bunch o' scamps, fer tradin', they said . . . if he ever comes home) . . . well, he'd best be gittin' home before dark, is all I can say! And if he comes home drunk, as I don't doubt, I'll have all the black divils o' Killarney on him, mark me words! Him gone lollygaggin' off to some Gentile settlement, and me here freezin' me hands to the bone, washin' his dirty shirts fer him! When did ye get in?" She switched topics without losing a stroke.

"Last night."

"Then ye prob'ly don't know yet . . ." She lowered her voice to a hoarse croak. "Know what?"

Gale wasn't sure she wanted to "know what," but Sister Muldoon didn't wait for an answer.

"*She's* in this company!" She reared back on these words of doom.

"Who?" Gale was irritated by this woman's continual scandal-mongering stories not quite true to facts.

"Who indade! Now who do ye think would be follerin' Pat Muldoon around the country, tryin' to get next to him every chance she gets? Who but that hussy from Boston, Addie Voak!"

Gale surprised herself by bursting into laughter. The thought of Addie Voak, horse-faced and independent, following anyone around the country, but

126

most preposterous of all . . . Pat Muldoon, whom she scorned with a scorn worthy of even Addie Voak. The thought was too ridiculous. But seeing the hot red rising in Sister Muldoon's face, she tried to smother her amusement.

"Ye'll be laughin' outa the other side of yer face when she sets her cap fer *yer* man, Miss Smarty!"

"Forgive me." Gale erased the smile. "It's just that I'm sure Addie isn't setting her cap for your husband, or anybody's husband. I don't think she even likes men. You needn't worry."

"It's easy enough fer *ye* to be givin' advice . . . when ye know there's no chance o' a husband like yers bringin' another woman into yer home!"

Gale's face blanched as she stumbled back, as though to avoid a blow, but Sister Muldoon didn't notice as she continued pounding the clothes with violence.

"Pardon me, ma'am," a childish voice at her elbow aroused Gale and she turned to find young Susannah Nickols, smiling shyly. "My sisters and I saw you here . . . and thought if it wouldn't be too rude . . . we were afraid we might miss you . . . We're in that wagon over there, and Mother asks to have you drop by for a visit when you have the time."

Gale smiled with gratitude.

"I'll be delighted to come at once. I was just now leaving anyway. Good-bye, Sister Muldoon."

Her farewell was ignored.

Sixteen

Next morning while most of the Saints were still at their breakfasts, messengers hurried from one company to another, announcing that Brigham had arrived and was requesting that every Saint meet at the upper ford at nine o'clock. Startled looks passed from one to another as they hurriedly packed their dishes, fed and watered the chickens in their coops on the sides of the wagons, banked the fires, drove the stock to the creek to water, and fed them their daily ration of elm and maple twigs.

By nine o'clock every Saint was crowded into the space around Young's wagon, some five to six thousand of them, anxious and alert, their breaths steaming. Young was stern in certain rules of behavior, and punctuality was one of them. Exactly at nine the wagon flaps of his wagon flipped sharply open and he stepped up on the wagon seat, looking over the multitude below him.

Gale understood why he had so naturally succeeded Joseph Smith as leader of the Saints. Stately and imposing, he looked considerably taller than his medium height. His eyes were cool and his lips were firm, lips that could smile encouragement to the weary, or curse those who displeased him. One had only to look at him to know the indomitable will that made him a master of himself and of those about him.

A hush fell on the crowd. His voice rang out through the frozen trees, out across the sea of lifted faces.

"Attention! The whole camp of Israel!"

There was a pause, although every ear was already straining to catch his words.

"The Lord has been with us in times past, yea, since our beginning, however singular has been His method of proving it. And He shall be with us in the future, through all our trials. Remember, it is through fire that steel is made strong, and the Lord God is testing us in the blast furnace of persecution." He sounds like Father reading the Bible, Gale thought.

"But let Him test us, and find us strong! Let us march from our homes and into the wilderness with our heads high, and not go skulking off like a pack of beaten dogs! We shall go gloriously! We shall sing, and the wilderness shall ring with our singing! We shall march, and those who see us pass will be glad for having seen!

"Where our march shall take us, it is not within human power to say. His empire, and the empire of His people, is established, and the powers of hell cannot prevail against it. It is established, and one day it shall blossom forth to the amazement of all the peoples of the earth. Where it shall be, I cannot now say. But we shall march onward to Zion, and when we reach that Zion, I shall know it, be it in a desert or on a mountaintop. And there we shall settle, to build up the Empire of God!

"And now, my Brothers and Sisters, go and prepare your wagons. We shall break camp immedi-

130

ately and set out for the West. May God be with you, and speed you on your journey!"

With dramatic precision he turned and disappeared into his wagon. For a moment after he was gone, there was a deep silence in the open woods. There arose a vast shout, as with one breath, a thunder of emotion unleashed from thousands of throats.

"Hosanna to the Lord! Hallelujah! Hallelujah!"

"And then someone began singing, loud and clear!"

"We'll find the place which God for us prepared,
Far away in the West,
Where none shall come to hurt or make afraid;
There the Saints will be blessed.
We'll make the air with music ring,
Shout praises to our God and King;
Above the rest these words we'll tell—
All is well! All is well!"

And then the multitude swiftly broke up into men, women, and children. People hurriedly went back to their wagons, beating their mittened hands together to drive out the frost. Their eyes brightened with fresh inspiration, they were no longer a sea of faces.

There was a new lightness in their step and an eagerness in their hands as they stowed their belongings in the covered wagons, struck their tents, and brought the stock out of the temporary corrals.

By noon the first company was under way, its members shouting and cheering, the wagons lumbering away across the rolling hills of Iowa, with dogs barking and bands of sheep and hogs noisily bringing up the rear.

Company eighteen was the third to pull away from camp, with its captain, Isaac Eldridge, riding at its head, his broadcloth riding coat and polished boots as black as the ebony mare he rode. Those in

131

the wagons yelled and jeered gleefully at those who yet remained behind, for it was a race to see which company would be the next to take to the road.

Toward the front of the company was Pat Muldoon, lashing his frightened oxen into a trot, his face red with excitement, his wife clutching the seat beside him with considerable anxiety. A few wagons farther back rode Addie Voak, settled among the many children of Ad Jenkins. She was content at last, accepted as an equal, and happily unaware of the jealousy raging in Sister Muldoon.

Behind came the Nickols family with the schoolmaster, Barret Nickols, driving his forlorn team of horses as though he were driving the family carriage to church on a Sunday morning. His lips were drawn down in his customary anticipation of impending catastrophe. As usual, Sister Nickols bobbed about with bird-like movements, torn between anxiety over the road ahead, and concern for the welfare of her five daughters.

Bringing up the extreme rear of the hundred rumbling wagons came Jeddy Tavenner, his wagon a hodgepodge of chicken coops and puppies, dirty bedding and children. Tillie Tavenner, not to be set into swift motion by man or God, had barely managed to retrieve the last twin and throw in the last sooty cooking pot before the final wagon of their company had pulled away. She now grinned at those they passed as though she and Jeddy alone had been responsible for company eighteen's swift getaway. Again heavy with child, she held baby Edna on her lap, muffled in an old quilt, while the four older children whooped and waved at those they were leaving behind.

Midway in the train was the Simons' wagon, with Edouard and Cassie seated alone on the seat. There was a slight line between his brows, but he rode as usual with his hand on the jerk line of the oxen. There was a look of fear in Cassie's face.

Behind them in the shadows of the wagon there was a sharp moan, and then low voices talking until the interruption of another stabbing cry. They were the voices of Gale and Sophie Eldridge. When another of the pains had passed and Gale had wiped the sweat from the woman's face with a cloth, Sophie went on talking, staring at the wagon cover above her.

"I'm sick, Gale, but I have to talk. It helps a little to let off some steam. I've kept it shut up in me for so long, being with people I hate, that it seems good to be with someone I don't have to hate." She let out a long quivering breath. "I'm sorry I've just moved in on you like this, without more than asking your leave. But I couldn't have the baby in Grace's wagon. She wouldn't stand for it."

"Sophie! Don't think such horrid thoughts!"

"If she can't have one of her own, she isn't going to be very happy to have mine around."

"She's kind enough to the Meier children. I wouldn't worry."

"You can be sweet and generous about her! It's easy for you! You don't have to live with her!"

Gale didn't answer. A cry was wrenched from Sophie, and Gale wiped her wet icy face. The spasm passed and the sufferer relaxed a little to give her body to the rough jolting of the wagon. When she spoke again, her voice had lost some of its strength.

"This marriage though, is better than last time. At least Isaac treats a girl like she wants to be treated. Jock didn't. He was a good man, in his way, but he didn't have any feelings, and he didn't expect anyone else to have, either . . . O–o–oh!" The cry of agony withered and again she spoke. "Isaac . . . he's kind . . . and polite . . . and treats a girl like she *is* somebody. But I hate him because I know he doesn't really mean it. He'd treat any dozen other girls just the same."

Sophie's bitterness made Gale a little sick. She began to feel defensive about Eldridge. Sophie wasn't being fair. Hadn't he taken in the entire troop of Meier children and given them affection and security? Sophie seemed overly emotional.

"Sophie hush, you mustn't talk. Rest now."

"I have to talk . . . as long as I'm able. I haven't had a chance to talk for so long. And when I'm talking, I'm not waiting for the next pain." She shivered beneath the heavy quilts, and her eyes closed wearily. After a time she went on. "I'll have the baby, and take good care of it, even though I don't want it. I've hated it ever since I first knew. But I'll be a good mother."

She broke off in a cry. But then she went on again, her voice faint above the creak of the wagon, her eyes closed, dark crescents in the pallor of her face.

"I have its clothes ready . . . still in Isaac's wagon." Another cry. "If we didn't have to have babies . . . it wouldn't be so awful. But a man gives us a home . . . We don't have any choice. He expects *something* . . ." A pain shot through her monologue.

Gale wanted to cover her ears with her hands. The hard words twisted at her vitals. Sophie continued to mumble, but her words were now too weak to be understood. Gale smoothed the hair back from the woman's wet forehead. Poor Sophie, Gale mused. She was becoming warped by two unhappy marriages, entered into for the sole objective of ref-

134

uge. For a moment Gale could feel herself in Sophie's place, and in Cassie's, and all the other second wives. It's better to be a first wife. At least she's sure of love in the beginning. But a second wife . . . She shivered.

The pains were coming very fast now. Sophie's hands tore at the covers with her straining. Talk ceased. Her lips twisted in agony. The voice that came from her throat was not Sophie's . . . not a human's. It was like the death cry of a wild animal. Fear knotted Gale's stomach. What if things went wrong? What if Sophie . . . She looked at the meager array of equipment laid out on top of the water keg. Was everything there? Until an hour ago she hadn't known the least essentials of birth. She knew that women bore babies by some agonizing miracle, but in her sheltered existence there had been no discussion to enlighten her. And Sophie's instructions had been hasty.

There was a clean blanket for the baby. There was thread for tying the cord close by the baby, she'd said, and again a little farther on. And there were scissors to cut between.

Gale crouched on her knees. The moaning ceased. There was the rough whistle of breath. The pains welded together into a grand finale of torture, with no rests between. A last tearing conclusion of labor. Every muscle in the stiffened body was rigid in a terrible symphony of effort.

And still there was no baby. Helplessly, Gale stroked the knuckles which stood out white in the harsh knotted hands. What should she do? There must be something. Instinct told her that it was time for the baby to come . . . past time. Still nothing happened. On rolled the wagon, thumping and lurching through the rutted snow, up across slow

135

climbing hills, down into frost-glittering swales, on and on.

Sophie's face became a distorted mask. Her lips were drawn back, leaving her teeth naked. Could she be dying? She must have help. Gale scrambled to the wagon seat and clutched Edouard's arm.

"You'll have to stop! I need help . . . the baby won't come. Sophie's dying!"

"There's not a doctor in the company," Edouard spoke thoughtfully. "Nor in any of the other companies, as far as I know. Who can I get? With the wagons strung out like this, our only hope is a nearby wagon. Sister Eldridge is just behind us."

"Yes . . . yes!" She would have to ignore Sophie's wishes. "Stop . . . quickly! Get her!"

She turned back into the wagon. In the dim shadows she peered into the woman's face. It was different. The tightness was gone. In its place was a kind of strange tranquility. The wagon stopped.

In the silence there was a faint sound beneath the quilts. The muffled wail of a baby.

"No, Edouard . . . don't stop!" she cried. "We don't need Sister Eldridge . . . now." And she added to herself, "Sophie wouldn't have wanted her."

Beneath the covers she wrapped the clean blanket around the wet squirming form of a baby. It mustn't be chilled. She brought the bundle out and rocked it in her arms. Her mind was sucked dry. She was startled by a faint sigh, and looked down to find Sophie faintly smiling.

"Is it . . . a boy?" she whispered.

"I don't know yet," Gale spoke, then laughed in inutterable relief. "It's too cold to look."

So that's what it's like, having a baby, she thought.

136

Seventeen

Eldridge rode back along the trail, giving the order to break up into formation for the night. The train divided into two groups, the lead wagon of each swinging out to form a wide circle.

Eldridge rode up to his own camp fire beside the wagon which Grace had maneuvered into position. Gale, glancing up from her own fire a few steps away, saw him lean easily over his saddle horn and address his wife.

"How did Sophie make the trip today?"

"I don't know," Grace answered evenly. "I haven't seen her since we left Sugar Creek."

"Haven't seen her!" Eldridge was startled. "Where in the devil is she?"

"I think she's with the Simons. Ask them." Her face was expressionless as she bent over her cooking. The children huddled near the fire with worried eyes.

"Simons! Why?" For the first time, Gale heard anger in his voice.

"I don't know. You'd better ask her."

Isaac shifted in his saddle to face Gale. "Is Sophie with you?"

She felt a tremor of fear, but her voice sounded calm. "Yes."

He jumped from his horse and strode to the Simons' wagon to jerk the blanket curtain aside. Gale sprang to her feet and put a restraining hand on his arm.

"She's awfully sick. The baby is here . . . but she had a bad time."

Eldridge shot her a quick look and dropped the blanket.

"Oh." He paused, staring at his boots. Then he raised the blanket again and disappeared within.

Sale tried not to listen, but there was only the thin canvas between the Eldridges and herself as she stooped over the fire. Isaac spoke softly.

"Sophie, are you awake?"

"Yes." Her voice was faint.

"How do you feel?"

"Not bad, considering. You ought to try having a baby some time. It would be something you'd never forget!" Then the flippancy was gone, and in its place was a tremulous pride. "It's a boy."

"Sophie!" Something of Sophie's pride deepened his voice. "A boy! We'll call him Isaac!" They were silent a long time. Then Gale heard him speak again, quite low. "No, Sophie. Let's not name him that. Let's wait. There might be a real Isaac, some day . . . a son of my own."

He climbed out of the wagon and addressed Gale curtly.

"Where's Edouard?"

"He's taking care of the oxen."

"How soon will he be back?"

"Here he comes now."

"Edouard, old man, lend a hand here, will you? I'm going to carry Sophie back to my own wagon."

Edouard glanced at Gale uncertainty. She turned to Isaac.

138

"Do you think you should? She's lost so much blood . . ."

"She belongs in my wagon." He spoke with sharp finality. "Simon, are you going to help me?"

Gale knew remonstrance was futile, so with awkward gentleness the three of them lifted Sophie and the baby from the wagon on the featherbed and carried her to the Eldridge wagon, with Cassie and the children looking on wide-eyed, and Grace over the cooking pot, ignoring the whole proceeding.

"I'll be over to see you in the morning," Gale whispered, smiling at Sophie in encouragement. Sophie shrugged and turned her face away.

As the wagon trains continued to move across Iowa, the weather began to moderate, but instead of adding to the comfort of the travelers, it made things worse. The most cruel of the cold weather had passed, during the last week of February the thaws came, with alternate days of rain, and sleet, and melting sunshine.

Shortly after they crossed the Des Moines River, the Saints all stopped for the first great rendezvous since Sugar Creek, with company after company pulling into camp. On the evening of March first they gathered in a wide clearing for prayer meeting. To listen to them, one would have thought they were gathering for a social. There was shouting and laughter, loud jest and playful jostling.

Edouard entered the throng with Gale and Cassie. Cassie looked like an angelic child wearing the blue snood that Gale had made her for Christmas.

Gale walked tall and proud. There would be no one to say behind a hand, "Have you noticed? Sister

139

Simon is looking mighty sour these days since her husband got himself a new wife, that little Cassie Meier." She'd show them. Even with Cassie hanging on his other arm, she'd show them. She knew, as none of the rest of them knew, that the girl was a wife in name only. As the three of them walked through the crowd, several men turned with approval to stare at the tall proud girl.

On a ridge a mile or so to the north, a small group of Indians sat their horses and listened, wondering at the thundering of a thousand voices raised in hymns. They sounded joyful. Yet these people were being driven from their old hunting ground. But this was no war song! White man was indeed strange.

After the closing hymn there was dancing. The multitude broke up into smaller groups about the fires while musicians began tuning up their strings and warming the brass of their horns. The Simons, with the rest of company eighteen, gathered around the gay lilt of Ad Jenkins' banjo and Bub Leary's accordion. Having tuned to his satisfaction, Jenkins burst into the rollicking strains of "Whoop 'er Up Cindy!" Feet began to tap and hands to clap in unison.

Bub Leary's fingers moved tenderly over the keys of his accordion. He stared off at the stars as though examining them closely.

"Get your partners for a quadrille, folks!" someone shouted.

The crowd fell back, and couples took their positions, stamping their feet and shouting. Before Gale knew what was happening, Eldridge had her by the arm and was swinging her out into dance formation, gaily shouting the dance calls as he went.

"Chase the rabbit!
Chase the squirrel!
Chase the pretty girl 'round the world!
Chase her through the sandy land!
Chase her home and back again!"

Gale wanted to be angry with him, angry because he had taken her so unceremoniously for granted, and because he had no right to the first dance. The first dance always belonged to one's partner. But in spite of herself she was caught up by the infectious hilarity of the music and the laughter of those about her. Lightly she whirled through the patterns of the quadrille, her feet skipping joyously over the frozen ground. Her whole body seemed to be singing, and she found it hard to remember her anger.

"You shouldn't have done that!" she scolded when the dance ended.

"Why not?"

"The first dance belongs to my husband, you know. Or don't you observe proper manners here in the West?"

"You don't have to worry about your husband," he teased. "One wife is all he can dance with at one time."

Quickly her eyes sought the spot where she had left them standing. Her heart gave a happy leap. They were still there . . . not dancing.

"Where is Sister Eldridge?" she asked, to mask her small pleasure.

He shrugged airily. "Back in the tent asleep, I suppose. She left right after the singing. She doesn't care much about dancing anymore." He took her back to Edouard.

"Why weren't you dancing?" she asked breathlessly.

"My first dance is with you," he said quietly. But it was enough to send her spirits soaring.

After her dance with Edouard, her partners came thick and fast, for it didn't take long for the word to spread that Brother Simon's wife was a merry and light-footed dancer. She laughed away the shadows and amused her partners with lively retorts. Once she stood, watching Edouard waltz with Cassie, but her jealousy was muted. A sharp elbow jabbed her ribs.

"Have ye seen Pat?" Sister Muldoon hissed.

"No, not recently." She was glad she had been fortunate enough to evade him.

"And have ye seen our barmaid?"

"Addie, you mean? Yes, she's dancing. With Olaf Pederson, I think."

"That was last dance. She's not there now!" She peered among the dancers. "Leadin' decent men off into the dark, like as not. Why we tolerate her amongst us is beyond me!" She craned her neck in anxious search.

"Please, Sister! Addie Voak is a good girl!" Gale was surprised at her own temerity. "Just because she had to work as your barmaid to earn a living in Boston doesn't mean a thing! Remember, I had to work as your maid once, too."

"And may I be askin', Miss," Sister Muldoon sniffed, "who is the little blonde yer man is waltzin' around tonight?"

Gale recoiled. When she recovered her composure, she managed a laugh, cool and brittle.

"Oh, didn't you know? That's Cassie. She and Edouard have been married for a couple of months now. She and I have been friends ever since I came to Nauvoo," she lied blithely. She cringed at the deceit, but she'd not let the other gloat over her misery.

"Ye mean . . ." Sister Muldoon stared with disbelief in her pale blue eyes, "yer a plural wife . . . and *like* it?"

"Why not? Cassie and her mother were the first friends I had in Illinois. Since her mother died, she's made her home with us. Both Edouard and I were glad to have her." She marveled at her new-found conciliation.

Mary Muldoon opened her mouth to launch a fresh barrage of questions. The questions were never uttered, for at the moment Pat appeared, headed straight for Gale, unconscious of his wife's proximity.

"Hey, girlie, this here is our dance, ain't it?"

Gale made a quick decision. Pat seemed preferable at the moment to the piercing questions of his wife.

"Why yes, if you like," she answered sweetly, and was swept away among the dancers.

But her relief was short-lived, for Pat's arm tightened heavily around her waist, and his breath, smelling of whiskey, was hot on her face. She pulled as far away from his as she could, but his arm was hard and insistent.

"Yes." She turned her head away, and pushed away as far as possible against the pressure of his arms.

"Sister, come down off yer high horse! Get friendly, can't ye? Ye act as if ye hadn't never been my hired girl, waitin' table and carryin' slops fer me!"

She was tempted to slap him and leave him where he stood, but common sense cautioned her against it. She looked in desperation for Edouard.

143

A clumsy hand fell on Pat's shoulder, and he whirled belligerently to face Bub Leary.

"Pardon me, suh," Bub addressed Muldoon, but his eyes were on Gale. "I think this is the dance the lady promised me." He twisted his hands in his coat pockets.

"Yes," she reached out and took Bub's arm, "thank you!"

"Say, what is this?" Pat's red face swelled. "Run on sonny, and play your music box!"

"I'm sorry, suh, but Ad Jenkins told me to dance this one." His manner was apologetic, but firm. He drew Gale away, and they were lost among the dancers.

"How kind of you, Bub!"

"That's all right," he flushed. " 'Twasn't much." They stumbled along awkwardly, for Bub's sense of rhythm lay in his fingers and not in his feet. He swallowed twice before he spoke. "I been wantin' to ask you . . . do you reckon 'twould be all right if I was to ask Cassie to dance . . . once? Would it be fair, I mean?"

Gale smiled, and her eyes were motherly. Somehow Bub always inspired in her a maternal instinct, although she couldn't be any older than he. Poor Bub! His lashes concealed the hurt in his eyes.

"Why, yes. I think it would be fine!"

"Thanks, ma'am."

When he returned her to her place where Edouard and Cassie stood, she found eleven-year-old Louisa Nickols waiting for her, her face tense with anxiety, her hood askew, her coat unbuttoned.

"Please, ma'am, could you come to our wagon? Mamma is very sick and Father says to get help. Could you come?"

She turned to Edouard. "I'll go with the poor child."

He squeezed her hand and smiled. "If you need help, send one of the children. Or should I come with you now?"

"No, there's no need. You may as well stay until the dancing is over."

She and Louisa left the fires and the music and stumbled through the darkness. Here and there a light glowed dimly through the canvas, but generally there was silence and darkness. They came to a tent where there was light and the sound of muffled sobbing. Louisa parted the flaps and ushered her in. Four girls huddled about their mother, who lay in a bed on the ground. When she entered, Barret Nickols turned and nodded briefly, then turned back to his wife. The children were crying, while the eldest, Susannah, was vainly trying to comfort little Nabby. Gale came close to the bed. Mrs. Nickols' face was swollen and her eyes dull. She tried to smile. When she spoke, her throat was choked.

"I'm sorry we spoiled your good time. Mr. Nickols gets so upset when I'm ill. I wanted him to wait until the dancing was over, but he was so nervous . . . and you're the only one I feel I really know here."

"It's quite all right," Gale smiled and took the woman's hand. "If there's anything I can do . . ."

"It's only a bad cold, nothing really." But her hand was blazing hot.

Barret Nickols interposed. "She is finding it increasingly difficult to breathe. I consider it a matter of serious consequence."

"I wonder if you could get the girls off to bed," Mrs. Nickols croaked. "Father has been so upset . . ."

145

With a lighted candle Gale followed the five girls out of the tent and into the nearby wagon. They were sniffling quietly as she set the candle on a keg. They sat like a row of small birds and began unlacing their shoes.

"I want my Mommy!" Four-year-old Nabby burst into sudden weeping.

Gale gathered the child into her arms.

"Hush, Nabby baby . . . hush." She rocked her and brushed the soft hair back from the little face.

"Why can't I sleep with my Mommy?"

Susannah answered her, jerking at the stubborn knots in her shoelaces as she spoke. "Don't be foolish, Nabby! You know why you can't."

Nabby lay quiet, staring at the canvas cover above her. Gale's fingers traced the soft tendrils around the child's temple and ear. If she ever had a baby, she hoped it would look like Nabby Nickols, from her fair hair and elfish smile to her dainty prancing feet.

"Is Mommy going to die tonight?"

The question frightened Gale, but she forced a light retort. "Mercy no, child! What makes you ever think such a thing?"

Susannah looked up, her serious eyes questioning.

"But Mamma is really terribly ill, isn't she?"

"Not terribly ill, dear," she tried to sound convincing. "She'll be much better in the morning . . . after I've put an onion poultice on her chest." She picked up the candle. "Everyone in bed?" she asked cheerily. Everyone was. She tucked Nabby in tenderly beside Susanah. "Good night, little ladies."

Blowing them a kiss, she went back to the Nickolses' tent.

Eighteen

Dawn was spreading over the camp when Gale left the Nickolses' tent. Sister Nickols lay sleeping fitfully, and her husband had promised to lie down beside her until the children would awaken. Gale hoped it was not lung fever as she feared, but the onions were a precaution.

Gale strode through the morning, breathing deep of the cold air. She had a sense of strange solitude as she walked between the silent rows of tents and wagons. Elation filled her, as though she alone of all these sleeping people were alive to the beauty of the waking world and this morning's dawn was her own special possession.

As she walked the camp began to come alive. A rooster crowed and a hen murmured answer. She heard quiet voices inside the canvas city, and somewhere a baby cried lustily until it was given its morning breast. The dogs sleeping beneath the wagons uncurled themselves, stretched, and lifted their noses to detect any news on the morning breeze. Before she had reached her own wagon she met two or three sleepy-eyed pilgrims climbing down from their wagons or bending over the buried coals of last night's fire.

Edouard would be still asleep, for it was very early. She would slip into the wagon as quietly as possible and perhaps could get a little rest before it was time to begin the day's activities.

As she reached their wagon, she saw the flaps of Cassie's tent opening. She heard a man's low voice. She stopped in her tracks, her heart pounding in her throat. Edouard appeared, smoothing his tousled hair and donning his hat. She never knew how long she stood there. An eternity passed, with the blood draining from her head and numbing her heart, leaving her as stiff as a snow image. Her mind burned with only one thought. Edouard had spent the night with Cassie! In Cassie's tent, in Cassie's bed!

She must not let him see her. Her thoughts raced wildly. *Hurry! I must escape. If I slip among the shadows of the wagons, he'll not know I was here. I must get away! Anywhere, so I won't see the guilt in his face.*

"Wait!" he called. "Gale! Where are you going?"

She pretended not to hear. *I can't go back. There will be shame in his face, and I can't bear to see it. I'll go on.*

"Gale! Wait a minute!"

She could hear his feet hurrying after her. She stopped. She turned slowly and waited.

"What's the matter? Where are you going?"

She didn't answer.

"Have you been up all night?"

Against her will her eyes were drawn to his face. She searched the dark familiarity of his features, half afraid. Then she dropped her eyes. A cold detached part of her mind told her that Cassie was his wife . . . that he had the right. But that part of her mind was a long way off. Her face began to burn with the shame that he did not seem to feel.

148

"You look terrible. Were you up with Sister Nickols all night?"

"Yes."

"Haven't you been to the wagon yet?"

"No. I mean, I thought you wouldn't be awake." She wouldn't tell him that she was running away.

"Where were you going?"

"I . . . I just thought I'd walk around a while . . . until you'd be awake."

"You need some breakfast and a good sleep." He led her toward the wagon. "Come."

She had the furious impulse to shake off his hand, the hand that a short time before had been caressing Cassie. Instead she submitted passively.

"How is Sister Nickols?" His voice sounded as usual.

"Better."

"What's the matter with her?"

"Lung fever, maybe."

She couldn't bear to share the long days ahead in the wagon with Edouard and Cassie. Cassie and Edouard. The thought nauseated her. She couldn't return to the wagon.

"I can't stay!" She pulled away and stopped. "I . . . I must go back to the Nickolses!"

"Go back? What for?"

"I . . . I must go back . . . now. I . . . I only came to change my bonnet and cloak. They need me."

He turned her squarely to face him. "You know I spent last night with Cassie," he spoke accusingly. "Is that it?"

"Yes," she whispered.

"Cassie is my wife." His voice was cold and hard. "I thought you understood that. It's not the first time, either."

149

She had no answer. She wished that he would let her go. He dropped her arms but continued speaking.

"Remember, Gale, I love you, more than anything in the world." He was very unlike the Edouard she knew. "But Cassie is my wife, and if you choose to act childish about it, that is your privilege. But it will not change the fact." He turned away, adding over his shoulder, "We are breaking camp this morning. Will you be riding in my wagon?" The cold anger of his words shocked her, like a stinging blow across the face.

Her head came up swiftly, and she looked straight into his eyes. Her tone matched his own, cool and hard. "Yes. Where else would I be riding?"

But when the train resumed its trek, Gale was not with her husband. Shortly before company eighteen pulled out of camp, Louisa Nickols came flying, her black hair whipping out behind her.

"Oh, please, ma'am!" she cried. "It's Nabby! She can't catch her breath! Mamma says to run!"

When Gale arrived the child was in her father's arms, struggling for life, her small face blue. Sister Nickols was trying to pull her coat on over her nightgown.

"It's the croup," she croaked, turning to Gale. "She can't breathe!"

The wagon train started, and Gale rode in the Nickolses' wagon with Nabby gasping in her arms. Edouard and Cassie rode alone, far ahead in the long crawling train.

Mid-afternoon of the second day out, a cold wind sprang up which cut through the early spring warmth, a wind that carried the smell of rain. The leaders whipped their teams into a trot, with those behind pushing to keep up, for they were crossing a desolate unbroken stretch of prairie with no camping facilities, and they hoped to reach a creek or at least some brush or fuel before the storm overtook them.

There was nothing to be seen but wagons and prairie and sky. The earth stretched away in every direction in a trackless mud-colored sea. Gale had the sensation of being adrift in mid-ocean, lost in the limitless vacuum between sky and sea. The wagons were small and foolish, hurrying ahead. To what?

Nabby, resting in an uneasy stupor, lay on a makeshift bed beside her mother. Gale wet the child's parched lips occasionally with a wet cloth. The mother dozed. The older children rode, silent and apprehensive.

Then the rain struck, a blinding torrent. Where a moment before there had been the brown matted prairie, there were now only dense sheets of white rain. It was almost impossible to discern the wagon ahead. Someone on a horse rode back along the train, shouting. His words were lost. But without hearing, the drivers swung their wagons out into a circle, fighting their teams into the face of the storm. Quickly the camp was formed. The stock was driven in the corrals formed by the wagons. The men, drenched to the skin, crawled shivering into their wagons for protection. Water dripped from them in disagreeable puddles.

The rain lashed at the miserable animals, their heads lowered, their tails against the storm. It drummed on the wagon tops, making speech impossible. The prairie began to collect little pools, pools which rapidly spread into wider pools. Before dark fell the entire prairie seemed under water, with only here and there the hump of an island showing above the surface.

Fires were out of the question without fuel, and so the Saints crouched through the night, wrapped in soggy quilts. Rivulets began leaking through the wagon tops. The wretched occupants ceased trying to find a dry spot, and slumped where they were, rain dripping down their necks, awaiting a morning that seemed never to come.

In the Nickolses' wagon the rain was a blessing, for the cold wet air cooled the fevered faces of mother and child. At the first blast of thunder, Nabby had awakened wailing, but now she had relapsed into silence. Barret Nickols unearthed a faded green umbrella and he and Gale took turns holding it over the sleeping mother and child.

A bright morning tried to erase the effects of the storm. A few men wandered out to see how the stock had fared. The horses and oxen huddled in groups, their coats caked with ice. Hogs wallowed in the frozen mud, squealing at the tops of their lungs. The animals suffering most were the sheep, for their thick pelts had become water-logged. Two or three of the weaker ewes lay stretched in the mud, dead. Several more were down, and it was evident they wouldn't be on the westward trek. They were slaughtered for immediate use.

Gale found the temperatures of Nabby and her mother again rising. The chill of the night had not been as beneficial as she thought. By turns Nabby thrashed in delirium, or drifted off into a stupor. Her little body shook with her labored breathing. Gale sponged her face and stroked the tumbled hair back from her fevered brow.

Watching these two, Gale almost forgot the burden of her own heart. Bringing it out into the light occasionally and examining it made it seem almost trivial, measured against the struggle for life that she was witnessing. The only sleep she had was as she drowsed beside Nabby, slumped against various bulges in the baggage.

Next morning the Saints broke camp. Like a barometer, their spirits rose. They shook out their damp bedding, folded it away, ate the last of their supply of cold food, and harnessed up. As they set out once more, it was with jesting shouts and loud singing.

As the wagons started to move, Nabby and her mother awoke, cool and clear-eyed. Gale offered them some apples and a drink of cold water from the keg.

Nabby pushed it aside impatiently. "I want some 'tato soup!"

"We haven't a potato to our names," Susannah murmured, "even if we had a fire to cook it."

"Neither have we," said Gale. "Ours were either frozen or eaten long ago!"

"I want some 'tato soup!" fretted Nabby with a sick child's insistence.

"Maybe we'll be passing a farm soon," Sister Nickols spoke hopefully. "Mr. Nickols says we'd soon be in the farming country. Perhaps . . ." her voice trailed off.

"Girls, which of you will be the first to find a farm house?" Gale took up the idea with great cheerfulness. "Let's play 'I spy'!" She turned to Nabby. "As soon as we come to a farm, we'll get a potato and make you some soup!"

The girls hurried to the seat beside their father to watch for the improbable appearance of a farm house on the western horizon.

Nineteen

Fires blazed around the circle of wagons that night.
With rejoicing the women stirred up great batches of
bannock bread and baked them in heavy iron spi-
ders over the coals. They fried plates of ham and
boiled pots of hominy and onions, while the older
children spread the damp bedding and clothing near
the fires to dry.

While Gale cooked supper at the Nickolses' wagon,
the girls went around the camp asking to borrow a
potato. Gale had the meal ready before they returned, their faces long with disappointment. Not a
potato was available.

Gale prepared plates for the invalids. In the dim
light of the wagon she held the plate for Nabby.

"Look!" she said, coaxingly. "A nice hot supper."

The child turned away.

"No," she said, then remembered her manners,
"thank you."

"Please, dear. Try some of this broth."

Obediently she took a sip, then turned away, her
face twisted with distaste.

"Nabby needs milk," Gale said abruptly. "Who
has a cow?"

Barret Nickols looked at her vaguely. "Why . . .
I'm sure I don't know."

"Don't the Tavenners have a cow?"

155

"Tavenners. Tavenners. I'm not sure. Should I . . . do you think I should ask?"

"No, finish your supper. I need the walk."

Gale started along the long curve of wagons that led away into the night. At every fire, the families gathered at their supper called out a friendly greeting to the girl who hurried past, and more than one asked about Nabby, who was a great favorite with the group from Boston. She stopped occasionally to inquire about the location of the Tavenners. At the Jenkins fire where Ad and his stout wife were eating supper with Addie Voak and the children, Gale paused.

"What business you aimin' to carry on with the Tavenners?" Ad parried her question.

Gale smiled as she answered, for his inquisitiveness was simply a part of Ad Jenkins, and no one resented it.

"Nabby needs milk, and I thought maybe they had a cow."

"Yup. They have. But it won't do you no good. She's dry, been dry for quite a spell now. And if she don't snucker up to the company bull some day soon, she won't come fresh till we get to the Land of Zion!"

"Who does have a cow, do you know?

"Pederson, the tall yeller-haired Swede, you know. He's only a couple of wagons off. I'll go with you."

Olaf and his wife were piling dishes into a pot of hot water by the fire. He came to the visitors, a smile on his pleasant face.

"This here's Sister Simon," Ad spoke. "She wants some milk for little Nabby Nickols, who is mighty sick. Have any to spare?"

"Good evening, ma'am. Sister Simon and her

156

good husband took in my family one night last September. We shall be forever grateful." Pain shadowed his face at the memory and he turned quickly to cover his emotion. "Mamma, can you fix up a jug of milk for Sister Simon? She needs it for the little girl."

"*Ja!* Sure!" She nodded vigorously and prepared the milk.

Gale knew that they needed it for their own children, for food was getting scarce, but neither hesitated a moment. Gale felt a comfortable warmth in their generosity.

On her way back Gale was startled when a man stepped out of the darkness into her path. Edouard spoke quietly. "I'm sorry if I frightened you. I was tending the stock and saw you passing."

"It's very dark. How did you know me?"

"I couldn't mistake you."

She did not answer.

"How are Nabby and her mother?"

"The same."

"Then . . ." there was uncertainty in his voice ". . . then, you won't be coming back . . . soon?"

When he spoke again, he seemed to have mastered his doubts, for there was a firm question in his words. "After they are well, then?"

For a long moment she stood, swaying again with the nausea of that morning when she had found him coming out of Cassie's tent, his hair rumpled. Cassie . . . and Edouard. Edouard . . . and Cassie. It would be like that for the rest of their lives.

Suddenly a feeling of indomitable strength rose up within her, a power that would keep even Edouard from knowing the fear and jealousy in her heart. She steadied herself on the rocking earth and raised her chin high.

"Of course I'm coming back," she said crisply. "I must be going now." She brushed aside the hand she felt reaching for her arm.

The mud-splashed wagons labored through heavy woods. On every side towered black-trunked sentinels, frowning down on the pioneers who were forcing their stubborn way through the thickets. The sky was blotted by a tangle of branches, heavy enough to keep out the sun, but not dense enough to keep out the rains which made the woods a bottomless morass.

Birds and squirrels screamed their alarm while the sweating Saints cut limbs from the trees and laid them across the mud to keep the stock and wagons from sinking out of sight. Occasionally the wagons rumbled through a small clearing where some early settler had built a rough log cabin in a field of fire-blackened stumps.

As they fought their way ahead, almost ready to abandon their wagons in the swamps of early spring, Brigham Young came riding out of the woods. He had left the company up ahead and had come back to cheer another band through the hopeless slough.

There was something magic in the man. He rode along the train, shouting words of encouragement to those who were ready to give up. Occasionally he dismounted and hoisted on a wheel that seemed permanently mired down. The cursing ceased, and in its place the songs of Zion began to ring out among the trees. Somehow with Brigham Young there, the way seemed easier and the mud not quite so deep.

In the Nickolses' wagon there was no singing, for Nabby was delirious, crying out for the potato soup that had become an obsession with her. Barret

Nickols' horses staggered on, their thin shoulders straining against worn collars. Suddenly Sybil turned and clutched Gale's hand.

"Look . . . quick! There's another cabin! Maybe someone lives there! Maybe they have a potato!"

Gale and Susannah clambered down and made their way up the muddy path to the shabby dwelling. There were fresh tracks in the damp earth, footprints of adults and children. Gale saw a wisp of smoke from the chimney.

"They're home," Susannah said quietly. "I hope they don't know we're Saints."

Gale rapped firmly on the door. Her heart was pounding. They were taken aback by the suddenness with which the door was flung open, and by the angry countenance of the woman who faced them. Several towheaded children crowded around her skirts, but she pushed them back with a rough shove.

"Whata ya want?"

Gale managed to summon her voice.

"We have a little girl in our wagon who is awfully sick, and she keeps begging for potato soup. We thought perhaps . . . if you had one you could spare . . ."

"Begging, are ya? You Mormons are too good-for-nothin' to settle down and make respectable citizens of yourselves! Ya go traipsin' around like a passel o' gypsies, thievin' and beggin'. You ain't gettin' a potato out of *this* house!" Her face was as red as a turkey gobbler's.

Gale tightened her grip on Susannah's frightened hand, speaking with dignity.

"We're not begging, ma'am. I can pay for the potato."

"Beggin' or buyin', it don't make no difference!

You lechers don't get a thing offen this place without you kill us and steal it. And you're liable to try that, too. But I'm ready for ya!" She pulled an old gun from behind the door and swung the muzzle up into the girls' faces. "Now! Start walkin' down the trail! And no back talk!"

Gale saw her finger twitching nervously at the trigger. She felt the hair crawl on the back of her neck. She turned, with Susannah's hand tucked firmly under her arm, and walked sedately down the path.

"Don't run," she whispered, holding the terrified girl back. "It would frighten them at the wagon."

The girls greeted them, wide-eyed.

"Wouldn't she give you a potato?"

Gale's eyes met Susannah's. Nabby was very quiet.

"They didn't have any," Gale lied.

"Was that woman mad at you?"

"Didn't she have a gun?" Louisa chimed in.

"A gun!" Gale laughed, and Susannah tried to echo her. "Heavens, what eyes you girls have! What would a woman want with a gun?"

The girls settled back in disappointed silence, and as the wagon moved on, they again peered through the trees for another cabin. Above the creak and groan of the wagon Gale thought she could hear the songs of Zion drifting through the darkening forest.

That night the Saints camped wherever they were when darkness fell, and tethered their stock to nearby trees. There were no stars, and the tiny fires seemed lost along the muddy trail.

Toward morning as the birds began twittering drowsily in the branches high above, Nabby Nickols died.

Twenty

They were going to bury Nabby before the wagons resumed their journey, but Sister Nickols, rocking back and forth, wouldn't let them take her. She was like a tigress when Eldridge and Edouard came for the body.

"No! No! You can't have her!" Her voice was hoarse. "You can't bury her here in this dark and wet! I won't let you! Nabby wants sunshine, and flowers, and singing!" She pressed her face against the cold of Nabby's cheek. But there were no tears in the bird-like brightness of her eyes.

Edouard and Isaac turned toward Gale for help, but she only shook her head slightly and motioned for them to leave. Barret Nickols sat on the water keg, seemingly unaware of what was going on. He kept shaking his head and muttering as he stared at his thin white hands. Gale had taken the other girls to her own wagon shortly after daybreak, and now Barret and his wife were alone, with Gale wondering how to comfort them.

"I knew God was going to punish us," she could hear him mumbling. ". . . I've seen God's revenge coming . . ."

Gale, knowing that there was little that she could do now, left quietly and made her way along the trail to her own wagon. She met Jeddy Tavenner carrying a wooden chest.

"Sister Simon . . . I been waiting to see you." His soft voice was husky. "I was wondering . . . do they have a coffin for the little girl?"

Gale shook her head.

"I thought they wouldn't. And I was thinking . . . how would I like to bury one of my kids without something to lie in." He became very busy examining a hinge of the chest. Then he straightened, trying to sound very matter-of-fact. "This is the box I've kept my tools in ever since I took up the trade of ship's carpenter. It's been on many a long voyage . . . went clear around the world once. But I don't have much use for it now . . . and I was thinking these folks might want it."

"Thank you, Jeddy." Her heart swelled in gratitude. "I'll tell them."

She was cooking breakfast when Cassie came to the fire. There were tears on Cassie's cheeks as she stood, sniffling miserably. The Nickols girls were silent on the wagon tongue, a row of sparrows. Gale shot a quick glance at the younger wife. The tears on her face irritated Gale.

"What's the matter?" Gale whipped the pancake batter vigorously.

"It's just . . . I've been thinking about Nabby."

"Why, you don't even know her!"

"I knew her well enough to . . . to want my little girl . . . to be exactly like her!"

"Your . . . little . . . girl . . ." Gale let the words fall from her lips, one by one, separate from one another like stones.

Cassie turned and walked off into the woods. She didn't return until it was time for the wagons to start.

* * *

At last the caravan emerged from the damp of the big woods. They came out on the edge of a rolling prairie. Isaac Eldridge passed along the word that they would halt for the funeral. The day was golden with spring sun. Grass was springing green across the land, and birds trilled in the willows along the creeks.

Addie Voak came running back along the train, her sorrel hair flying in the March wind. She came to Gale who was helping the Nickols girls down from the wagon.

"Oh, I was afraid I might be too late," she panted. "Would it be proper if I was to offer them this . . . to wrap around Nabby?"

She held out the white loveliness of a silk shawl, with delicate flowers in Chinese embroidery gleaming in the sun.

"Oh, Addie, it's beautiful!"

"It's . . . well, a friend gave it to me in Boston. He brought it from China."

"If you want to give it," Gale was gentle, "I think it would be very proper."

"Maybe Brother Nickols . . . you know he's awful particular . . . maybe he wouldn't think I was good enough." She cast an uneasy eye at the children and her voice dropped to a whisper. "Some folks think I'm not . . . a lady."

Gale smiled and pressed her hand.

"Addie, I think you're very much a lady."

Nabby Nickols stayed to sleep in the prairie beside the deep ruts of the Mormon trail, a trail that was to be marked with many more graves before the Saints reached their Zion. It was a brief ceremony, with Isaac Eldridge speaking a few low words beside the opened earth. A few friendly Pottawattamie Indians, curious and properly solemn, joined the crowd about the grave and stood staring at the fair-haired child in the battered box.

Just before the ceremony, Cassie crept close and slipped a bunch of spring beauties into the small hands. Gale flushed in shame. That was what she had been doing in the woods. Gale felt humble. Someone threw a shovelful of dirt on the box in the shallow grave. The sound was final.

"I'll try to be kinder to Cassie, from now on," Gale thought.

Twenty-One

In April Brigham Young, fondling a clod of rich black soil, announced that the entire body of Saints was to spread out across Iowa, break up into bands and form settlements. They were to plow the soil immediately and sow all the seed they had. They were to make gardens, and fields of corn and wheat. As soon as the crops were well up, they would again go on and leave the harvesting to those coming behind.

It was a gigantic scheme, with ten thousand Saints playing their roles. On April 27 the first settlement was begun at Garden Grove, and as if by magic other settlements sprang up until they stretched like a string of beads on a leather thong across the breadth of Iowa.

Isaac Eldridge called the captains of company eighteen together during the noontime stop in order to discuss the news that a messenger had brought from Brigham Young. The long string of white-topped wagons extended across the green sea of prairie, with the stock hungrily munching the grass close to the trail, the children herding them as they ate their own lunches of cold biscuit and bacon.

Eldridge, with Edouard and Olaf Pederson, captains of the fifties, and the others who were captains of the tens, met in the narrow strip of shade on the north side of Simons' wagon, as it was midway in

165

the wagon train. As they ate, they talked of when and where they should stop to build their settlement.

Gale sat on the wagon seat with her knitting needles flying at feverish speed and scarcely heard them. Her mind was smoldering with the increasing complexities of her life. Edouard had not told her about the baby, and Cassie never spoke of it again, but they didn't need to. She knew, in the whiteness of Cassie's face, and the smug little smile she wore when she was not being ill. She knew, in the odd light that flashed up in Edouard's eyes when he looked at Cassie, and in the added gentleness of his voice when he spoke to her.

It was at night when Gale knew her real torment. Whether he spent the night in Cassie's tent or beside her in the wagon, it meant burning torture. When he was with Cassie, she would lie alone in the center of the bed with a pillow over her head, trying to shut out the sounds of them, and the thought of Cassie in his arms, his lips against her yellow hair, his hands caressing the white childishness of her body. When he slept in the wagon, she lay far to her side of the bed, her face almost against the canvas, her body rigid and fiercely unresponsive. If he reached out and tentatively touched her arm, she would pull away with an aloofness that was almost hatred.

"We're stopping at the next creek." Edouard was climbing onto the wagon seat beside her, his voice vibrant with eagerness. "We'll spend the next few weeks there, plowing and sowing. This is fine weather for planting. I hope it lasts."

The wagons creaked into motion.

"I hope so," she responded shortly. Why did I say that? I don't care if it lasts or not. Rainy nights are no worse than clear nights. Rain, when it comes down hard enough, can help blot it out for a while.

166

Even the rain, thundering on the canvas and dripping through on pillows and blankets, is better than just thinking.

One afternoon in mid-May Edouard came from the woodland along the creek with his axe in his hand. He dropped to a seat on the sod beside Gale, who sat in the shade of the wagon, her fingers busy over the willows that lay in her lap. Willows along the creek were plentiful, and boys with knives were eager to supply the women with fresh wands for their new and flourishing business of weaving baskets. Someone had suggested that they make the baskets to trade at the Gentile settlements for merchandise which they badly needed. The idea took like wildfire and women could be seen everywhere sitting with a pile of slender red saplings beside them, fashioning big baskets and little, round ones and oval, baskets with lids and baskets with handles, some dainty and neat, meant to sit on a parlor table with a lady's sewing inside, others heavy and sturdy enough to carry a bushel of potatoes from the field.

"Eldridge just now tells me that I'm to take my wagon and go south with Luke Reynolds for several days of trading. We're to collect all the baskets tonight and get an early start in the morning."

Fear gripped her. Edouard going out among the Gentiles! Memory slashed through her mind of the woman with a gun in her hands and hatred red in her eyes.

"Oh, no!" Involuntarily she clutched his arm. "Why must it be you?"

He looked startled, and then pleased. It had been weeks since she had touched him.

"I guess I have a reputation as something of a trader," he grinned. "I did enough of it last fall."

167

"Won't it be dangerous?"

"Eldridge says the settlements to the south are fairly friendly." They sat in silence for a time. Then he spoke again. "Where's Cassie?"

"In the tent."

"Why isn't she helping you with the baskets?"

"I don't know."

"Doesn't she ever help you?"

Gale shook her head, her eyes guarded by a thick fringe of lashes. She kept her lips locked tight for fear of the burning words that might come tumbling out. In spite of her bitterness, she still felt some of the same reverence for Edouard that she felt for God. She must never appear petty and mean in his eyes. She would go on being cold and aloof . . . she would keep herself from him, for she couldn't force herself to share his love with another . . . but she refused to be childish. She wouldn't let him know how much Cassie irritated her.

"You'll have to share the tent with Cassie while I'm gone, since I'll be taking the wagon. I hope to bring back a load of seed potatoes."

Dew was heavy on the grass as Gale lifted his bacon, sizzling, from the frying pan. He ate hurriedly, for he had the oxen hitched and waiting.

The tent flaps opened and Cassie stepped forth, wearing her blue challis dress and Gale's black bonnet, which she now considered her own. She was smiling with bright charm and looked as though she were about to go to Sunday morning church. The two stared at her in astonishment.

It was Edouard who spoke. "Why . . . what are you doing?"

"I'm all ready to go with you," she said, smiling happily.

168

"Cassie! Have you lost your mind? Of course you're not going!"

"Please, Edouard . . ." The smile was gone and her soft lips began to tremble.

"Why, Cassie dear . . . you're not able to go. There's no road . . . and no telling what kind of people we'll have to go through. No, you'd better stay here with Gale."

"I don't want to stay here! I'm sick of it here!" she stormed like a petulant child. "There's nothing but the hot sun in the day and the mosquitoes at night! I want to go with you . . . and see people and everything. If you leave me, I'll just . . . just die!" Tears rolled down her cheeks.

Edouard set his plate and cup aside uncertainly and turned his troubled gaze to Gale. "Do you think she should go?"

Before she could answer, Cassie broke in shrilly. "Don't ask her! Of course she'd say no! She wouldn't want me to have you to myself that long!"

The red in the east was fading into clear daylight. Edouard got hurriedly to his feet. He spoke firmly.

"I haven't time to argue. Luke is waiting for me and I must go. Even if I thought you should go, there wouldn't be time to pack your things. I'll be gone several days, you know."

He turned and walked quickly to the wagon. Cassie stooped and caught up a bundle just inside the tent, then ran after him.

"You don't have to wait!" As quick as a monkey she climbed to the wagon seat. "I'm already packed!"

He stopped, his foot on the hub. His face was dark with anger. "Cassie, let's not have any more of this foolishness. This trip is no place for you in your condition. Get down!"

Again her bright face crumpled into weeping, and even Gale watching in disgust could have felt pity if it had been anyone but Cassie. Edouard shrugged hopelessly and mounted the seat. Gale watched them move off, her whole body blazing with anger.

She was startled by a step behind her and a friendly voice. "Good morning. Did I frighten you? You jumped like a startled doe." It was Isaac Eldridge, smiling.

"No, but . . . I wasn't expecting anyone this early."

"I came to see if I could help Edouard get off, but I see I'm too late."

"Yes."

"Didn't I see our blonde friend on the seat with him?" He was gaily mocking.

"Yes." She turned away, pretending to look off after the wagon.

"Why didn't you go, too? You don't impress me as the kind of woman who would sit back and let her rival take all the honors."

"I . . . well, Edouard didn't plan to take either of us."

"Oh, she slipped in, huh? A stowaway!" he laughed. Then he looked at her searchingly. "You'll probably be pretty lonesome here by yourself, won't you?"

His words unsteadied her, but she managed to meet his gaze with a level one of her own.

"No. I think not."

He stepped close and caught her hand in a firm grip. Now all the gaiety and mockery were gone from his handsome face, leaving only a deadly earnestness. "Gale, will you promise to marry me . . . if Edouard does not return?"

She jerked away and stared at him.

170

"Are you crazy? Certainly not!" Rage made a blackness of her eyes. "Get away from me! Get away, I say! How dare you . . . !"

Then his earnestness left him, and his eyes lit with laughing mockery. "Well, it did no harm to try. I thought perhaps, with things as they are between you and Edouard . . ." He shrugged. "Oh, well. Better luck next time, maybe."

Sudden horror struck her. "You . . . you scum! You sent him down there to the Gentiles on purpose! You *wanted* something to happen to him!" Her fists knotted at her sides. She shook with murderous fury, but her voice was very low. "Leave me, before I . . . I . . ."

He laughed again.

"You know . . . you're quite a magnificent woman when you're angry. You're even better than in your natural state of saintliness." Then he was serious again. "Don't worry about Edouard. He'll be back . . . and Cassie with him." He turned to go, and called back over his shoulder, "If you're lonely while they're gone, come over and see Sophie and the baby. She's lonely."

Twenty-Two

Gale couldn't be sure that the sound of wagon wheels was real or imagined. He had been gone so long. She could hear the dogs, and the shouting, and the laughter. Before she could place the Dutch oven on the fire to heat, he was there. A crowd of shouting, excited Saints surrounded his wagon as he leaped down. Trying to answer everyone's questions and welcoming cries as he came, he made his way toward the fire and the woman who stood there, tall and still, just as he had left her. Cassie still sat on the wagon seat, pouting and tired and dirty.

That night after the supper was over, and the noisy crowd had departed with their fresh provisions and seed potatoes, Gale made up the bed in the wagon once again. The neighbors had stayed late, pumping Edouard of news . . . about the trip, the roads, the weather, the Gentiles, and all other news of the outside world. Cassie retired early to the tent, eager for the softness of her featherbed.

As Gale unlaced her shoes, Edouard watched her in silence. Then he took a bundle from beneath the wagon seat, and she could hear the crackle of newspaper. He knelt at her side and laid in her lap a bolt of calico, starched and gleaming in its newness, gay with tiny blue sprigs of flowers. She caught her

173

breath and looked up at him, pleasure glowing in her face.

"Do you like it?"

"Oh . . . it's lovely!"

It had been so long since she had seen anything that spelled civilization, or shops, or new dresses. And now this, a whole bolt of it!

If he had taken her into his arms then, he could have kissed her, and she would have melted into his embrace, holding him tight against her, remembering all the long lonely nights while he had been gone. Perhaps much of the old breach would have been healed. Instead he pulled off his boots, sighing wearily.

"I'm sorry, Gale, about how it turned out. Sorry and ashamed. I should have made her go back. But I was so pushed about starting on time, I didn't take time to argue with her. A thousand times on the trip, I wished I'd asked you to come, too. But that morning it didn't enter my mind. Can you forgive me?"

The magic moment was broken. She laid the calico aside and bent over her shoes.

"There's no need to talk about it. There is nothing to forgive."

On an evening in early June, company eighteen reached the high bluff overlooking the Missouri River. Their crops were planted, the settlement built for those following after, and now once again the Saints were on their way West. The sun had just set as the Simons arrived, and the whole sky was dyed with Indian yellow, giving Gale the unreal sensation that for a moment life hung suspended in a huge golden ball.

The wagons broke into irregular formation along

the bluff, their arched tops reflecting a soft halo of yellow, with horses and oxen looking like figures carved from gold. Even the faces of the Saints were gilded by the sunset.

Early next morning Edouard, riding a borrowed horse, helped drive the stock across the river. Cassie moaned and whimpered, clinging to Gale in terror as they watched the sucking, treacherous current, and the heads of men and beasts bobbing through it.

Suddenly one of the horses, jerking about in fright, reared and threw his rider into the river. The man reappeared far down stream, floundering helplessly.

"Oh, it's Edouard, it's Edouard!" Cassie screamed. "He's drowning and my baby will never have a father!"

At another time Gale would have jerked away, saying, "We don't know who it is, at this distance." But she was rigid with fear. It could be Edouard.

Cassie stopped sobbing and whispered, "Is he drowned . . . yet?"

Gale spoke with difficulty, for she was struggling with the man in the river, struggling for life.

"No . . . he's trying . . . to . . . swim. He's . . . drifting."

Cassie uncovered her eyes.

"Look! Someone is helping him! God knew I couldn't bear to have him drowned while I am in this delicate condition!"

It was not Edouard. Gale went to finish her preparations.

As the wagons lined up for crossing, Simons found the Muldoons' wagon directly ahead of them. Pat Muldoon, his eyes uneasy, drove out into the river with his wife sitting strangely silent beside him. Gale rode on the seat with a thrill of excitement flashing in her eyes. Cassie rode in the back, unable to consistently hide her face, or to cling to Edouard's neck in terror. She did both.

Edouard had lashed logs to the wheels for a float, and the wagon rode high and dry as he had hoped. Although the vehicle swayed uncomfortably, and the sucking waves crept up higher, the odd craft remained upright, with the oxen swimming steadily for the far shore.

Ahead, the Muldoons' wagon careened wildly in the current like a bobber on a fishline. The wagon was loaded unevenly, and tipped dangerously, like the list of a sailboat in a bad storm. Then it flipped over, with a sickening splash.

Pat's curses were extinguished. Soon he bobbed up, floating on the current. But Mrs. Muldoon was nowhere to be seen. The oxen, after Pat's jerking and shouting had ceased, began to pull once more in unison. It didn't matter to them if the wagon was upside down or not. They swam toward solid ground.

Suddenly a great shout of laughter went up from the crowd gathered on the opposite bank. Sister Muldoon, dripping and offended, slowly crawled from the floating hodgepodge of possessions inside the wagon. She grabbed one of her precious hens, which at the moment perched on the edge of a cooking pot.

"Come here, ye stupid beast!"

Her bonnet hung limply over one ear, and her sandy hair streamed over her face. Gale laughed at the resemblance between the woman and her wet hen.

A great square object wrapped in burlap floated down the river.

176

"Ye gads!" yelped Mary Muldoon. "There goes Uncle Andy!"

It was the portrait of the old sea captain that had hung in the Muldoons' parlor in Boston.

Twenty-Three

Day after day more Saints crossed the wide Missouri, from the high cliffs known as Council Bluffs in Iowa, to the encampment growing in Indian Territory on the west bank, soon dubbed Winter Quarters. Brigham announced that the main body of Saints were to remain for the winter, while an advance guard would travel west to search for sites for a permanent empire.

Work began at once. Winter Quarters resembled a nest of ants, pulling, cutting, carrying, toiling incessantly in the heat of July. Streets were laid out, and lots assigned. Log cabins began to rise, and sod shanties; excavations were dug by those who felt an earth dugout would be more snug during the cruel blasts of a prairie winter.

To Gale, sitting in the shade of the wagon carding wool, the activity on all sides was mildly stimulating, like the strains of music heard vaguely in the distance. Her attention was caught by the thunder of a horse's hoofs. A horseman galloped up the street, sending dust and bits of turf into the air. She caught the glimpse of the uniform of an army officer. An army officer . . . in Winter Quarters! What could it mean? She recalled the militia of Illinois and her heart froze. The horse looked worn, as though he had been ridden long and hard.

She put the wool back into the old muslin sheet and tied the four corners firmly together. She stood and gazed down the street.

"Gale . . . are you there?" It was Cassie's plaintive call from the tent.

"Yes."

"Who was that . . . riding by so fast?"

"I don't know. A stranger."

"I wish he wouldn't make such a clatter. It woke me up."

As she thrust the bundle of wool inside the wagon, Edouard came up out of the excavation which he was digging. He stood beside her, wiping the sweat from his face.

"Who was that? Did you see?"

"A stranger. An army officer." Her voice was not steady.

He laughed gently, seeing the fright in her face. "Don't look so fearful. It's probably just a messenger on his way from the fort in Kansas Territory. Dear heart, you look as though you'd just seen a band of attacking Indians!"

"Sometimes I'd prefer Indians." She took a deep breath.

"I think I'll just walk down and see what it's about."

Then they heard Brigham Young's signal bell.

"It must be important after all!" He started off.

"I'll go with you." Gale ran to keep up with his swift strides.

"Will Cassie be alright alone?"

"Of course." Her reply was sharp.

A crowd already gathered around Young's half-built cabin. Sister Reynolds was there, the wife of Luke who had gone south with Edouard.

"What in the world is it all about?" she asked

180

Gale, her face bright with excitement and the heat of the sun. "He's an American soldier, isn't he?"

The stranger talking with Young was little more than a boy, looking weary in his travel-stained uniform. They talked earnestly for some time. Then Brigham Young climbed the logs of his cabin to address the crowd.

"Brethren, this gentleman who has just arrived in Winter Quarters is Captain Allen of the United States Army. He comes from Fort Leavenworth with an unhappy message. A message which brings an ending to some of our plans. My Brothers and Sisters, the United States has declared war on Mexico!"

He stopped. Few of the Saints knew much about Mexico, and they cared even less. How could this affect them?

"Washington asks us to raise five hundred men at once to send to the fighting in California!" Young's voice rang out over the crowd.

There was a stunned silence. Then the tension broke. Angry shouts erupted from the crowd. Young stood listening intently.

"They wouldn't lift a hand to protect their citizens in Missouri or Illinois, even when we wrote to Washington for help!"

"They let us be kicked clean outa the country, didn't they?"

"Now they come askin' us for volunteers! Let 'em toot!"

"Five hundred men! Why, that's almost every young, able-bodied man in camp!"

"We wouldn't have nothin' left but women, kids, and old men!"

"It's a put-up job, that's what it is!"

"They're aimin' to take away all the men, and

181

leave the women and old folks alone and unprotected here in Indian Territory!"

"Yeah! We've heard citizens of the old US talk before! Weren't they the ones that swore they'd drive all the Mormons into Nauvoo, and all Nauvoo into the river?"

Some laughed, a loud raucous bray.

"Yes, and since we didn't sink in the Mississippi, they're trying to cook up a new stew for us!"

"The government probably figures this is the one sure way to wipe us out. This will be the end of the Saints!"

Pat Muldoon, growing over-confident with the shouts of those around him, bellowed, "Say the word, Brigham, and we'll toss the captain in the river where he belongs! He'll get a mouthful there that he can take back to Leavenworth with him!" He swaggered, forcing his way forward in the crowd.

Brigham Young's face darkened with anger, and a penetrating look from his cold gray eyes stopped Muldoon short. He raised his hand, and the shouting ceased. When he spoke, his tone was hard and direct.

"Men, I've let you talk, because I wanted to hear your thoughts. Now I know. And you're wrong, absolutely wrong. This is no trick. The government needs men badly, and they're asking us to help. They're asking everyone to help. Captain Allen tells me that you men will go at once to Fort Leavenworth, receive supplies there, and go on to California by way of Santa Fe. You are to enlist for twelve months, and at the end of that time you can return to your people and keep your arms. Upon enlistment each man will receive forty dollars, an amount which I need not remind you would be mighty welcome to your families at this time.

"I recommend that five hundred volunteers be raised immediately! Let's see the hands of those who will go."

That was all he said. It might have been the common sense in his words, or it might have been the imperative earnestness in his manner. At any rate, the men who had been shouting angrily only a moment before, now looked at one another uncertainly for a second, and then one by one their hands were raised. Pat Muldoon raised his arm high and coughed noisily so that Young would not miss him.

Gale felt a sinking certainty that Edouard would go, from the moment that Young began to speak. But when she saw his hand raised, a sense of doom struggled with a thrill of pride. Of course Edouard would go.

It took two weeks for Young to ride back along the Mormon trail, meeting other bands of Saints to fill the battalion of five hundred men. The night before their departure the Saints had an open-air ball in the square of Winter Quarters. Around the square, the hulks of half-completed cabins loomed in the warm moonlight. The square itself was bright with flares made of cattails soaked in oil and set in pots of sand.

The ball was gay with that intense artificiality that always marks celebrations on the eve of sending soldiers off to war. The music was spirited, and the ladies sparkling, dressed in their party dresses which had not been worn since the parties back in Nauvoo. They laughed and chattered with bright animation, but no one seemed to notice if some wife's eyes were suddenly brighter than they should be. It was a gala farewell, and nothing must mar its gaiety. But how long would the partings be? Forever . . . for some?

Gale danced the whole evening, laughing with breezy banter at the least excuse. Edouard was leaving, maybe forever . . . leaving her alone with Cassie. She danced as lightly as ever, but the music was only in her feet. None of it reached her heart.

She was wearing her best dress, the white one with bright blue buttons and the blue velvet bands around the skirt. She still thought it the loveliest dress she had ever seen, the one she had made for her graduation from Lockwood Seminary for Young Ladies. As she danced with Isaac Eldridge, she felt the intensity of his gaze.

"You know, you're really very beautiful tonight."

"Yes, I know," she answered coolly. "Edouard mentioned it."

Eldridge laughed at the pointed thrust.

"All right. We'll forget your charms for the moment. Any other suggestions for conversation?"

She looked at him with eyes on a level with his own, both of them mocking.

"It's heartbreaking to think of you leaving us." Antagonism was threaded through the brightness of her tone.

"Oh, but I'm not going."

"Not . . . going?" She thought he was teasing until she saw the seriousness in his eyes.

"No. Brigham Young needs me here."

"Needs you!" Anger flashed in her face. "Why should he need you any more than Edouard, or anyone else?"

He shrugged airily. "My pleasing personality, perhaps?"

Her lips tightened. "I believe you're lying. I don't think he wants you at all."

"Oh yes, but he does! We've had a long talk about it."

She felt that he was baiting her, ridiculing her in a subtle way, but she couldn't be sure. There was always light laughter in his voice and politeness smooth on his tongue. It infuriated her, but she hoped he wouldn't know.

"Why, even Barret Nickols is going, and he's not nearly as able-bodied as you are."

"Lady, are you trying to make me ashamed?"

"No, I don't think anyone could do that. I'm merely calling you a traitor." She had her anger in check, but the edge of it was a well-honed knife.

"A traitor!" His brows raised. "My dear lady, that's an ugly word to be coming from such a pretty mouth. Do you mean it?"

"With all my heart."

"Oh, well, we won't spoil the fun tonight by going into the subject. We'll have plenty of time later. By the way . . . the music has stopped . . . or had you noticed?"

She was embarrassed to discover that they were standing alone in the center of the arena. "Take me back to Edouard . . . instantly."

Later Bub Leary left the musicians' platform to dance with her. His face was creased with worry. They hobbled about awkwardly. "Does she hold it against me, Miz Gale . . . my not goin' tomorrow?"

"Why, Bub, I didn't know you weren't going."

"Yes ma'am . . . but it ain't my fault! I volunteered . . . but Brother Young says I ain't old enough. I'm seventeen, but he won't believe it. Do you reckon she'll think I'm a slacker, ma'am?"

"No, Bub, I don't think she will. I'm sure she won't." She didn't say that Cassie would probably never think of Bub at all.

185

"I know it isn't very patriotic," he brightened perceptibly, "but now that I come to think of it, I'm glad I'll be around to help if y'all should need something. With Brother Simon gone, you'll need a man."

It was well past midnight when she overheard a conversation that sent her mind spinning. The dancing had ceased for the moment, and women were passing plates of sandwiches and cakes. This farewell party was to be a bright memory in the days ahead, and nothing had been spared to make it a glorious affair.

Gale was standing with Edouard and Cassie when she heard the women talking behind them.

"How I envy Sister Muldoon and Sister Voak, leaving with the battalion in the morning!"

"Me too! I almost wish I didn't have a family of children to keep me here!"

"Well, a family doesn't keep some women here. Sister Nickols is going along, you know."

"No! With all those little girls?"

"Yes. You wouldn't catch me volunteering as a laundress in the army if I had to take along a family of girls! But . . . we're not all made alike, thank goodness!"

The last of the conversation was lost on Gale. Women could go! Why not she? She turned excitedly to Edouard. "Edouard . . . did you hear? Women can go along! I'm going with you!"

He shook his head. "No, my dear. I'm afraid it is not for the best." Finality was in his tone.

A chill of disappointment hit her. "Edouard . . ."

He shook his head again and thanked the woman who was passing him a plate of cake. To spend the rest of the night dancing, laughing, making gaiety of disappointment . . . She couldn't do it! When

186

Edouard turned for a moment to Cassie, Gale slipped away through the crowd, carrying her plate.

She walked out into the silence of the empty prairie streets, with the half-shells of houses around her. She threw the plate of cake away, hurrying through the moonlight, with the music growing fainter behind her. She walked down the street that led to their dugout, but when she reached it, she knew she couldn't stop. Sleep was impossible. She must walk . . . fast and far.

It was some time before Edouard overtook her. She was standing on a little hillock, her eyes staring miserably at the prairie that shimmered away into a distance of green moonlight. When she heard him coming, she turned slowly. He was breathing hard, as though he had been running.

"Gale darling . . . I didn't want to hurt you. Please forgive me. I could have been kinder in my refusal."

"You still refuse?"

"My dear . . . I must! It isn't that I don't want you . . . you know that."

"Why then? Other women are going. I have no children to keep me here. Why shouldn't I go?" Her voice was trembling with anger.

"You will know if you only stop to think. What about Cassie?"

"What about her?"

"She isn't able to go. You know that. And we can't leave her alone, dependent upon strangers, at a time like this. It is bitter medicine, I know, leaving you to care for her when you feel as you do. But it is the only way I know. Believe me, I have thought about it a good deal. There is no other way."

"Of course there is no other way!" Rage struggled for expression. "You married that little girl, and forced me to share everything I own with her . . . my meals, my clothes, my husband, every minute of my life! And then you go off to the ends of the earth and leave me to nurse her while she has your baby . . . *your* baby!" The pent-up emotions of the past months erupted like a volcano. "It should be *my* baby . . . mine, do you hear? But no . . . it's dear little Cassie having the baby, while I have to stay here to console her in her loneliness!"

Then the tears came, a tempest of tears which for so long had been dammed behind a mask of cool aloofness. And with the tears came the warm security of Edouard's arms. She did not push him away. She had almost forgotten the sheer delight of his strength, and the feel of his lips against hers. It had been so long.

Toward morning she drifted off to sleep in the circle of his arms, with the sweetness of prairie grass under their heads. The moon slipped out of sight on the western horizon. For the first time since that long-ago Christmas, she knew the tranquility of love fulfilled. She would not think of tomorrow.

Twenty-Four

With the Mormon Battalion gone, affairs at Winter Quarters settled down to the routine of daily living. Bub Leary began work immediately on the Simons' dugout, but it was well into August before he could complete it. One day when he was sure that Gale was alone, he motioned toward Cassie's tent.

"Is she . . . sick or somethin'? I know it ain't any of my affairs, but I been wonderin'. I never see her around workin' or nothin'."

"No, Bub, she's not sick. But she's just . . . just not feeling very well these days."

"You mean . . . ?" Comprehension dawned in the boyish face.

"Yes, Bub. It's a baby."

"A baby! Not that!" his exclamation was a whisper. "Why . . . she's nothin' but a baby herself!"

For a moment Gale saw her with Bub's eyes, and she shared a little of his horror at the prospect of impending motherhood for the little girl. He didn't refer to Cassie's condition again, but Gale often saw the torment in his heavy eyes.

With Edouard had gone the tensions built between the two women. Now they could live together with cool amiability. Gale was surprised to realize that she no longer felt anger with everything that

189

Cassie did. There was no particular affection for her, but the hatred was gone.

The day Bub finished the dugout, he asked both girls to come to see if it was all right. Gale had looked in often during the building process, but she had not seen it completed. Cassie had not seen it at all.

Cassie emerged from the tent looking like a porcelain doll, for none of the summer's sun had touched her skin. Bub stared, for in contrast to the wind-bronzed faces of the other women, she was a vision of pale gold and pink. Gale, who had faced the sun and wind for months, looked swarthy beside her.

"Well! What are we waiting for?" Cassie said with impatience. She was beginning to be self-conscious about her figure. Although her condition was not obvious, Bob's intense gaze made her uncomfortable. "I thought you said we were going to see the new house!"

Bub's eyes dropped and he flushed. To relieve the tension, Gale slipped her arm through Cassie's and the three of them walked to the dugout. Bub pushed open the heavy plank door and they went down three shallow steps in the dim interior. For a moment they were blinded by the darkness. Cassie shivered and leaned against Gale, who was breathing deeply of the sweet odor of newly turned sod and the fragrance of green lumber. The coolness of the earth was refreshing after the glare of the August sun.

When their eyes had become accustomed to the dark, Cassie looked around her. The disappointment in her face showed that she had expected something much finer. "Why, this isn't anything but a potato cellar!" she exclaimed.

Bub's face dropped, and his ears glowed brick-red.

"Oh, Bub, I think you've done a splendid job!" Gale interposed. "I don't know how we'll ever repay you for all this! I just wish Edouard were here to see it!"

"I didn't do it for pay, ma'am."

"I know you didn't. And that's all the more reason why we should be grateful. Oh, Bub . . . that fireplace! I hadn't seen it since it was finished. What a fine job you've done! I can't wait to start cooking in it! I didn't realize how tired I was of cooking on a windy camp fire until I see this fireplace!"

The lad brightened a bit. "Yeah, it ain't bad. I tried a fire in it the other day, and it draws real good, don't smoke a bit."

"And the shelves! A place for my dishes and pans! Oh, and this table! Look, Cassie, a table! Won't it be grand to sit down to a table again?" She patted the rough planks admiringly. "No more holding our plates in one hand, or trying to balance them on our knees."

Her elbow gently nudged Cassie's ribs, and after a pause the younger wife responded, unwillingly.

"Yes . . . yes. It will be nice."

"Now, as soon as we get the walnut bed unpacked from the wagon, and my cedar chest moved in, and I make new blue calico curtains for the shelves, it will look quite elegant! Oh, Bub . . . we're so grateful!"

"It wasn't nothin', Miz Gale. Do you want I should move your bed and stuff in now?"

The two young women had been living in their new home almost six weeks when the last straggling refugees from Nauvoo began pouring into Winter

191

Quarters. They came on foot, often limping in without shoes, crippled with rheumatism from exposure and weakened by fever. As the autumn drew on, many of them were seriously frostbitten. These were the ones who had clung stubbornly to the comfort of their homes, either because of the reluctance of old age, or because of some serious illness of a member of their family.

Each day Gale went to the community storehouse where all the provisions were kept and brought home flour which she made into great crispy loaves to be distributed among the new arrivals. This sudden influx of the starving and homeless worked a severe hardship on a settlement already handicapped by the absence of many of its young men. The food shortage in the coming winter would be acute, and Brigham Young immediately ordered rations reduced.

When Gale wasn't baking bread, she was spinning yarn or knitting stockings which were so badly needed. Little realization of what was going on in Winter Quarters touched Cassie in her refuge in the dugout. One day she arose languidly from the bed where she was reclining and volunteered to card the wool, if Gale would show her how. For a moment the older woman was speechless, but recovering, she showed Cassie how to do the work, displaying a gentleness she had not felt since that Christmas Day long ago.

It was almost the middle of September when Gale made an astonishing discovery. Something had gone strangely awry with her bodily functions. She had been hoping so long for a sign to tell her that she was to have a baby, that she had forgotten that such a thing was still possible.

With a sudden burst of hope, she began a rapid

mental calculation. Slowly she dropped the loaf of bread she was kneading back on the table and stared at the dough clinging to her hands. It was true! It must be true! She swallowed a sob of joy. How silly to cry now! She wiped the tears from her lashes with a surreptitious movement of her floured hand. The memory of Edouard's last night in Winter Quarters still lay warm in her memory.

After that day, life in the settlement on the bank of the Missouri took on a glorious significance for Gale. She laughed at the news of cut rations, news that sent most of the others away grumbling. Her singing could be heard drifting from the door of the dugout on fine days. Hearing it, women raised their eyebrows, and the men shook their heads. It didn't seem right somehow for a young wife to blossom forth in such happiness with her husband gone off to war.

She didn't tell Cassie of her hope, but guarded the secret while it was so fresh and new. She now felt a warm kinship with the girl who shared her own condition . . . having a baby for Edouard. They would go through all of it together.

In October the Sutlers came. Gale had given up looking for them, and so when she saw them one day on her way from the storehouse, she could hardly believe her eyes. She would not have recognized them had it not been for Cliff's peg leg. She ran and caught him by the arm, dismay almost blotting the gladness from her face.

"Oh, Cliff . . . Cliff! You've come!"

He turned a yellowed mask of a face toward her. There was no immediate recognition in his eyes.

"It *is* you . . . isn't it?" she said hesitantly.

He wore nothing but a tattered filthy pair of

193

trousers and a ragged shirt. His one foot was bare, and he had no coat, although the day was chill. His once ruddy cheeks were hollow and his blue eyes cavernous. When he finally spoke, it was with effort.

"It's . . . it's Miss Gale . . . ain't it?" he quavered. Gale's heart went sick for the old man before her. She remembered him hale, hearty, and vigorous, his bright eyes twinkling like a boy's.

"Yes. Oh, Cliff . . ." She tried to find suitable words for this thin beaten creature. She asked softly, "The girls, Cliff . . . where are they? And the baby . . ."

He turned and indicated a grotesque scarecrow in the group. Over a ragged dress she wore Cliff's faded old pea jacket.

"There's Debby. Aggie . . . and the baby . . . is dead."

She took them home with her, and while Cassie made toast over the fire, Gale boiled two precious eggs and made hot tea. She brought out the tiny pat of butter that Sister Pederson had shared with her that morning. She served the simple meal on a white linen cloth spread over the rough table. Neither of the guests had spoken while the preparations were being made, but sat huddled close to the fire, greedily soaking in the heat.

At sight of the food, a light almost like madness glittered in their eyes. Gale watched with pity as they gulped and crammed the food like a pair of ravenous animals. Could this wild, unkempt creature with the long dirty nails and hair about her shoulders be the prim, meticulous Deborah Wilbe? Could she have been the girl reared in the refined seclusion of a Boston mansion?

After they devoured everything on the table, they relaxed a little and crept back to the warmth of the fire. Some time later, Cliff startled them by speaking in a mild voice.

"Miss Gale, them was mighty tasty vittles."

"I'm glad you enjoyed it. It wasn't much, but we'll have a better meal tonight." She didn't tell them that she was afraid to give them more after so long a starvation. "They butchered some sheep this morning and we're going to have mutton stew for supper."

"Mutton stew." He rolled the words over his tongue, tasting them hungrily. Gale heard Debby swallow hard. "Mutton stew. Miss Gale, do you know how long it's been since we've had any meat?" Then he stopped, and the others were surprised to hear him laugh, almost like his old self. "Well, I don't recollect as I know myself, now I come to think on it."

Gale smiled. They would be all right now. The hot food, the fire on the hearth, the warmth of the dugout, the coziness of the room with its walnut bed, patchwork coverlet, and linen-covered table, all this was helping to drive the wildness from the hollow eyes of the old couple.

"I wonder . . ." Deborah raised her head and spoke timidly, "Do you have a pair of scissors I could borrow? And a comb? I left mine in Nauvoo. And some hairpins?"

"Of course," Gale smiled and got the requested articles.

And while Deborah retired delicately to a corner to improve her appearance, old Cliff began to talk. The words came slowly and painfully at first, but soon they began to flow in a great rush of terrible drama.

"Most days, I didn't think we was goin' to live to set down to a table again, or set by a real fireplace,

195

without the cold gnawin' into your back." He pulled his one bare foot under him, embarrassed by its nakedness. " 'Twas early in the spring that the mobs started tormentin' us again, robbin' chicken coops, settin' barns afire and raisin' hell in general. I didn't let on to the girls, 'cause I knew it would scare 'em, and we wasn't leavin' till after the baby come, anyhow.

"We was lucky for a spell. Then one night they come. They caught me and tied me to a tree right in front o' our house and took off all my clothes. Then they laid the whip to me . . . When I come to the next day, Aggie was screamin'. The baby was comin'. Pore Debby was purt' nigh outa her mind."

The story broke while Cliff stared into the fire, stroking the sole of his bruised foot. When he spoke again, it was a whisper.

"We buried Aggie as soon's I could get around. The baby was porely from the start, but Debby done wonderful by him. We got a she-goat from a feller acrost town, and the baby got so's he'd take milk outen a spoon real good. Then the mobs come again.

"This time they meant business. They was an army of a thousand or so and they'd come to make war. They brung a battery o' six pounders and fired on the town out on the east side, but they didn't do no harm. Next day, come daylight, they tried to take Nauvoo by storm, but Cap'n Anderson and about thirty-five o' us held 'em off. They had to use eight . . . ten rounds o' grape shot 'fore they drove us back. When dark come, they let up, and all that night we worked, buildin' up a breastworks o' cornstalks. The next day . . . well, it don't do no good to talk about it.

"Day after that was Sunday, and the mob didn't
196

fight, bein' such good Christians. But they sent us word that ever' last one o' us had to cross the river before night or be kilt. By this time we saw it wasn't no use fightin' 'em. Everybody just grabbed whatever come to hand, a loaf o' bread and a blanket and set out for the river.

"A bunch o' the devils was hangin' around the river, watchin' us leave. One of 'em grabbed a-holt o' me and says, 'Let's baptize the . . .' well, what he meant was, 'Let's baptize him.' Then they throwed me in the water, face down, sayin', 'The commandments must be fulfilled, Goddam ye!' Then they fished me out and throwed me in the boat with Debby and the baby and some others. They shot up the water all around us, just to give us a fast start, I reckon."

Cassie sat up on the bed and listened intently.

"When we got acrost the river, we was a sorry lookin' crew. About six hundred and forty of us there was, mostly women, children and sick folks. That was late in September, and the nights was gettin' cold. It wasn't no picnic . . . we had no grub, no shelter, and no clothes but what we wore. Folks just laid there in the rushes and docks and died with the rain beatin' 'em in the face.

"We wasn't there long before the baby died. He mighta had a chanc't if we'da stayed in a warm house and kept the goat. But all we had for him was water offa boiled wheat. He didn't last long, pore little chap."

Cassie flung herself back on to the bed, sobbing into the pillow. But Cliff didn't seem to notice, and Debby continued her task of making herself presentable. They had heard too much of weeping already.

"All any of us had was parched wheat, and not much o' that. Once the good Lord took pity on us.

A whoppin' big flock o' quail had set out to cross the river, but a storm drove 'em back, and for a while they fell around us like hail, too tired to lift a wing, and we picked 'em up by hundreds."

Gale listened, wondering at the courage of this old seaman, and the matter-of-fact manner of his telling their story. There was no self-pity, merely the recounting of an experience.

"As fer as I recollect, that was the last bit o' luck we had on the trip. Most of us set out walkin'. There ain't much to tell about the trip. To tell you the truth, there ain't much I remember. Just seems like we walked forever."

Abruptly he leaned back and stretched. His story was told. He looked across the hearth at Deborah, who now sat primly, her hair combed smooth, her nails trimmed, and her face and hands clean, revealing the thin parchment of her skin. She looked a bit more like the Deborah Wilbe of Boston, except that she was pathetically older.

"Debby, ye look right purty."

She smiled faintly.

Twenty-Five

When the first shrill blast of winter swooped down on Winter Quarters, it found a tottering, shaken settlement. The pestilence had come.

No one knew what it was. No one had ever seen anything like it. One day a man would be plowing the prairie sod, walking the black furrow in robust health . . . the next day, tossing in a delirium of fever. Within a week, his wife and children would be weeping beside his grave, if they were not already stricken with the malady themselves. A mother would get breakfast for her fanily, humming a familiar tune; by night she was unconscious, her face bloated with fever.

It struck young and old alike, the weak and the strong. No one knew where it would strike next, nor what to do to ward off the disease. Some kept a handkerchief steeped in camphor at hand, to be sniffed frequently, and they escaped the malady. Others kept a handkerchief steeped in camphor handy, and they died within forty-eight hours. Some slept with a soiled stocking tied around their necks at night. Some wore bags of vile-smelling asafetida beneath their undershirts. Others swore by the drinking of hot ginger tea at bedtime. Still others soaked their feet night and morning in a blistering bath of mustard, others in baking soda. Some, re-

199

mote from neighbors and exposure to the disease, fell ill and died. Others lived among whole families laid low, and remained hale and hearty. No one could explain it.

The Sutlers stayed on in the Simon dugout, as there was no other place to go, and Gale was glad to have them, especially after the advent of the plague. For Cassie's sake she was glad, because the young woman was terrified of being left alone. Cassie was like the leaves of a tree, quivering with every passing wind, while Gale was the trunk, knowing the fear down into her very roots, yet standing strong and tall in spite of it. When the first news of the plague reached Cassie, she went frantic.

"The plague! And it's almost time for my baby!" She cried hysterically. From that moment she refused to go near the door. When it was opened by one of the others, she cringed away to a corner and held her breath until she felt the danger of the outside air was past.

Gale, believing that one either got the disease or one did not, went out daily to do what she could for those who were stricken, leaving Cassie in the company of the Sutlers. As the epidemic gained momentum, family after family went down, and healthy Saints who were willing to help were at a premium.

After a time the deaths were so numerous that graves couldn't be dug fast enough in the frozen sod of the prairie graveyard to accommodate the corpses. Not everyone who had the disease died of it, but to those digging graves, it seemed so. The rows of ice-clodded mounds lengthened day by day, until those digging graves at last took sick, and for a time there was no more burying. The bodies were taken to the cemetery and covered lightly with snow until sufficient health should return to the settlers to enable them to dig more graves.

Gale was working from morning till night, going from house to house, preparing food for those who were still able to eat, bathing the faces of the sick, straightening their beds, caring for small frightened children whose parents were ill, comforting parents whose children were dying, carrying messages, bringing food from the warehouse, bathing babies, and putting pennies on the eyes of the dead.

It was a time to strike dread to the hearts of the most robust. Gale's singing was forgotten. She knew only a continual aching fatigue from which she felt she would never recover. She arose in the dark of winter morning, as tired as she was when she went to bed the night before.

Thoughts of her baby were so far in the back of her mind that she almost forgot it. At night when she got home, Deborah always had a cup of hot mint tea and a plate of toast waiting for her. After that she tumbled wearily into bed, and then, only for a moment, she could bring the lovely thought out into her conscious mind. It seemed to give her strength for the coming day. Before she drifted off to sleep she always thanked God for two things . . . that her baby would come after the epidemic had run its course, and that Edouard was far out of reach of the dreaded horror.

Cliff hobbled out to work on the shanty he was building with the help of Jeddy Tavenner. It was on the river in the area of the settlement known as Misery Bottoms. Many believed that the Plague had started here where the shallow water was stagnant. But Cliff scoffed at the idea and went on with his building.

201

"We'll be outa yer way by the first of December!" Cliff told Gale. "It's comin' right along."

"But Cliff," she insisted, and meant it more than he knew, "we don't want you to leave! The dugout will be much more comfortable than the little house this winter. Besides, I *want* you to stay!"

"That's what ye say, child, and it's mighty kind of ye to say it. But Debby and I've pestered ye enough already, movin' in on ye thataway, and we aim to move into our own shack as soon's we can."

"Cliff, you're *not* in the way! I really need you."

"When Cassie gets that new baby, ye won't want a couple of old cronies like us settin' around in the way."

"We *love* you and Deborah. It's wonderful having you here!"

"That's all right, Miss Gale. Ye been mighty fine, makin' us feel at home and all, but we ain't settlin' down on no young folks to be burden on 'em."

She knew he cherished his wiry independence, and so she said no more, although she dreaded the day they would leave, and Cassie's baby so near. She knew they had no idea of the sense of security they gave her.

One night Olaf Pederson roused her out of a drugged sleep by his pounding at the door. "Please, Miss Gale," he panted. "Can you come? I think Mamma's dying."

When they reached the log cabin, the children by the bed were clinging to the hand that was already growing cold. The room swam in the haze of Gale's tears. Then Sister Pederson opened her eyes and looked up at her husband.

"Good night . . . Olie."

That was all. Gale knew that she was gone. The

202

lips, which only a strong will had forced to keep moving, drooped in final repose.

"Take the children to my house," Gale whispered, taking Olaf's arm. "It's better for them to remember her . . . alive."

Hastily she helped bundle them into caps and coats. Their father moved about like a man asleep. Gale picked up the baby, Hulda's baby, now twice an orphan, from the cradle where it was sleeping, and wrapped it in a quilt from the bed. The older children, now realizing the full import of what had happened, were crying softly with the utter grief that only childhood can know.

When they went out into the bitter moonlight behind their father, Gale closed the door and went back to the bed. Gently she closed the eyes, eyes which had looked for the last time on her babies . . . and her Olie. A sudden terrible sob arose in Gale's throat. She sank to her knees beside the bed.

"Oh, God," she prayed, "must it always be like this? How could I *ever* have believed that this life was good . . . and beautiful?"

The candle flickered low in the silent room.

Twenty-Six

The Simons had not known the Sutlers' decision to move was due largely to the impending birth. Since Aggie's death, Deborah lived in profound fear of childbearing. Her world was filled with fears of every variety since the Nauvoo experience. No one but Cliff knew of the nightmares which terrorized her at night and haunted her during the day. She kept it all locked behind her prim lips.

After they were gone Cassie implored Gale not to leave her alone, even for a moment.

"Cassie, I'd like to stay, but I can't. There are dozens of people who are sick, and need food and water carried to them, and wood for their fires. And there are so few who are able to help."

"What if you get the plague and die? What'll become of me? Then I'll get it, too . . . and I'll die, and my baby! Then Edouard won't have a soul left in the world! How can you be so heartless?" She was crying.

Gale smiled a little. "Being with those who have it doesn't seem to make much difference. I'm not any more liable to get it than—" she caught herself before she said "you" "—than anyone else."

"But you can't leave me. I might have my baby any minute! And if I had it . . . and died, while you were gone . . . you'd never forgive yourself!"

205

"Don't worry. Babies don't come in a minute. And I'll come back every little while to see how you are."

"Are you sure you'll come back . . . often?"

"Of course." She knew that it would add miles each day to her exhausting work, but she promised. Cassie was a lonely child, clinging to her for sustenance, and Gale would do all she could.

Christmas Day was warm and bright, with the sky an immensity of turquoise over the white prairie. Gale remained at home all the forenoon, baking hot fragrant loaves and boiling a great iron pot full of soup. The man at the storehouse had let everyone have extra rations because it was Christmas, and the pot was brimming with bits of beef, ham, mutton, and a variety of all the vegetables grown by the Saints in the summer gardens of Iowa.

As she worked over the table and hearth, she remembered a year ago this day. How different it had been, with the snow falling in heavy whirling flakes. She had been young, and light-hearted and very gay. She pushed the memory from her. So much had happened. She felt infinitely older. She glanced at Cassie, who lay drowsily across the bed, content that she was not alone. She too, must feel a great deal older.

Gale put on her cloak and started on her rounds, laden with warm loaves and a pail of soup. Many times during the afternoon, she came back home to replenish her pail and to reassure Cassie. Each time she found the girl across the bed, half drowsing, her childish body bloated. She's so young to go through the ordeal of having a baby! And yet . . . she's sixteen.

As Gale walked through the streets of Winter Quarters, with the sun warm on the copper of her hair, and the snow blazing in her eyes, she could almost feel cheerful. Everyone, even the sick, brightened to her cheery greeting of "Merry Christmas!" And there had been no new deaths. Could the pestilence be nearing its end?

When she came back for the last pail of soup, it was dusk. She found the dugout dark and getting cold. As she hurried to light a candle from the dying coals on the hearth, she heard a moan from the bed. It seemed that the candle wick would never flame. Finally it caught, and she hurried to the bed to find Cassie doubled up, her face hidden in her arms.

"Cassie! Are you sick?"

"Yes," she moaned through clenched teeth. "Go get help!"

"We don't need help," Gale tried to sound more calm than she felt. "I can do everything that's necessary. How long have you been having pains?"

"Since you left last time. But what if I should die? Get somebody!"

"Hush! You're not going to die. Healthy girls like you don't die." But did they? Her fingers were stiff with fear. Maybe Cassie was too little to have a baby. She had wondered.

The girl cried out again, a sharp cry of agony. At the same time there was a knock at the door. Gale went to answer it, resenting the intrusion at such a time. Who would be calling?

It was Isaac Eldridge, smiling and debonair, handsome in spite of the fact that he had only recently recovered from the epidemic. His had been one of the earliest cases, but it had been rather mild. Gale had not seen him since the morning that the battalion had left. She held the door open only a crack, for her mind was on Cassie, and she didn't want the room to become any colder.

207

"What do you want?" she asked bluntly.

"What do I want? My dear lady, how can you be so rude? Here my first thought when I am able to be up and about is to see how you and your little friend are getting along. And when I brave the chill night air, and the chance of a relapse, what do I get for my pains? A 'What do you want?' and not even an invitation to come in out of the cold. Are you going to let me stand out here all evening, and then go home and die for my thoughtfulness?"

She opened the door with impatience. "Come in, then, for heaven's sake! I don't want the house to get any colder! And shut the door!"

"Cold is right! Good heavens, Sister Simon, haven't you any wood? Why didn't you have someone get you some?"

"Someone does, thanks. Bub Leary keeps us well supplied. I have been gone all afternoon, and Cassie is sick."

"Sick?" He looked quickly toward the bed. "Plague?"

"No."

"What then?"

"She's having a baby. Now if you'll kindly leave . . ."

He raised one brow. "A baby! Well blow me down! Congratulations, Edouard!"

Something about the way he said it jangled against her already over-strained nerves. It was an effort to keep her voice low. "Will you please go now?"

Cassie uttered another cry, and when the pain had subsided, she cried, "Send him for help! Hurry!"

Eldridge grinned a little. "She sounds worried."

"Could Sister Eldridge come?" Gale asked, ignoring the lightness of his tone. "Or Sophie?"

"Sophie is in bed with the plague. And Grace has her hands full with the baby and the other children."

"Well, I guess I can manage." She took a long breath and slipped off her cloak. "I must get the fire going."

"Go ahead and get things ready," he spoke over his shoulder. "I'll take care of the fire."

Disagreement seemed pointless, so she hurriedly collected the necessary articles and placed them on the table. It struck her suddenly that the baby didn't have a stitch of clothing. She had been too resentful even to think of the child; and then had come the epidemic. Why in the world hadn't Cassie made something? She had been too concerned with her own welfare to think of her baby.

Cassie's moans were coming with alarming frequency, so while Gale helped her undress and get into bed, Eldridge took off his coat, rolled up his sleeves, and washed the soup pot so that it could be used for heating water. While they worked, there was the sound of heavy shuffling about outside the door. Gale straightened up.

"That's Bub, bringing us wood and water. The water pail is dirty. You'll have to wash it."

After he cleaned the bucket, he asked, "Do I have to deliver it to him, too? Doesn't he know enough to come in and get it?"

"He never comes in!" She spoke sharply. "Or hardly ever. Hurry and take it to him! We need the water."

Eldridge grinned at the look of blank astonishment on Bub's face when he opened the door and handed him the bucket. The boy had no words for the amazement that gripped him at the spectacle of Isaac at home in the dugout, his sleeves rolled up, and a tea towel tied about his waist for an apron.

"Hello son." Eldridge broke the silence. "Won't you come in?" It was evident that he was enjoying the lad's discomfort, and was going to do nothing to help the situation. Gale resented his soft chuckle.

"It's Cassie's baby, Bub," she said from the bed. "Can you hurry back with the water?"

"Is . . . is she in a bad way, Miss Gale?" he blurted anxiously.

She shook her head and motioned him out the door. Cassie was uttering soft moaning sobs, punctuated at frequent intervals by piercing cries.

Eldridge returned to the fireplace and stretched luxuriously on one of Bub's homemade chairs, his back tactfully toward the bed. "Anything I can do?" he asked.

The girl's moaning suddenly ceased, and she said in a strangled voice, "Get me something, quick! I'm going to throw up!"

While she retched and strained, Isaac Eldridge sat uneasily at the fire his head in his hands. If Gale had seen his face then, she would have seen him without the gay sophisticated mask. She would have seen pity in his eyes, and sadness about his mouth.

Instead, she was looking for the first time at Cassie's baby . . . Edouard's and Cassie's. She looked with wonder at the tiny, black-haired boy and held him reverently for a moment before she wrapped him in the waiting blanket. He looked so like Edouard, even then.

When Bub returned a few minutes later, puffing and panting from his run to the nearest well, his eyes went instantly to the bed. Then he heard the thin wailing of the baby.

"Cassie has a beautiful boy," Gale smiled. "She's resting now."

She saw his lips form the words, "Thank God!"

Twenty-Seven

Gale felt a fierce love for the baby, as though the child were her own, the baby she was expecting, the child created by hers and Edouard's love. Never for a moment did she resent him. She felt that he was a beautiful miniature of his father, from his dark head to his arched feet.

Gale gave up her work among the sick until Cassie would be able to be up and about again. She couldn't think of leaving him untended with no one to answer his first wavering cry when he awoke, so for a fortnight she enjoyed a heavenly respite, while her weary body recuperated from the past grueling weeks.

She bathed baby Edouard and warmed his pink toes before the fire. She and Cassie spent delighted hours watching the miracle of the tiny man-child, the funny little yawns and the pleasant crinkling of his face that they were sure was a smile, the owlish roving of his dark eyes, and the jerky groping of his little hands.

Cassie was inordinately proud now that he was here. Before his birth, her only thoughts had been of her own condition. But now that he was a third member of the family, a real person, she became acutely aware of her responsibilities as a mother. Almost at once she asked Gale to show her how to make some clothes for him. Because the birth had been so easy, and her strength not depleted, Gale let her sit up in bed to sew. Gale cut out the garments from one of her own muslin petticoats, and guided Cassie's awkward fingers in the intricacies of seaming and hemming, tucking and button-holing.

One day as Cassie lay with the baby curled in her arm nursing, she gave an exultant little laugh. Then she grew suddenly grave. Gale looked up questioningly from the hearth where she sat, drying her freshly washed hair before the fire.

"Gale, I was just thinking. If . . . if Edouard should not come back, you'll never know how wonderful it is . . . having a baby."

Gale flushed. "Cassie, dear . . . I should have told you sooner. But I'm going to have a baby, too."

The girl on the bed was silent for an incredulous moment, her blue eyes wide. "You . . . are?"

"Yes. I've been sure of it since late in the summer."

Cassie's lips drew into a petulant pout. "Why didn't you tell me? Why should you keep it a secret?"

"At first I didn't tell you because . . . well, because I just didn't want anyone else to know for a while. Since the epidemic it didn't seem as though the time was ever right. But now I'm glad you know."

"Yes it is nice," Cassie admitted rather grudgingly. After a time she repeated more heartily, "Yes it is nice, Gale. It will be fun having our babies together. Let's see, when do you expect yours?"

Gale answered softly, her face hidden by the bright cascade of hair. "About the middle of April, I think."

They became accustomed to a diet of bread and cornmeal mush, cornbread with flour gravy, and parched wheat porridge. Gale consoled Cassie by the observation that perhaps they were sharing in the privations that Edouard was suffering. Her concept of war was vague, but he was always in her thoughts. She wondered where he was and what he was doing, but when she thought of the grimness of a battlefield she could only turn her thoughts away. She could think of him as hungry, or dirty, or weary from miles of marching, but she refused to think of him as wounded . . . or dead.

The two women, like the other Saints, grew thinner each day with cheeks more hollow and eyes set deeper. In spite of her pregnancy, Gale could fold over a good two inches of her waistband. But it was with a sort of stubborn pride that they went without mentioning their constant hunger. Others were hungry too.

They could forget their troubles as they watched baby Edouard grow more lovable. The day he was a month old, they were positive that he smiled at them, although Sister Jenkins told them that babies couldn't even *see* until they were two months old, let alone smile.

"He's just exercising his face," she told them bluntly.

After that remark, Cassie hadn't even tried to be polite to their caller. Sister Jenkins left soon after. When the door closed on her, Cassie exploded.

"Baby Edouard not see! Why the old simpleton! Can she remember when she was a baby? The stupid busybody! You *can* see can't you, angel baby?"

"I don't think she knows," Gale took his wee hand in her fingers. "You smiled at us didn't you, little man?"

215

She bent and kissed the soft sole of his naked foot, while he curled his toes in delighted response. He was probably the most openly adored child in Winter Quarters.

Next evening Gale was taken ill. She had spent the afternoon in the fetid Tavenner dugout doing the thousand odd jobs that are to be done for a large family. The slovenly happy-go-lucky mother was in bed with the plague, which had attacked her just as she was recovering from the birth of a new baby. The twins had taken sick simultaneously and shared their mothers tumbled bed with the new baby.

They were all delighted to see Gale, and after the greetings were over, she set herself vigorously to the task of doing two months' work in one afternoon. She washed dishes caked with several weeks' food, picked up soiled garments from piles which littered the room, swept bones and scraps from a floor which had not been swept since they moved in, carried water from the nearest well a quarter of a mile away, washed clothing, and much to their awe, washed the children. Her last task had been to bake a great pan of biscuits and make a pan of bacon-grease gravy and set it before the famished brood. When she left it was with a light heart, although she was painfully weary.

That night as she sat by her own hearth knitting a shawl for her baby, she suddenly doubled and buried her face against her knees. She stifled a cry and remained silent. When she straightened, her face was almost gray.

"Cassie . . . I wonder . . ." she tried to sound casual, "could you go get Sister Jenkins . . . or someone? I think I'm going to be sick."

216

Cassie jumped up, terror-stricken. The baby grunted disapprovingly.

"Is it the plague?"

Gale shook her head. It was a full minute before she could speak.

"No. I'm afraid . . . it's . . . the baby."

"Oh, dear God . . ." Cassie began crying. "What will I do? What will I do? Oh, Gale . . . if you'd stayed home, this would never have happened . . . Oh, dear God . . . What will become of us?"

"Go for help," Gale said thickly. "Hurry. You can't manage it alone."

Cassie returned ten minutes later with Sister Jenkins. They found Gale unconscious, sprawled near the hearth. A little past midnight her baby was born dead.

Gale's recovery was slow. During her long days in bed, she persistently kept up a front of calm, but no one was ever to know the rebellious bitterness that stormed through her thoughts.

Was this all one could expect of life, she brooded. Suffering . . . death . . . disappointment . . . anger . . . grief . . . jealousy? There was so little of loveliness and beauty, so little of what she had expected from the creed of the Saints. She remembered the words of the young missionary speaking in a meetinghouse in New England so long ago. She could still hear Edouard's deep voice telling the congregation of the faith of the Saints. "If there is anything virtuous, lovely, or of good report or praiseworthy we seek after these things."

One morning in May back in Lockwood Seminary, Gale Smith had looked forward with assurance and eagerness to the great adventure that was life. Life was glorious, life was beautiful. Now Gale Simon,

217

lying ill and hollow-cheeked in a dugout in Indian Territory, wondered if anyone could possibly go through a lifetime of feeling that life was worth the struggle.

It was early March before Gale was strong enough to venture outside the house. She was dizzy as she climbed the steps to the open world, and was astonished to hear a meadowlark calling its sweet song from the prairie. The plague was past . . . and spring had come to Winter Quarters.

So gradual had been baby Edouard's decline that the girls were not conscious of it. Although both were perpetually hungry themselves, they supposed that he was being nourished by Cassie's milk. Because of his good nature, they hadn't noticed his lack of weight gain. His responsive smile and happy gurgling had lulled them into a false sense of security.

One day when Cassie exclaimed in alarm that her milk was gone, they awoke to the truth. They discovered in a panic that his arms and legs were actually thin.

Gale felt a dreadful premonition that he might be taken from them, but she pushed it aside with the wrathful determination that she would not *let* him die, if she had to kill or steal to save him. Surely, she reasoned, there would come a lull in the long stark parade of tragedy that marched with the Saints. Was life to be nothing but a succession of deaths, heartbreak, agony?

When she saw that he was getting no better on a diet of thin flour gruel, the rebellion in her spirit centered against the Church of Jesus Christ of Latter-day Saints. It can't be chance . . . all this waste of life . . . all this suffering. I know God just didn't *let* it happen, without some reason. It's the fault of

218

the leaders, with their stupidity and lack of foresight in dragging thousands of people out here to freeze and starve in the wilderness! If the leaders had led decent moral lives, she raged inwardly, we would still be in our homes in Nauvoo, safe and happy and well-fed . . . living at peace with the people of Illinois.

Hot with anger, she put on her cloak. She was unnoticed by Cassie, who crouched by the fire trying to soothe the now feverish child. Gale snatched a comforter from the bed and knelt by Cassie.

"Let me have him," she said gently but firmly.

Cassie shrank back. "What do you want to do with him?"

"Don't worry, dear. I'll wrap him well so he won't catch cold. It's not cold today anyway."

Cassie clutched him tighter. "No. What do you want him for?"

"I'm going to Brigham Young. If there's any way, in God's name, of getting food for you and the baby, I'll get it. Let me have him now."

Brother Young was more than a little surprised by the strange manner of the young woman at the door, a terribly thin young woman with a wild hostility in her dark eyes. Something about the brightness of her hair struck a chord of memory.

"Good morning. Let's see, you're Sister . . . ?"

"Simon," Gale said icily. "My husband is Edouard Simon, who you shipped off to California to be killed with the rest of the Mormon Battalion, while his family is left here to starve!"

"Oh . . ." For a moment Brigham Young was taken back by the suddenness of the attack. "Won't you come in?"

Inside the house she ignored the battery of curious feminine eyes, and pulled the covers away from

219

the baby's fever-flushed face. She began without ceremony.

"See! He's dying! Starving to death because his mother is too undernourished to feed him! We're all starving . . . but I don't care about the rest of us! I've seen so many die this winter that I'm getting numb to death! But I'll not have this baby die . . . not if I have to *kill* to save him!" The intensity of her voice shattered the air of the small room as though it were glass. "I've lost *my* baby this winter, through starvation and overwork during the plague . . . and I'm not going to lose this baby! I'm going to get food for him . . . do you hear? Food!"

A baby started crying in another room of the cabin, but Gale went on unhearing.

"You brought us here . . . here to the end of the earth! Seven hundred of us have died, so far, and five hundred others you have sent off to war! You're doing well, Brother Young, very well! By the time you get to this Zion you talk about . . . you'll have probably half a dozen followers alive to help you build your little empire! You've brought us here to follow *your* bidding! The least you owe us in return for our allegiance is food! . . . And life for the babies!"

Brigham Young shook his head wearily. There was a bleakness in his haggard face. "My dear, believe me, I would help you if I could. But if I would let the people eat all they need, within a week our storehouse would be entirely empty. Remember, we would be hungrier next week without a mouthful, than we are today with only a little."

Gale scarcely heard him. She stared at him with stony anger.

"Save your fine talk! I don't believe you! You

wouldn't sit by and let one of your own children starve!"

He turned to one of the awe-stricken women. "Bring our baby here, my dear."

What Gale saw then was a dash of cold water on her fury. The baby was very like Edouard except that he was older. He was hot with fever, and his little face was thin and wizened. Young took him gently from the woman, and Gale thought for a moment that she saw tears in his deep eyes.

"Sister Simon," he said very gently, "my baby is dying, too. I could rob the storehouse, and perhaps save his life, for the present, at least. But it is because of you, and hundreds of others like you, that I don't. Sister Simon, we share alike, our food and our suffering. We can only continue praying for a brighter day in the Land of Zion."

Slowly Gale pulled the covers back over Baby Edouard's hot face. Her anger was gone now, and there was a droop of desolation in her shoulders as she turned to the door.

Nothing then could save him . . .

Twenty-Eight

They stood together beside the open grave to watch Bub and Cliff lower the tiny bundle wrapped in Gale's silk patchwork quilt. Funerals had long since ceased to be a ceremony during this tragic winter among the Saints. And so there were only five of them standing there in the parched prairie grass of early spring, Gale and Cassie, Bub and Cliff and Deborah.

Back at the dugout, Gale was startled by a timorous tapping at the door. It was Deborah. Her face was pale, and Gale, despite her own emotions, thought she saw something like terror in the woman's eyes.

"I . . . I must speak to you!"

Gale motioned toward a chair. Deborah shook her head, motioning to Cassie who lay face down on the bed. Gale went ahead with folding and putting away the tiny garments that she had just laundered. Deborah bent close, whispering.

"I . . . I don't know quite how to start." Gale, waited.

Deborah watched her nimble hands on the baby clothes. "Perhaps I shouldn't have come to you . . . but I can't tell anyone else. Child . . . I need help, desperately!"

Gale knew that if the proud and reserved Debo-

223

rah Wilbe came asking for help, her need was urgent. "What is it?"

"I'm . . . well . . . I'm afraid I'm expecting."

"How wonderful!" Gale smiled, but her lips quivered.

"Oh, don't you see . . . I don't want it . . . I *can't* have it! I simply can't! And I wondered if you knew . . . if you have ever heard of anything . . ."

Gale's eyes narrowed in anger. "You mean you want me to tell you what to do *not* to have it? Is that what you mean?"

"Yes . . . oh, I know it sounds clumsy . . . and heartless. But I simply can't go through with it! You see, I watched Aggie die . . ."

Gale took a deep breath before she could try out her voice. It was shaking. "Do you know . . . there are some who would gladly risk their lives to have a baby! How can you dare to admit that you are too cowardly to face it?"

Deborah covered her face with blue-veined hands. "I shouldn't have come . . . I know I shouldn't . . . not today, anyway. But I was afraid to wait any longer. In God's name . . . tell me, if you know anything! I'd rather die now than go through what Aggie did!"

The prim mask was gone, and for the first time since Gale had known her, she saw the real Deborah Wilbe, a frail terrified girl, grown into middle age without having lived life. Gale reached out and took one of the bony hands. Her eyes softened.

"I can't help you, because I don't know how. But if I did, I wouldn't tell you, because I think you're safer as you are, going ahead with it. Don't be afraid. Don't think about Agnes. Just because she had a bad time doesn't mean you will. I think you're

224

the luckiest woman in Winter Quarters right now! Does Cliff know?"

"No. He was so pleased about Aggie when we first knew, I hate to disappoint him again. He was so proud of his son . . . even though it cost Aggie's life."

"He will be proud again, and you will, too."

Deborah raised doubtful eyes. "I don't know . . . I'm so old."

"You're not too old. Now hush. Help me fold away these clothes. Tomorrow I'll bring down some muslin and we'll start some sewing for you."

Deborah's hands were shaking as she picked up some of the small shirts, but a little of the fear was gone from her eyes. Gale's hands were shaking too. Perhaps only Cassie, lying quietly on the bed, knew what an effort Gale's words had cost her.

With spring, hope and activity began to revive the inhabitants of Winter Quarters. Early in April, Brigham Young organized a group of men who would accompany him westward to blaze a trail for the rest to follow. Even now, they had no idea what their destination would be, as their knowledge of the country ahead depended wholly on conjecture and hearsay. Zion might lie somewhere in the mountains, or perhaps in California, where they would meet and join up with the battalion when the war was over. At times Brigham even spoke of the Oregon Territory, of which such splendid tales were being told back in the States. This idea, however, met with distrust among those who knew that hundreds of Missourians, their erstwhile enemies, were flocking to that land.

The pioneer company, with Brigham at the head, set off early one morning, one hundred forty-eight of them. Included in the party were three women, one of them a wife of Young, and two little boys. Almost the whole of Winter Quarters turned out to see them off.

Gale and Cassie stood among the excited crowd, watching the wagons roll away, one by one, across the prairie. Cassie looked more than ever like a wistful-eyed child, her yellow hair tumbled loose about her thin shoulders. Beside her Gale looked tall and infinitely older. Those who knew her found a subtle change in the beauty of her classic face, a change they could not quite define. It might have been the added hollowness in her cheeks, or perhaps it was a faint hardness about her mouth. Only her eyes were the same, very dark and with a sadness which even her thick lashes could not conceal.

The two Simon women stood quietly, sharing none of the wild enthusiasm which this event produced. Cassie shivered, although the morning was warm.

"I wish we could leave, too. I hate this place!"

Unconsciously Gale's eyes wandered in the direction of the cemetery. A harsh shadow seemed to cross her face.

"We're going . . . with the first company to leave!" There was certainty in her words.

This decision was carried out in June. After the pioneer company left, the remaining Saints set to work plowing and planting on the flats near the river. But when the spring work was done, the monotonous waiting irked them beyond endurance, and so they determined to set out after their leader, although he had told them to wait until he should send back for them. They knew that he was leaving markers along the trail, and that they would have no

226

trouble in finding the way. With eager impatience they organized into companies and made ready to leave.

Thus it was that in the year 1847, on June 12, Gale and Cassie Simon left Winter Quarters and the graves of their sons. They rode together on the seat of their own wagon, with Bub Leary walking alongside, driving the oxen. Once more they found themselves members of Brother Eldridge's hundred, no longer the old company eighteen that had left Nauvoo, but a new group known simply as Eldridge's hundred. Gale felt a terrible heaviness in her chest at the thought of how many were staying at Winter Quarters, in the long rows of mounds in the cemetery. Determined to become cheerful again, she pushed the thought quickly to the back of her mind.

Cassie was in a state of feverish excitement the morning of their departure. In place of her customary listlessness was a sparkling vivacity which turned more than one head in her direction as the wagons assembled to leave. She chattered incessantly, and her laughter rang out clear and bright through the hubbub. Two spots of color burned in her cheeks, accenting her blue eyes, which this morning were the exact shade of the wide June sky.

Even Gale found herself staring at her more than once, with a mixture of wonder and bewilderment. She could scarcely recognize this animated girl as the pallid child with whom she had spent more than a year and a half. Cassie, usually so reticent, was calling from one wagon to another, and clapping her hands with delight and excitement. As Bub adjusted the yokes of the oxen, he looked at her with ill-concealed adoration. In spite of his ever-ready presence during the winter, he had caught few glimpses of her, and he was looking forward to his task of driving the Simon wagon with secret joy. He was further elated by her gay greeting to him this morning, the first direct attention she had ever given him.

The enigma of Cassie's strange behavior was blotted from Gale's thoughts in the final flurry of departure, and she didn't examine it again until they were well out on the prairie. She was thinking only of the future, wondering what it could possibly hold for them. Suddenly remembering Cassie's actions, she glanced at her.

The animation was gone, and her face was white and drawn. The blue eyes were gray, and she was leaning wearily against the bow of the wagon top. Gale stared at her anxiously.

"What's the matter, dear? Are you all right?"

"I'm tired. Do you mind if I crawl back in the wagon and rest a while?"

"Mind? Of course not! But are you sure you're all right?"

"Yes. Just tired."

It was fully five miles farther on before Bub Leary could summon courage to turn and steal a look back over his shoulder toward the wagon seat. A sharp disappointment showed in his face when he saw Gale riding alone, her sunbonnet pushed back from her hair. She was knitting as usual.

Twenty-Nine

Once more on the road, with the rumbling wagon beneath her and the swinging blue sky above, Gale found it easier to cease remembering the past winter. It was a beautiful June, the prairie brilliant with wild flowers. The grass was lush and green, in some places growing as high as the oxen's bellies. In spite of the long days of travel, the animals began to grow sleek.

Cassie resumed her air of customary languor, riding by turn on the wagon seat or on a bed in the wagon. When she was on the seat she was a delightful, spirited companion, a new Cassie. For the first time Gale discovered that the girl had a keen sense of beauty, often pointing out lovely spots in the wide landscape before Gale herself was aware of them. Then suddenly, in the midst of a conversation, she would grow quiet and soon would retire to the inside of the wagon to rest.

On the third day, the company stopped to noon on the bluffs on the eastern banks of the Elkhorn. As they ate, the Saints amused themselves by guessing the depth of the river whose golden-black bed appeared to be deceptively near the surface. Ad Jenkins mildly squelched the ensuing arguments by remarking that it had been about four feet deep when he passed this way several years back.

As they sat in the shade of their wagons, eating lunch and letting their animals graze a bit, they were startled by a cry.

"Indians!"

Two young Indians rode out from the cottonwoods on ponies, with their hands held high in a gesture of friendliness. Almost immediately they were followed by six or eight others, running out on foot from the shadows of the trees. The young braves, their dark faces grinning, started systematically at the head of the wagon train and indicated boldly that they desired gifts.

Gale's curiosity outweighed her fear as she watched them with interest. Cassie jumped up with a cry, but Bub caught her by the arm and pulled her down on the grass beside him.

"Don't let 'em know yer scared," he warned, "or they'll go on with the pleasure of devilin' ya. Set quiet, miss. They're friendly and won't do us any harm. They're just after a handout. They're the whoppinest beggars on earth."

Gale rose leisurely when they reached the Simons' wagon despite the pounding of her heart, and got a small bag of cornmeal from the back of the wagon. This gift left their own store pitifully meager, but Brigham Young's orders had been to keep peace with the Indians at any cost.

As the group passed gleefully on, carrying their growing load of loot, Cassie's strength collapsed, and she fell insensible to the grass. Some of the wagons had already resumed the journey when she finally regained consciousness. She caught Gale's hand to her pale lips.

"Oh, Gale," she whispered, "you are so brave and strong. Don't ever go away and leave me."

Bub lifted her as he would a small child and laid her gently on the quilts in the wagon. Gale gave her a drink of water, and Bub led the wagon out into the train of moving vehicles.

That night Isaac Eldridge ordered a heavy guard to be kept around the camp.

Slowly and steadily the train moved westward, following the ruts left by Brigham Young's advance company earlier. Gradually the landscape changed. The groves and green grass gave way to mile upon mile of sandy bluffs and desolate river bottom, with the Platte River spreading its wide water across a vast breadth of quicksand. Cottonwoods were less numerous. Grass was becoming scarce, and what little there was was harsh and coarse, cutting the tender feet of the oxen. Eldridge ordered all wagons drawn by horses to go in the lead in order to tramp out a trail.

As June melted into July, and the earth grew drier and sandier, the wheels of the wagons and the feet of the stock threw up great clouds of dust, which hovered over the entire train and were visible for miles. It was a choking, penetrating dust which almost suffocated both man and beast. Mothers wet cloths and spread them over their babies' faces as they slept, to keep them from strangling on the sand.

Cassie developed a dry persistent cough which began to worry Gale, although she would not admit it even to herself. Everyone was coughing and sneezing through the long dusty days. Even the teams of oxen were beginning to cough.

Perhaps it was not the cough which bothered Gale as much as did Cassie's erratic behavior. She

231

was seized occasionally by the fear that the girl was losing her mind. Young mothers did, sometimes . . .

As July blazed over the sandhills, the lure of the open road lost its enchantment for the Saints, and once more they began to allow their thoughts to dwell upon the specter of starvation which had haunted them since early the past winter. Their hoarded supply of flour and meal was running terrifyingly low. And as yet they had found no game along the trail to supplement it.

They were tantalized by the fact that they were now in buffalo country. Buffalo signs were everywhere. Dried buffalo chips lay thick and were their sole source of fuel. Mammoth white skulls bleached in the sand along the riverbank. Frequently large circular depressions were sighted along the trail, landmarks which Ad Jenkins told them were buffalo wallows. Everywhere along the river could be seen the tracks of great cloven hoofs.

But there were no buffalo. Apparently the Pawnees, either by malice or accident, had driven the entire buffalo herd far into the south. And so the Saints pulled their belts even tighter and traveled on through the heat and dust, their red eyes smarting as they peered among the bluffs for the dark forms that would mean food.

One morning as Gale was frying some pan bread over the fire, Cassie climbed down from the wagon wearing the yellow sprigged dress that Gale had made for the barbecue at the Bowery two years ago. The sight of it, with its hem torn and stained, brought back vivid memories of that night's disaster. She stared at it, and at Cassie, speechless. At last she found her voice.

"Cassie . . . what in the world are you doing?"

Cassie shrugged a bare white shoulder and tossed the light curls back from her neck with a flourish.

"I'm not doing anything. I'm just tired of wearing those old faded ginghams and calicos! You've had this in your chest for ages and you never wear it. I don't see why you should mind if I wear it."

"Why . . . it isn't that I mind, Cassie. But it's . . . it's unsuitable."

"Why?"

"It's made for evenings, and parties. You know no one wears low necks like that for everyday. What can you be thinking of, child?"

"Don't call me 'child,' for heaven's sake! And I'm not thinking of anything . . . except that I'm sick and tired of everything . . . dust, and living in these lumbering old wagons, and always being hungry! I'm sick of it all, I tell you!"

Gale spoke patiently. "But dear . . . riding through these sandhills in an evening dress won't help matters any. Your neck and arms will be burned to a blister!"

"No they won't! I'm going to use your parasol!"

She turned and reached the parasol down from the seat of the wagon where she had placed it in readiness. It was the white silk parasol Gale's father had given her just before he sent her to Lockwood Seminary, shortly before his death. Cassie snapped it open coquettishly and laughed. She's gone mad, Gale thought in terror.

"Cassie," she tried another line of reasoning, speaking gently, "are you sure you want to wear it, torn around the hem and pulled loose at the waist? I've never had time to mend it since that picnic at the Bowery."

Cassie smiled serenely and took a few mincing

233

steps of dance through the sand, holding the full skirt up with the tips of her fingers.

"Oh, I don't mind. It won't show while I'm riding. You know . . . I wish we'd have a dance some time around the camp fires, like we used to last summer. I wonder why they don't?"

Gale handed her two thick slices of bread, their entire food ration until evening, when they would be allowed two more pieces. "I suppose it's because most of us don't feel much in the mood for dancing."

Cassie ate the bread, staring into the sky absently. When she had finished, she wiped the crumbs from the unusual redness of her lips and adjusted the velvet ribbon at her neckline.

"I have a notion to go this very minute and mention it to Brother Eldridge. If he knew we really wanted to dance, I'll bet he'd say we could."

Gale tried to keep the concern from her voice.

"But Cassie . . . do you think most people really want to dance? The men are so tired after walking through this hot sand all day . . . none of them feel very gay when night comes."

"If you don't want to dance, that's your bad luck." She turned and started through the milling action of the corral made by the circle of wagons, where the drivers were rounding up their own animals with shouts and curses, the usual early morning confusion.

"Cassie! You can't be going through there . . . dressed like that."

"I don't know why I can't! Men have seen you in this dress! I don't know why they shouldn't see me!" She flounced off with her ruffles swishing.

Gale watched as she picked her way through the hubbub of men and animals. What in the world was the matter with her? She felt oddly responsible for her welfare, and her strange actions were more than she could understand. She saw her disappear in the swirling dust, holding up the too-long skirt that was dragging in the dirt and sand burrs.

Bub had just finished hitching up the oxen and was swinging the wagon out into line behind the others when she returned, her eyes bright and her cheeks brilliant. She caught him by the hand and squeezed it excitedly.

"Oh, Bub! We're going to have a dance tonight! Aren't you glad?"

Bub let his hand rest in hers, his face burning dully. His attention seemed to be riveted on the left hoof of his lead ox.

"Isn't it just too wonderful!" Cassie crowed.

"Why . . . yes . . . mighty fine, miss." He was almost as surprised as Gale was.

She dropped his hand and climbed up on the wagon seat. Then she leaned down and called softly, "If you're a good boy, you may have a dance with me!"

That night Gale sat on the hot sand with her back resting against the wagon wheel and watched the dancers whirling against the bright glow of the camp fires. Bub Leary and Ad Jenkins made the warm night sing with their rhythms. Isaac Eldridge came to where Gale sat and dropped to the sand at her side.

"Isn't this our waltz?"

"I told you a few minutes ago . . . I'm not dancing."

"I know. But I thought you were being coquettish." He laughed. "But you can see now how much I really want to be with you. I have left the festivities to seek you out a second time. Will you dance?"

"Isaac, don't be silly. I've told you, no!"

"Being loyal to the honorable Edouard?"

"You wouldn't understand what loyalty means."

"You know, of course, that there are many lovely señoritas in California," he taunted, laughing. "And that an American soldier is quite an attraction."

"Don't be hateful! I'll not dance with you, so stop bothering me!"

"Hmmm! You sound as though you meant it. Oh well, you can't hold out forever. By the way, what is this crazy transformation that has come over our little friend?"

"Cassie?"

"Yes. She seems suddenly to have cast aside her cloak of childish innocence. What happened?"

Gale felt all at once the need to share her burden of anxiety with someone. She burst out in desperation. "Oh, I don't know! I'm afraid she's . . . well, do you think she could be losing her mind . . . over her baby?"

Eldridge laughed softly. "Her mind is all right . . . what there is of it. And I don't think it's the baby that's her trouble. She's after a man. She's tired of waiting."

Gale drew in her breath sharply. "I might have known what to expect of you! I hate you!"

"I find Cassie's metamorphosis quite attractive, don't you?"

"Why did I expect any help or understanding from you?"

"I'm sure I don't know . . . unless it's my fatherly face." He caught up her fingers and kissed them lightly, and then bounded to his feet. He was gone before her anger could find words, calling softly over his shoulder, "My noble widow, you rebuff me; I'll seek out another of Edouard's wives. She is not so cold!"

As he strode toward the fires, she heard Cassie's laughter ring out clear above the voices of the others.

Thirty

The following week, Cassie lay in white listlessness inside the lurching wagon. She had no desire to leave her bed, and Gale didn't urge her. Her only interest was in food. When Gale brought her ration of bread in the morning, her eyes gleamed bright and she devoured it hungrily. After a few days she began to eye the other accusingly.

"Where is the rest of it?"

"The rest . . . ? There isn't any more, dear. You know we're allowed only two pieces morning and night. And it's true, they are much thinner pieces than they used to be. The flour is almost gone."

"Two pieces? I didn't have two pieces, did I?"

"Yes darling."

"Of course I didn't! You're keeping it for yourself!"

Gale stroked the cool, clammy forehead. She knew it would be burning with fever by night. It always was. "Dear little Cassie."

"You're eating my share! Yours and mine, too!" She burst into a storm of hysterical weeping.

Gale knew then that Cassie was ill, desperately ill. She was starving to death. Terror fastened itself to Gale's innards. She went out to get her own bread ration which she had kept in a heavy pan to keep it from the dogs. Even the dogs were starving. She took a mouthful, and took the rest in to Cassie. Cassie raised herself on one elbow, and stared at the bread with delight.

"So there *is* more! I knew there was!" She ate it with the tearing and gulping of a famished animal. Then she settled back, content. "You'd better go and eat your own breakfast now."

Gale turned away quickly, because she couldn't stop the quivering of her lips.

As the days went by, the possibility of replenishing the common larder with buffalo seemed as remote as ever. Daily hunting parties went out from the train and scoured the sandhills for game, and each night they came back to camp empty handed. Great wolves began to make their appearance. During the days they could be seen trotting along parallel to the train, but just out of shooting range, lured by the scent from the wagons, following along in hope that there would be something edible that these strange creatures might leave behind. At night their shrill, weird howling surrounded the camp, creeping in closer under the cover of darkness.

Inside the Simon's wagon, Cassie would crowd close to Gale, her thin fevered body shaking in terror. As she wasted away, her hunger grew.

"I'm sick of bread," she moaned pettishly. "If I could only have some meat . . . or some soup . . . I think I'd get well."

One night as soon as they broke for camp, Gale climbed into the wagon with a pan of water from the Platte River. She would sponge the invalid's face. The gray dust of the road lay heavy over everything. Even Cassie's face, as she lay with her eyes closed, was dusted with the color of cold stone. Something about the utter quiet of her and the pallor beneath the grime brought terror to Gale's heart.

She slopped the water wildly as she set the basin down.

Cassie opened her eyes and smiled. "What's the matter? Do I look that bad?"

Gale sighed in relief and began fumbling with the towel to cover her fright. "It's that dirt on your face! You should see yourself!"

Cassie wasn't asking for food. Her quietness was more frightening than her childish whining. As soon as Gale finished the girl's sponge bath, she hurried out to seek Bub Leary. Her mouth was grim with determination. It couldn't go on like this! She had listened to Brigham Young and let baby Edouard starve! She would not let Cassie go the same way, even if they killed her for it!

She found Bub outside the camp where they had the oxen staked out in the sparse grass. He was bathing a sore neck on one of the animals, where the yoke had worn through the tough hide. She came close and spoke quickly.

"Bub, I need help badly. It's for Cassie. Will you help me, even though you're liable to get in deep trouble for it?"

The boy dropped the rag in agitation. "Is . . . is she bad?"

"Yes, Bub, I'm afraid she is. She's starving." She spoke with harsh, cold bitterness. "She's starving . . . just like her baby starved. We're all starving . . . but most of us can stand it. But Bub . . . Cassie is *not* going to die! I won't let her!"

His face was working. After a time he regained a semblance of composure. "Is she really that bad?"

She went on hurriedly, glancing over her shoulder to see that no one was near. "Get Cliff Sutler and Ad Jenkins . . . tonight at ten. I know we can depend on them. Bring what knives and things you'll

241

need. We're going to kill one of our oxen. Out here where no one will see. Can I depend on you?"

He nodded. Gale knew he would give his life for Cassie if need be.

After the camp was wrapped in sleep, Gale crept out through the softness of dark where the cattle were grazing. The herd was guarded against wolves and marauding Indians on three sides, but the side toward the wagons was open. She had made a clear mental picture of where her cattle were tethered, and so she moved with cautious assurance. The only light was from the stars, a light that was swallowed in the gloom that lay in the valley of the Platte. The wolves were quite close, their eerie howls breaking up into a thousand echoes through the bluffs and sandhills. Gale swallowed her fear and forged ahead into the night. They would have to hurry, for Cassie was alone, and afraid.

Figures, a little blacker than the night, loomed before her.

Cliff spoke softly, "That you, Miss Gale?"

"Yes. Bub told you what I want?"

"Yes'm, but air ye sure this is what ye really want to do? Ye know this will cause a mighty big fuss when folks find out about it."

Her answer was sharp. "Are you afraid to help?"

"No, it ain't that. But I'm thinkin' o' *you*. Ye know it's agin the rules to kill animals . . . without permission from the elders."

"I know that. But I also know they wouldn't give me permission if I were to ask them. They'd say we're short of stock now. But these animals are mine . . . Cassie's and Edouard's and mine . . . paid for with the home we bought with our own money, and if I choose to kill one of them to save

242

the life of someone I love . . . that's my own af-fair."

Old Cliff was silent, but Ad Jenkins spoke up with his toothless lisp.

"Have you stopped to think, ma'am, what's going to pull your wagon after you've killed this ox?"

A growing desperation was goading Gale's deter-mination. Why did they have to stop to argue, to waste valuable time? She'd do it, if she had to do it alone! "The other three, I suppose."

"Three oxen don't pull good, ma'am. It'll take two teams to get through the mountains."

Bub spoke for the first time, "I've already got the other critter spoke for. One runnin' loose in the big herd, belongs to Rogers."

Gale reached out and pressed his hand in silent thanks. A wolf howled close by, and the animals moved about restlessly. "Can't we hurry?" Her words were a plea, almost a prayer.

Without another word the men turned away, and in another minute she heard a shuffling, and a short moan. Then there was the heavy gurgle of hot blood running into the sand. Cassie would have food.

Discovery came quickly. Gale had arisen at dawn and made a steaming bowl of beef stew, which she gave Cassie. The girl sniffed at it uncertainly, and then began to eat it eagerly. But after a mouthful or two, she sank back on the pillow and pushed the bowl away.

"Can't you drink a little of the broth, dear?"

"I'm so *tired* . . . I think I'd rather rest."

Gale had just finished putting the rest of the soup in a gourd and concealing the meat beneath the blankets in the wagon when Luke Reynolds approached the fire where she was busy with her own toast. He cleared his throat and eyed her uneasily.

"Good morning, Luke." She knew what was coming.

"Good morning, ma'am. I . . . I'm sorry, ma'am, but I wonder if I could bother you to come down camp a way? The elders are having a little meeting, and . . . and . . . could you come down a minute?"

Gale took a deep breath and set her teeth in her lower lip. She arose silently and laid her toast on the wagon seat.

A knot of men were gathered before the Eldridge wagon. They stopped talking when she and Luke approached. They turned and watched her with ill-concealed curiosity. She held her head high and returned their looks steadily. Only one pair of eyes met hers. They were Isaac Eldridge's. There was no expression in his hard handsome face, nothing in the steely blue of his eyes. Bub Leary was in the center of the group, twisting his hat.

Eldridge spoke. His voice was curt. "Sister Simon, one of your oxen was butchered last night. Did you know it?"

"Yes."

"Bub says he did it. Is that true?"

"He . . . he helped."

"He helped? Who else, then?"

Her eyes sought Bub's. He looked at her dumbly, but in the slate-gray eyes, she could read the message. 'Jest let's bear it, you and me, ma'am. Let's not get the others in trouble. Jest you and me. We'll do it for Cassie.'

"No one else. Just Bub and I."

"You!" For a moment his surprise lifted the mask from Eldridge's face, but then it was back again immediately. "No others helped?"

244

"No. No one," she lied glibly.

"Why did you do it? Didn't you know it was against the rules?"

His tone was hard and direct, with nothing to reveal the suave familiarity with which he usually addressed her. He might have been a criminal judge, sentencing a convict to life imprisonment, for all the harsh relentlessness in his face. Gale hadn't expected leniency, but she hadn't quite expected this. Her eyes wavered. She glanced desperately around the group, but nowhere did she find a friendly face. The men were all gazing with calm indifference at their boots. Lem Gibson looked at her a moment coldly, and then spat into the sand.

"Why did you do it?" Eldridge repeated.

Sudden anger flooded her face with color. She glanced around the circle with contempt. "I'll tell you why I did it!" she burst out. "I did it because Cassie is dying . . . starving! I've lost my own baby . . . and I've stood by and watched Cassie's baby starve . . . watched with my hands folded helplessly, according to the rules! Now I'm not going to see her die just because of your cruel, senseless rules! You can starve me, you can carry out your rules in any way you see fit . . . but I'm going to have the meat Cassie needs to save her life! It's our own meat . . . paid for with our own money!"

The silence following her ringing words was uncomfortably long. The camp was awaking to the chattering noises of the day, with chickens cackling in their coops, children quarreling and shouting, and the horses neighing shrilly on the end of their tethers. But inside the ring of men, the silence was absolute. Bub broke it by inhaling a great gulp of air. He thrust his hat in a wadded ball into his pocket.

"Brother Eldridge," he blurted, "I'll take the punishment, whatever it is y'all is aimin' to do to Miz Gale. I was the one who done the killin'."

"That's very noble, Bub," Eldridge's response was caustic. "Your loyalty to Sister Simon is overwhelming. Your bread ration will be cut in half for the rest of the week."

Gale caught her breath. The punishment was cruelly severe, for already the drivers, walking all day through the hot sand, were weak for the want of food. She sensed that Isaac was striking at Bub through his own jealousy. He had mistaken the lad's apparent chivalry for something more personal.

Eldridge turned to Gale. "Sister Simon, you will surrender *all* the meat, immediately. If you refuse, your wagon will be searched and the meat removed by force. That will be all."

In that instant all the hate and rebellion that she felt was centered on the tall immaculate person of Isaac Eldridge. All that hate blazed in her eyes, but her lips were shut tight. She could not say anything without saying too much. What she had to say, she could not say before all these men. So she turned and walked quickly back to her own wagon. As she went, groups fell silent and watched her pass with curiosity. So violent was the turmoil within her that she failed to note the effect of her passing.

Just before the train broke camp, several men came for the meat. She relinquished it with disdainful silence. It would do no good to object. Argument would only upset Cassie, who lay in a restless semi-sleep. It was useless to rebel against the relentlessness of fate. She watched them carry off the precious carcass, with white fury in her thin face.

All that day Cassie rode in a dull stupor, rousing only long enough to sip a little of the broth which

246

Gale hoarded in the gourd. The gray dust sifted in through the canvas and over the sick girl. Gale tried to keep it sponged from her hot face, but it was useless. And always, even when she slept, she was tormented by the dry, dust-nagging cough.

If it would just rain . . . enough to settle the dust. Gale rode beside her all the day, silently cursing the Saints, the dust, the unbearable heat, the insistent bleating of the band of sheep which followed behind them, even cursing the unjust God who would allow such things to continue.

Cassie coughed again. If it would only rain . . .

Thirty-One

Cassie was sleeping. Gale sat in the end of the wagon, breathing the welcome coolness of the night air and watching the great circle of fires waver and fade out as the camp retired for the night. All the sounds that arise from five hundred people and their dogs, chickens, cows, sheep, and horses . . . all dwindled away, sound by sound, until at last there was only the very distant crying of a wolf, and the muffled hoofs of the horses as they moved about through the sand nearby, grazing on the short wiry grass. Tonight the stars looked very small and remote, as though even their friendliness were withdrawn.

Gale felt she could not sleep, and so she paid no heed to the nine o'clock bugle which sent the rest of the Saints to their beds. She still felt restless and irritable from the helpless wrath which had burned in her since her trial that morning.

She was startled by a soft footstep in the sand close by, and a dark form appeared at the opening of the wagon.

"Who is it?" she whispered.

The man peered closer, then slipped a large bundle into the wagon beside her. He took off his hat and leaned easily against the wagon wheel near her knee. It was Eldridge.

"That's a piece of the meat that you made such a fuss about this morning," he said softly.

Astonishment choked back the anger that was on the tip of her tongue when she recognized him. Her mind dashed up and down various corridors, like an angry bee in a trap. But in spite of her indignation, her first thought was of the girl asleep behind her.

"Don't wake Cassie," she warned.

"Don't worry. I'm not here to wake Cassie. But aren't you going to thank me for the meat?" His voice was faintly impudent.

"*Thank* you?" For a moment she was so taken back by the man's insolence that she only sat, staring at him. Then all the hopeless fury of the day swept back over her, magnified a thousand-fold. Like a flash her hand leaped up and struck him across the face. "You . . . you devil!" In her anger, she forgot to keep her voice in a whisper.

Eldridge reached up and jerked her from the wagon, and half-pushed, half-carried her out across the sand away from the camp.

"You said not to wake up Cassie . . . and we won't!" he hissed in her ear.

A short distance from the wagons they stopped. He caught her by the shoulders and rudely whirled her around to face him. With equal rudeness she pulled away and stood panting in hot anger.

"Don't you dare touch me!"

"I might ask the same of you, my dear," he said, laughing. He rubbed his face where she had struck him. "Why all the fireworks?"

"Isaac Eldridge, you're the most despicable person I've ever known! Good night!" She whirled and darted back toward camp. In a moment he had her by the arm.

"I thought you had a lot to say to me this morning. Aren't you afraid you'll wake your little friend if you go shouting at me back at the wagon?"

"There's nothing to say about this morning. You showed me, in front of everyone, what friendship means." She was scalding in her simplicity.

All at once his impudence was gone and he was a small boy floundering for words. "Why did you ever think you could get away with it?" His distress was genuine.

"I thought I had explained all that this morning, very clearly."

"Yes, but you might have known you'd be reported. *Everyone* is hungry . . . and they won't sit by and see their neighbor with illegal food, while they obey the rules and starve."

"And I might have known my so-called friends would stick by me, come hell or high water," she said with heavy sarcasm.

"Gale dear, it isn't a matter of friendship . . ."

"No, evidently not!"

"I have the responsibility of being captain of this wagon train . . . and I have to maintain law and order, no matter whom it hurts. Can't you see?"

"Yes, I think I see it all." Those were her words, but her tone said, "No, I don't see! I know only that I hate you!"

At that moment the night was split with a sudden rifle shot, and a tongue of flame flared not far away. Instant pandemonium broke loose. There were the thunder of horses' hoofs, the frightened lowing of the cattle, and in quick succession, half a dozen more shots from various points in the vicinity.

Gale froze. After a stunned moment, her first thought was of Cassie and the terror she would feel on finding herself alone in such a nightmare.

Eldridge caught her wrist. "Good Lord . . . it's

251

the Indians after the horses! And I'm supposed to be on guard duty!"

Someone rushed past them from the wagons, cursing softly and trying to fasten his trousers as he ran. Another ran by, muttering fervently concerning the priming of his flintlock.

Gale pulled free. "I must get back to Cassie . . . before she misses me. She'll be terribly frightened."

"Are you afraid to go alone?" he asked gently. "I should get back to the guards before they discover I'm gone."

"No. It's not far."

"Hurry then. And don't let anyone see you."

While she ran back to the wagon, she could hear the voices of excitement shouting near the bluffs. She found Cassie standing at the front of the wagon, dressed only in her chemise. As Gale approached, the girl's knees gave way. Gale carried her tenderly back to her bed.

"Hush darling, hush," she quieted her whimpering. "I'm here now. It's going to be all right."

Between her sobs, Cassie coughed out incoherent phrases of terror. Gale cradled Cassie's head in her arms and stroked her tear-stained face until the last of the weeping subsided. Cassie grew quiet. Gently Gale lowered her to the pillow.

Outside the wagon, the camp was in hubbub. Returning from the skirmish with the Indians, the guards were telling various and sundry versions of the incident to a gathering audience. But Cassie was unaware of the excitement.

Gale found an odd stickiness on her hands. Her fingers had been wet with Cassie's tears . . . but tears weren't sticky. With sudden foreboding she struck a light to a candle and looked at her hands. They were red with blood.

She forced her eyes to look at Cassie. A thin trickle of blood started at the corner of her mouth and ended in a spreading pool on the pillow.

Next evening a mellow light that was half-day, half-night lay on the barren land. Sister Jenkins and Sister Gibson appeared at the Simons' wagon. They wore clean white aprons, which announced the fact that this was a formal call. Gale greeted them with scant enthusiasm, for they were women she didn't care about particularly. And besides, she was busy with Cassie. She was climbing down from the wagon with a basin of water with which she had just sponged Cassie's fever-racked body.

"Evening, Sister Simon," said the faintly oily Sister Jenkins.

"We just thought we'd call," said the other without warmth. "We thought we'd see how you and the other wife was gettin' on."

Gale had the feeling that they had a motive other than concern for the two women. She emptied the basin into the sand and waited. They peered curiously into the wagon.

"I'm fine," Gale said. "And Cassie is a little better tonight, I think."

"Better? So . . . she's sick?"

"Yes." She wanted to add, 'thanks to the Saints,' but she held her tongue.

"What's wrong?" Sister Jenkins demanded. "I'd better have a look at her. I'm something of a doctor." She was already pulling her mountain of flesh up on the wagon tongue.

"I'd rather you didn't go in, if you don't mind." Gale's sharp words stopped her.

The woman settled her bulk back to earth. A

storm warning shone in her heavy-lidded eyes. "You got something to hide?" she asked.

"What would I hide?" Gale flared. Then she remembered the bundle of beef concealed beneath the baggage, and her face turned crimson. She hastened on, "I've just got Cassie bathed and settled for the night, and I'd rather she wouldn't be disturbed."

"What's ailin' her?" said Sister Gibson.

Horror of the previous night flooded Gale. Even now she dared not admit her terror that Cassie might have . . . did have . . . galloping consumption. She pushed the words from her mind. "It's . . . it's starvation."

"Starvation, huh?"

The callers exchanged meaningful glances.

"If that's it, how come she's gettin' better? You said she's better, didn't you?"

"A little stronger, I think."

"I think I'll just hoist myself up and take a look," Sister Jenkins said, action following words. "No telling what's going on here."

Sister Gibson followed. Gale lighted a candle, which revealed the girl's white pointed face on the pillow, with enormous eyes staring at them.

"Cassie dear. These ladies have come to visit."

"That's lovely," she whispered. "I heard."

The women stared at her curiously. "What's the matter?" Sister Gibson said.

"Nothing. Nothing at all." It was an effort for her to speak. "I'm just . . . just resting."

"Humph! Do you get enough to eat?"

Then Gale knew why they had come. Rumors must be circulating about the sudden windfall of beef that was being distributed through the camp. Despicable! Prodding information from a dying girl! Cassie would innocently admit the possession of the meat, since she had not been warned to do otherwise. Besides, she was very ill and should not be disturbed for any reason.

"Please, Sister Jenkins!" Gale cried. "Can't you see she's ill?"

"Do you get enough to eat?" the woman drilled Cassie ruthlessly.

"Oh, yes," the girl responded with unwinking eyes. "Plenty. Gale goes out every morning and shoots me a buffalo before breakfast."

The women glared at her, then turned and crawled from the wagon. Cassie caught Gale's eye and smiled faintly.

"Blithering idiots . . ." Cassie whispered when they had gone. "Isn't that what . . . we call them?"

It rained. Gale's prayers were answered. It rained until there was no more dust swirling up under the wagon wheels. It rained until there was only the sodden earth and the Platte, muddier and wider than ever. It continued to rain, with the wagons drawing up in hit-and-miss formation against the downpour, horses tied to the wagon wheels, their tails against the rain and their heads drooping dejectedly. The insides of the wagons smelled of wet chickens, wet dogs, and wet clothing.

At twilight the storm cleared and the sky was a fresh bowl of apple-green. Little by little, a deep blue began seeping into it from the east, until at last it was a black setting for the diamond-clear stars.

That night the wolves howled closer to the wagons than they had ever come before, made bold by a gnawing hunger which the drought of July had brought. As they prowled nearer, Gale lay awake, keeping the blanket over the restlessly tossing Cassie, and holding her in her arms when she awoke sobbing in terror.

"Oh, Gale, don't let the wolves get me!" she moaned. "Don't let them get me . . ."

Gale was always there, with comforting arms and soothing words. All that night she kept the candle burning, although it was almost the end of her supply, and she knew that it was against the rules of the camp. She expected one of the watchmen to come by and order her to extinguish it, but no one came. Toward morning Cassie awoke, quietly, quite rational. For a long time she watched the candle fluttering in the cool night breeze.

"I've been thinking of Edouard . . . and the baby. It's queer I should think of them tonight, isn't it? I wonder if Edouard is . . . all right." Her voice was merely a breath, as low and soft as the wind which crept through the sandhills. Gale strained to hear her words.

"Gale . . . Gale . . . if I shouldn't ever see him again . . . if something should happen to me . . . tell him how much I loved him . . . please." There was urgency in her words. "Promise me! He never knew how I felt . . . he was all the time thinking of you . . . But I want him to know . . . I loved him more than anything else in the whole world."

Gale tried to control the steadiness of her voice. "I'll tell him."

Cassie clung to her hard, her thin nails cutting into Gale's flesh. Gale stroked her hair.

"Oh Gale . . . don't let me die! I'm afraid. I don't want to die . . . but I've known it all along . . . only I wouldn't let myself think of it. But I knew I wasn't going to get well. That's why I wanted to dance . . . while I still had time."

256

Then she pulled herself upright and flung her hair back from her face with the old familiar gesture.

"I *won't* die! This is a bad dream. Everyone else can die . . . Mamma . . . and the baby . . . and maybe . . . even Edouard! But it can't be me!" She turned to Gale, her eyes glittering.

Outside, the sky was growing a shade paler behind the stars. After a time, a wolf cried very close. Gale felt a cold chill.

Cassie sat rigid, listening. Her face was marble-white. Then she slumped forward.

"Don't let them . . . get . . . me!" she whispered.

A long time later, Gale wiped the warm red blood from the girl's lips and laid her body gently on the quilts.

Dear God . . . I have nothing left . . .

Thirty-Two

Just before the wagons started rolling on, they buried Cassie in a shallow grave dug hurriedly in the sand. Not far away two wolves watched the man hastily shoving the sand over the slender, blanket-clad figure. Cassie was so small . . . and frightened. They couldn't be doing this to her! Shoving sand over her . . . as though she were a bone that dogs were burying! Gale, still numb and unbelieving, stared at the men as they worked.

Nearby Bub Leary stood, desolation in his eyes. No one guessed, nor had time to care, that this tall ungainly lad was watching with a grief which tore at his guts. The others knew only that here was another grave. And graves were common now, too common to arouse much consternation. They knew also that the train was getting a late start, and that they must push on quickly toward the buffalo before starvation caught them all.

Almost the entire wagon train was under way when Gale turned from the grave. Her eyes caught sight of the gray shadows lurking near the bluff. She stiffened. "Look!"

Issac Eldridge followed her gaze. "Only wolves. They've been all around us for days. Come now . . . get in your wagon. Everyone has gone on."

"No! I'm not going! I can't go and leave her here

alone . . . with the wolves!" She broke into hysterical weeping. "Oh, no . . . I can't go . . . She begged me . . . not to let them . . . get her!"

Eldridge lifted her bodily and set her on the seat of her wagon. She struggled against him, her eyes still on the gray skulking forms. There were four of them now. The rest of the wagons had gone on. The wolves came down from the bluff a little way, sniffing the air.

"No . . . no!" Gale screamed. "I'm not going! I'll not leave her alone!" She tried to climb down, but Eldridge pushed her back.

"Drive on," he told Bub Leary.

The lad opened his mouth twice before he could speak. "I'll stay here today . . . with Miz' Gale . . . and dig a better grave."

Anger flushed Eldridge's hard face. "You'll stay nowhere with Gale! I'm the captain of this company, and I say you're driving on . . . *now*!"

Bub moved his weight from one foot to another. "I beg your pardon, suh . . . but I'd rather stay."

Eldridge glared at him for a single furious moment. Then he swiftly stepped forward and jerked the bullwhip from the boy's dangling hand. He laid it on in one cruel cutting blow across the lad's shoulders. He then flung the whip at Bub's feet. "Now . . . drive on!" he ordered curtly.

Bub stooped and picked up the whip, but he made no move to go. Desolation blotted all anger from his face. "If Miz' Gale wants that we should stay, we'll stay," he said tonelessly.

Both men glanced at Gale, who was staring in fascinated horror at the movement of the wolves. There were five of them now, and they sat on their haunches, waiting.

Eldridge turned back to Bub. "You young fool

. . . don't you know that you can't stay here? One wagon, alone, would never stand a chance against the Indians, and you know it, if you have half the gumption I think you have! Do you want to have both your scalps hanging on some Indian's belt? Now . . . get going, before I really whip you!"

Bub stared for a long time at the grave. At last he turned wearily and spoke to his oxen. Captain Eldridge mounted his horse and rode beside them.

After the wagon began to move, Gale made no move of resistance. She rode, slumped on the seat, her eyes shut tight against what they were leaving behind. She soon heard the snarling of the wolves, but she put her hands over her ears, trying to believe it was the wagon wheels, shrieking for grease.

Day after day she rode, unaware of what was going on about her. She never kindled a fire, and seldom ate unless Sophie Eldridge or Tillie Tavenner or old Cliff Sutler brought her a dish of their own supper and sat by to see that she ate it. She quietly refused invitations to join neighboring families in their suppers.

At nights she lay terrifyingly alone in the wagon, listening to the wolves and shuddering in cold sweat. Everything was blotted from her mind by the wolves and the horror of Cassie's ravaged grave.

July ground its cruel way into August. At last the Saints came upon the buffalo. There were thousands of them, grazing upon the short upland grass. Slaughter was easy. There was feasting, and thanksgiving, and meat in plenty. The Saints were almost wild with the superabundance of food after eighteen months of semi-starvation. After the men learned the knack of killing the beasts, they brought them into camp by the dozens. Finally Eldridge and his elders ruled that the hunters should kill only what they could eat.

There was liver, kidney stew, baked heart, full red-blooded steaks, and fragrant succulent roast, dripping with all the delicious goodness of which the emigrants had been dreaming for the past gnawing months. When they had all eaten their fill—a thing which many had thought they would never do again in this world—they cut the meat into thin strips and smoked it over the fires, or strung it on cords across the ends of the wagons to cure in the hot sun, storing up a supply for the weeks ahead.

But for Gale there were only the nights of terror and loneliness. She rode alone on the wagon seat, a gaunt lifeless figure, her shoulders drooping, her eyes black and staring, and a look of sudden age in the cruel hollows of her cheeks. Even the brightness of her hair seemed faded in a dry bushy mane beneath her sunbonnet.

Slowly but steadily the long caravan moved westward, and the Saints marveled at the strange wild land through which they were passing. The sandy bluffs gave way to rising cliffs of marl and limestone, cut by wind and water into fantastic shapes resembling towers and castles, cones and pyramids, and great tables with the underpinnings partly worn away. Here and there cedars and pinions dotted the cliffs with their dark stunted growth.

Then one evening with twilight settling over the camp, old Cliff came hobbling to Gale's wagon. She still sat on the seat, leaning against the bow that held the top, and stared blindly at the swooping circles that the nighthawks made against the mellow sky.

"Miss Gale . . . Miss Gale! Pardon me, ma'am, but can ye come with me? Right quick?"

She turned her face to him slowly. It was a full minute before she spoke. "What do you want?"

"Pardon me for botherin' ye, ma'am . . . but it's Debbie. She's bad took . . . with the baby comin', I think. She's awful sick . . . like Aggie when . . . when she died." There was childish panic in his quavering old voice. "Can ye come . . . right away?"

Gale sat silent, again watching the nighthawks. At last she spoke without expression. "Get someone else, Cliff. I don't want to see anyone else die."

"There's . . . there's nobody else she has faith in like she has in you. She's scared of ever'body else." He, too, was silent for a moment. Then he burst out in frantic plea, "Oh, please God, Miss Gale . . . she's dyin' there alone, and so scared! I . . . I jest can't lose Debbie! I can't let her go."

"That's what I've said . . . so many times. It doesn't help."

"Please, ma'am!"

Gale shrugged, as though shifting an uncomfortable burden on her shoulders, and climbed down. Cliff hurried away through the gathering dusk, while Gale followed behind with lagging steps.

Before dawn the baby was born, a healthy squalling boy, vigorous in spite of his parentage. And to Deborah's inexpressible surprise, she lived. She was weary and sore, but still living. And with the swaddled son resting on her arm, all fear of death faded from her mind.

Gale, riding again in her own wagon, became conscious of the world about her for the first time in weeks. Despite her long night of midwifery, her eyes actually saw. She stared with surprise at the country through which they were traveling. She remembered only monotonous sandhills, with the sluggish Platte winding among them. And now she found herself suddenly riding through a wilderness of high rugged hills, with a breeze from the icy mountains coming down on the morning air.

She shivered, and pushed the hair back from her face. She must open the big chest tonight and find some clothes for Deborah's baby.

Thirty-Three

It was late August when the Saints reached the ferry of the North Platte, high in the hills. They were ferrying the last of their wagons across when another party drove up behind and stopped at a distance. Both the Saints and the newcomers eyed each other appraisingly. The new company was small, consisting of but ten shabby travel-worn wagons, drawn by drooping animals. One of the drivers, a heavy bulk of a man, left his people and started toward the Saints. Suddenly he stopped and shouted back over his shoulder. His voice carried clearly to the wagons waiting at the ferry.

"These ain't no Missourians! They're the Saints! Come on!"

Bub Leary looked up at Gale where she sat, waiting their turn to cross the river. A slow grin lighted his face.

"That's Pat Muldoon, ma'am, shore's I live! No one else shouts jest like that. That's the battalion, come back!"

The battalion! Edouard! So suddenly intense that it hurt, a joy burst like a bomb within her. Edouard! And then as suddenly as it came, it was gone, leaving only fear. What was wrong? Were these all the Saints who were left . . . after the war? Then frantic

265

hope revived in her. Edouard *was* there, riding in one of the wagons . . . wounded, perhaps.

She leaped down and ran across the intervening space toward Pat Muldoon and the wagons. She flew as fast as her feet and the wings of her hope would carry her. She stopped, panting, before the grinning Pat.

"Edouard . . . Is he with you?"

"Howdy, Sister! Say, this *is* a reception! The way you chased out here to meet me, I thought you was aimin' to give me a kiss."

"Edouard . . . he has been . . . hurt? Isn't he . . . coming back?"

"Edouard? Oh, him? Well, I can't say about him comin' back. But he ain't hurt none. Leastways, he wasn't the last time I seen him. He was feelin' finer 'n frog fuzz. O' course, that was some time ago."

"How long . . . ago?"

"About a year in October, I reckon. Me and this bunch that's with me was laid up, sick in Pueblo for the winter, and didn't go on to Californy with the rest. Last time I seen 'im, he was feelin' right chipper. I wouldn't count too much on his comin' back if I was you."

"Do you think he's been . . . killed?" It was a whisper.

"Killed! Hell, no! But Addie Voak went along, and he ain't goin' to get lonesome. He might even settle down in Californy."

He slapped his thigh and bellowed with laughter. Gale turned unsteadily and walked back to her wagon. Her face went from icy pallor to a hot flush of anger and humiliation. She felt suddenly dirty, splashed with filth. Pat couldn't be relating facts. It must be his vulgar way of making a joke.

And yet . . . his words held the seeds of doubt

266

and anxiety that were to torture her in the days to come. Until that moment she had not once thought of Addie . . . and Edouard, together.

Gale was finishing her lonely supper of bread and dry jerked buffalo when a tall black-haired young woman hurriedly came to her wagon. They had traveled late that evening, and although it was almost dark, most of the families were just beginning to prepare their evening meal. Gale looked at the stranger curiously. She was almost beautiful, in a grave aloof way, but Gale could not remember having seen her before.

"Hello Sister Simon," she said huskily. "You don't remember me, do you?"

"No . . . I'm afraid I don't."

"I'm Susannah Nickols. Oh, Sister Simon, you can't know how thankful I am to be back again! You're the only friend we have . . . and this past year has been just . . . just awful!"

"Susannah! Why, child, you have become a lady! How you have changed! I hadn't the least idea who you were! Why, when you left, you were just a little girl!"

"Yes, and I wish I still were!" Gale was shocked by the vehemence with which she spoke.

"Sit down, Susannah, sit down . . . and tell me about everything. How are the other girls, and your mother and father? But wait! Have you had your supper?"

"No, I don't want any. I had to come over to see you as soon as I heard that you were in this company."

"Don't you want *anything*?"

"No, I'd rather talk while we're still alone. The

other girls will be here as soon as they've had their supper."

"I'll light a fire while you're talking. It will be more cheerful. I haven't had a fire since . . ." She broke off abruptly. "Come, tell me about yourself, and the rest of the family."

"That's it. That's what is so . . . so terrible. It's not the same family any more . . . not even the same name. We're 'Muldoons' now!" She spoke with cold anger.

"Muldoons!" Gale turned with a bunch of dried grass in her hand.

"Mother married Pat Muldoon." She spoke in hard clipped phrases. "Father died of the fever last winter in Pueblo. Mother hates Mr. Muldoon and hates being married to him. I know she does, but she tries not to let anyone know, not even me. She stands up for him when I try to talk to her about him. She thinks it's a wife's duty to be loyal to her husband, regardless. She only married him because we were stranded down there in the Mexican town alone . . . and he kept after her."

Gale sat on her heels, watching the flame climb up the dry grass she held, and then devour the sticks she had waiting. She was having difficulty grasping the full import of Susannah's swift story. Sister Nickols . . . the dainty little sparrow of a woman, the wife of the schoolmaster . . . married to Pat Muldoon!

"But . . . but what about Mary Muldoon?" she stammered.

"You mean why did she let Pat do it? I can't understand, either. But I think he'd married Mother before Sister Muldoon even suspected. She was so worried about Miss Voak, she thought her worries were all over when Addie went on to California with

268

the Mormon Battalion. But when she found out about Mother, she came to the little adobe house where we lived. It was awful. I thought for a while she was going to kill Mother."

Gale rose then and went to sit beside the tall black-haired girl, taking her hand in her own.

"I'm sorry, dear. I only wish there was something I could do to help you."

She could feel the girl's knuckles tighten and saw a storm gathering in her young face. She can be no more than fifteen, Gale thought with compassion.

"This isn't half of it . . . what I've been telling you. It's just an introduction to what I came to tell you." She took an unsteady breath. "Mr. Muldoon wants me to . . . to marry him!"

"Oh, no!" Gale gripped her hand. "No, Susannah! You can't!"

"That's what I came to ask you about. I can't get any help from Mother. I can see in her eyes that she doesn't want me to. But every time I try to ask her about it, she starts telling me all we have to be grateful to him for! Grateful! I'd rather have starved in Pueblo, or have lived forever with the Mexicans and Indians, than to be grateful to him for anything! But what can I do?"

"Do? Why child, you don't have to do anything. Just don't marry him. You needn't marry him if you don't want to."

"Oh, I wish I knew!" She buried her face miserably in her hands. "There's no reason why I should marry anyone, as far as I can see. But when he finds me alone, and starts telling me I *have* to marry him or he'll make me sorry, I get so frightened I don't know what to think. And he keeps after me all the time! Oh, dear God, I wish I had died in Pueblo!"

Gale brushed the girl's smooth head with her fingers, and watched the fire shimmering on the dark hair.

"I know, Susannah. I understand better than you think. You know, I once lived in the Muldoons' boarding house in Boston. Believe me, I know what fear and hate mean. But luckily for me, he was not seeking another wife at the time." She paused a moment, engulfed by memories of that dreadful summer before she married Edouard. "Oh, my dear, don't ever give in to him! Don't ever let him frighten you. You'd be miserable the rest of your life."

"I know. But with Mother on his side . . ."

"Hush child! She's not on his side! She couldn't be! Your mother will be proud of you for being strong, in spite of what her sense of duty tells her to say. I know it."

Susannah straightened and looked into the fire. Some of the storm had left her eyes. "Sitting here with you, it's easy to feel strong. But when he starts threatening me again . . . I don't know. I get so frightened."

"Hush now. Here come the other girls."

On up the Sweetwater River the Saints rumbled, up and up, with the sky above getting bluer, and the air each day more thin and clear. On they went through the wild highlands, where nothing much grew but sagebrush and cactus, on past rugged red bluffs and through occasional miry stinking sloughs. On they went past Independence Rock, a giant mound of solid stone where travelers paused to scrawl their names. They stopped, too, and inscribed their names with anything they could find, tar, red wagon paint, a bit of yellow house paint one of the Saints had carried along. Then on they went, past Devil's Gate, the picturesque chasm which the river cut from sheer walls of granite, on until they could see the Wind River Range looming up like phantom clouds in the sky. On the weary oxen plodded, up past groves of aspen, where the hoar frost whitened the grass each night, and the wind sweeping down from the snowy peaks was bitter cold in the mornings. On they went, with long days of travel and short nights of rest, hastening on to the destination, they knew not where. They must outrun winter!

And then one day, they met a small company of fur traders returning from Oregon with a pack train of pelts. The grizzled white-whiskered leader drew his Indian pony up beside Eldridge's wagon. "Headin' for Oregon country?" he inquired sociably. "If you are, you're not alone. There's shore a passel of wagons ahead of you!"

"I don't know where we're headed for exactly. We're just following the trail our leaders blazed for us earlier in the summer."

The trapper looked at him sharply. "You must be the Mormons, then."

"That's what folks call us."

"Well, I have some news for you then. Your leader . . . believe his name was Brigham Young, is only a day's travel behind me, comin' this way. Got his colony started, he told me, and is headin' back to some place he called Winter Quarters. Got quite a crowd with him . . . bunch of fellers they called the battalion . . . come back from fightin' with the Mexicans in Californy. Yep, we had supper with 'em last night up at Pacific Spring, top of south pass."

Eldridge's face lighted up as the other talked. Beside him on the seat, Grace Eldridge leaned forward, suddenly intense. Isaac spoke.

"Brigham Young, you say? Coming this way?"

"Yep, I reckon. Well, we gotta be moseyin' if

we're goin' to get these pelts into Fort Laramie before their fall shipment leaves for the States. Glad to
've met up with you, pardner." And his train of wiry
ponies clattered off.

The news spread like a prairie fire back through
the train, which had halted while Eldridge and the
trader talked. The Saints jumped down from their
wagons and gathered in excited groups. Immediately
plans were laid for a celebration for the morrow.
They would go on to the first available camping spot
and there make preparations for a feast to honor the
returning Pioneers and the battalion.

The next day, September seventh, dawned dismal
and cold with heavy black clouds sweeping down
from the mountains, and snow beginning to spit
down at the Saints. But the preparations went on full
tilt. The tables were laid in a great grove of trees
near the river, tables of planks and sawbucks, with
white linen cloths and "company" silver. It was a
great occasion, and the women vied with one another to see who could produce the finest appoint-
ments for the tables from their chests in the wagons,
and who could cook the most delectable dishes with
what they had on hand.

A fat heifer was killed, and all morning the ladies
stewed and baked, broiled and roasted, while their
feet grew colder and wetter with the snow that was
beginning to collect in thin white drifts. Their faces
grew redder from the excitement and the heat of the
fires.

By one o'clock everything was in readiness. Great
kettles of roasted and broiled beef lay in the coals to
keep hot. Pan after pan of fluffy biscuits were covered with flannel so that they would stay warm. Pies
and cakes were hoarded in various secret places in

272

the wagons, to keep them safe from the dogs and from the hungry fingers of the children. The long white tables were jeweled here and there with precious dishes of chokecherry and squawberry jelly, made from fruit picked in the early mornings and at noon stops, and boiled over the fires at night.

The older girls kept watch over the tables, brushing off the thin sifting of snow which drifted down through the trees. The younger children bounced about excitedly, dashing on frenzied expeditions up the trail to see if they could catch a sight of the approaching company, then dashing back again to report that no one was in sight.

A little before two o'clock, with the snow now falling heavily, the wagons of the pioneers rumbled into sight.

"Hallelujah! Hallelujah!" shouted the welcoming party, streaming out of the grove to the astonishment of their guests. It was a time of joyful intoxication, with wives greeting husbands, and children meeting fathers who were almost strangers, fathers whom they had not seen in more than a year in some cases.

Gale had kept feverishly busy all that morning, working among the others, trying to keep down the seething joy of anticipation which boiled in her veins. Once, not many days ago, she had been bitterly disappointed, she kept telling herself, and she must not let her hopes run away with her.

Now she ran with the excited crowd that rushed to greet the newcomers. She ran from wagon to wagon, peering into faces, searching. The last wagon rumbled in and came to a halt. He must be here! He had to be! But he was not. She had missed him in the crowd.

The hungry Saints surged toward the tables, clasping hands in loving greetings as they went, and shouting at one another in joy. The men sat, and the women rushed to serve the banquet there in the grove. Gale wandered silently among the tables, searching, her face strained. She must have missed him in the throng. She stood a long time at each table, staring into each face carefully. Then she moved on to the next.

At the last table she stood a long while. Realization settled over her. He had not come back from California!

Some time later she became aware that she was still standing, staring with empty eyes at the white linen cloths dusted with snow. She found Pat Muldoon staring at her, a leer hovering over his heavy mouth, greasy with food. Down the table Isaac Eldridge was gazing at her with curious steadiness.

"Didn't yer man come back, dearie?" Mary Muldoon was at her elbow, nudging her in sympathy. "Tsk! Tsk! Ye'd best be goin' back to yer wagon and have yerself a good cry. Ye look like ye'd seen a ghost! But I wouldn't worry about his bein' dead, if I was ye, dearie. Ye notice that Addie Voak wasn't with 'em as they come back, didn't ye? Well, *I* noticed! She's probably got him out there in California somewheres, thinkin' the moon is made of green cheese. But don't take it so hard, dearie! A man's nothin' but a torment, anyhow. Ye're better off without him!"

Gale turned away, trying to keep down the sobs that were rising in her. Sister Muldoon's sympathy was rubbing salt into her fresh wound. She felt Eldridge's and Pat's eyes on her. They were gloating. They were all gloating because Edouard had chosen not to come back. He had chosen to stay in California with the Boston barmaid, Addie Voak.

She walked away with her head proud and high, a bright unreal smile fixed on her lips. They would never know, any of them, how deep the disappointment was cutting. They'll never know, ever!

That afternoon, after the storm had cleared and the feasting was over, there was dancing. The music rang in the grove, and the dancers' feet trod the snow into the earth as they whirled and stamped and laughed.

And no one among all the Saints was quite as gay as Gale Simon, whose husband had not come back from the war. Watching her, the women shook their heads. The woman was crazy! Hadn't she gone into violent mourning for her husband's second wife? And as though that weren't strange enough, here she was on the day that her husband did *not* return, dancing until her face glowed, and her hair gathered in bright damp ringlets around her neck. One would think to look at her that she was glad!

Gale laughed and chattered, and made herself the most popular girl at the celebration. And no one but Gale Simon knew the bitterness that she was trying to conceal.

Thirty-Four

The Saints listened greedily while Brigham Young told them of the settlement the pioneer company had started in the valley of the Great Salt Lake. Another month of travel, he told them, and they should be home. Home! A great shout went up at the word. Home! They pounded one another on the back and laughed in joy.

He told them not to expect too much at first. The country was dry, and it was desolate, but it had wonderful possibilities. There was an abundance of water for irrigation, and there was timber in the hills for building. There in the desert they would build up an empire, a civilization of which the whole world would be envious. There would be great cities, and fine roads, and mile upon mile of splendid rolling farmland. It would mean years of work and hardship, but it was there, that empire.

Already they had laid out the capital city, Salt Lake City, so named because of a great saltwater sea nearby. There were to be wide streets, and a large plot of land for every Saint. No land was to bought or sold, but each man was to receive his share by drawing a lot number.

Although the pioneers had not arrived in the valley until late in July, they had plowed and planted potatoes, corn, peas and beans. Even before they left to return East, they were encouraged by the fine stand the young plants were making.

The Saints listened as their leader talked, listened with eagerness as he unfolded it all before them, and that night they went to their beds with a prayer of thanksgiving on their lips. Early the next morning Young and part of his company parted from their friends and continued on their way to Winter Quarters. Many of those pioneers, now that they were reunited with their families, were turning back to Salt Lake City.

Eldridge's company broke camp long before the sun tipped the treetops and set out for the Promised Land, far to the west. No other travelers were before them, but they learned from the swift-moving Indians and from a fur trader heading for Oregon that several other companies of Saints were on their heels. Winter was crowding them, and they were all traveling fast.

The old Gale Simon was gone, the one with the white tortured face and the dark brooding eyes. Edouard had chosen *not* to come back, but no one would see her shame. And so the new Gale was bright and alive and gay, too gay, with a clear brittle laugh and a feverish sparkle in her eyes.

She brushed her hair each night until the sparks snapped in the darkness, and once again it was as bright as a new penny. With reckless shears she slashed into the fresh crisp bolt of blue-flowered calico which she kept wrapped carefully in the big chest. During the noon stops and morning and night, her flying fingers stitched and fashioned three new dresses. Edouard was not coming back, and she must not let anyone see how terribly much it hurt.

No longer did she remain in the seclusion of her wagon with Susannah in the evenings, frozen and aloof. Instead she visited from wagon to wagon, romping with the children, talking jelly making and quilt patterns with the women, chatting and laughing about nothing in particular with the men. Edouard was in California with Addie Voak, but no one could see behind the bright mask of her face.

More than one man's pulses quickened with the lightness of her banter, and many a masculine eye followed with hunger the lithe grace of her figure. Of this Gale had no idea, so busy was she in playing her part. She gave none of them an opportunity to speak to her alone, for Susannah was at her elbow most of the time.

Now that it was common knowledge that Edouard had not returned, the men took it for granted that Gale was once more eligible for marriage. But no man, whatever his yearnings, could very well propose marriage to a girl in front of his wife and children. During the days she chatted volubly with Susannah and Bub, and at night she shared her wagon with Susannah, who accepted this arrangement with joy, eager to escape Muldoon.

Eldridge tried persistently to seek Gale out, for this sudden new role puzzled him and piqued his interest, but he found himself no more fortunate than his fellows. What was even more tantalizing, she often visited his camp fire to talk with Sophie, bouncing Isaac's adopted baby son on her knee, and singing gay little songs to him, much to the delight of the other Meier children. But never could he find her alone.

Into this brittle, dangerously balanced environment drove Charles Fairbanks, an elder from Philadelphia, short, rotund, bald, and perspiringly serious about life and everything in it. He drove at the head of his company of fifty, with his stylish

279

young wife at his side. His fashionable carriage was scarred and battered, his once-dashing team of matched grays lame and sore-shouldered. Brother Fairbanks had discovered long ago that their slender pacing legs were no match for the sturdy oxen which plodded along this trail, but at his wife's haughty refusal to ride in an ox wagon, he kept on, hoping that his horses and conveyance would hold out until they reached their destination.

Fairbanks' group overtook Eldridge's company shortly after the dangerous crossing of the Green River. The large company had stopped for the noon hour on a grassy meadow bordered on the riverside by dense clumps of willow and partly shaded by several large cottonwood trees, turned a golden yellow by the frost. The whole world, it seemed in this lovely spot, was tinged with the warm colors of autumn.

The newcomers approached, still wet and splattered with mud from the ford which they had just crossed. Although the day was quite cool, Charles Fairbanks was perspiring freely from the multitude of his problems. His young wife was just recovering from a spell of hysterics brought on as a result of fording the river, and was still reclining gracefully against the back of the seat, with a bottle of smelling salts to her nose. Behind them rode their black people, Jules and Fanny Ivory, who had come from Sister Fairbanks' childhood home in Philadelphia. With them was riding another black woman, handsome Oleander Harrison, who had been a laundress in Nauvoo. Sister Fairbanks had generously offered her transportation if she would do all the washing and ironing on the trip, a herculean task which Oleander did perfectly, to the resentment of the rest of the company. A colored maid to do the ironing, on a pioneer journey of this kind!

Charles Fairbanks' eyes were bulging and his lips compressed with the effort of trying to divide his attention between his fluttering wife and his skittish weary horses. At the same time he was endeavoring to appear staid and dignified before his own company and before these strangers. He was having a most difficult time.

At last he succeeded in maneuvering his team up to the resting group. Eldridge went out to meet him. He hastened his steps when he saw the fair china doll figure in the chic carriage. She was dressed in a gown and bonnet of heavenly blue.

"How do you do, friends!" Isaac greeted them. "Are you bound for Salt Lake City, too?"

"Yes sir, and by the grace of God . . ." On and on prattled the chubby Fairbanks, but Eldridge wasn't listening. He was looking at the blonde blue-eyed girl on the carriage seat.

She was returning his look with equal interest. She saw his wide shoulders, so different from those of her corpulent Charles. And then, quite without warning, she found that her fainting spell was returning. She half rose, then slumped slowly and gracefully over the side of the carriage into Eldridge's open arms. He looked down at her for one startled, unbelieving moment before he turned to shout.

"Grace! Sophie! Gale! Somebody . . . hurry! She's dying!"

Gale was the first one there, but already Fanny Ivory was brushing them aside with her capable black hands.

"She's not dyin', sir," she was saying. "I've seen these spells of hers before. She'll come around right

281

off if you stretch her out somewhere, and stop makin' a fuss over her. It's when folks pay her a lot of attention that she gets worse. She likes the fussin'."

Sister Fairbanks moaned feebly, and opened her eyes sufficiently to cast a fierce glance at Fanny.

"Fanny, leave me alone," she murmured weakly, but with proper sharpness. "Let them take care of me."

Gale, staring down at the pretty doll-like face, tried to think where she had seen it last. Then it flashed back with distressing vividness. She was in the library of Lockwood Seminary, with the Headmistress, Miss Hester Adams, questioning two frightened girls. And Julia Ann Roundy was saying with great innocence, "Why, yes, Miss Adams. Yes, of course, *I* went to church! No, I did not attend the missionary meeting in the schoolhouse. I don't even know what you're talking about."

Here was Julia Ann Roundy. A bit older, and a bit more extravagantly dressed, but most certainly Julia Ann. As Gale stared at the sham invalid, a wave of the old distrust swept over her. She had never liked Julia Ann, and after her duplicity following Edouard's missionary meeting which they had both attended, an action for which Gale had been expelled in disgrace, her liking for the other had not improved.

At that moment, Julia Ann raised her eyes to Gale's face and met the look of cold recognition. She fluttered her eyes a moment and then struggled to her feet.

"Why . . . you're Gale Smith, aren't you? How sweet, finding you out here in this ghastly wilderness! How perfectly sweet!" Then she turned to Eldridge. "Pardon me, sir, for appearing to be such

282

a tender soul . . . but it was that river, that dreadful river we just went through! It had me so horribly frightened . . . I still feel a little faint."

She rested her hand on his arm while she turned to Gale, "Imagine finding Gale Smith away out here, at the end of the world! My *dear*, tell me, what in the world are you doing out here, of all places? Are you married?"

She felt Eldridge's eyes upon her, but she answered firmly, "Yes, I married Edouard Simon. Remember, you heard him speak in the schoolhouse at Lockwood."

Julia Ann's eyes widened.

"Oh, that handsome young missionary? That day was when I first made up my mind to join the Latter-day Saints. But how in the world . . . ? Oh, I remember now! You ran away with him, didn't you? You heartbreaker!"

"No, I met him again quite by accident in Boston," Gale answered evenly.

"Oh, my dear, I'm so glad for you. And I'm really dying to meet him again! Although I'm sure he'll never remember little old me. I'm so plain, people scarcely ever notice me." She adjusted the bonnet strings under her chin, and looked slyly at Isaac.

Gale took a deep breath. Julia Ann would have to know sooner or later. Better tell her now, than to wait until someone else told her. She would rather have waited until they were alone, or at least until the crowd about them had ceased listening to their conversation with hushed interest. The circle of Saints had increased until they were the center of a large, news-hungry group who flocked to greet this band of strangers. Gale glanced about her with a feeling of desperation. Eldridge was watching her with keen interest.

"Well, where *is* your Edouard? You don't mind my calling him Edouard, do you?" Julia Ann babbled like a mountain stream. She too looked around, searching for the handsome young missionary who they had both risked severe punishment to hear. Charles Fairbanks sat in the carriage in perspiring silence, and watched the tall bright-haired girl with whom his wife was talking.

Trapped, Gale searched for an answer. "He went to California to fight in the war with the Mexicans," she said, straightening her shoulders. "He didn't come back."

The other's face melted in syrupy sympathy. "Oh, you poor darling . . . a widow! I'm so sorry . . . if I had known, I wouldn't have . . ." Her eyes slid down to Gale's gay blue-flowered dress. Widows wore black. Her brows went up.

Gale read the look. She laughed, a light ringing laugh. "Widow's weeds are so unbecoming, don't you think?"

Julia Ann's face showed chagrin, and her full red lips fell open in amazement. Then she turned sharply to her husband.

"Charles, let us be on our way! What are you sitting there for?" And before Eldridge could help her, she had hopped numbly into the carriage. In some vague way she felt that Gale had scored against her before all these strangers, and her anger glowed in the pinkness of her cheeks. She switched her voluminous skirts about her feet irritably.

"Charles, drive on!"

Charles Fairbanks wrenched his gaze from the tall smiling girl who stood by the carriage. "Yes, dear . . . I mean, I'm sorry, but I can't. You see, this is the company we're going on to Salt Lake with. We have to wait until they're ready to leave."

He took out a white handkerchief and mopped the sweat from his shining head. For another short moment, he let his eyes wander back to the woman named Gale. Funny, her being a friend of Julia Ann's.

Thirty-Five

Closer to the valley toiled the train, following the twisted road laid out by the pioneers, along narrow rocky ledges, down through deep black canyons where the road was a constant crisscrossing of roaring streams, up over mountains so steep that often the teams had to be doubled in order to get the wagons across.

One afternoon as the company was nearing the mouth of Echo Canyon, Charles Fairbanks' fears were realized. As his carriage crossed the rocky creek bed for the tenth time that day, the left front wheel was wrenched against a boulder and the flimsy spokes crumpled to splinters.

For the past three miles, Julia Ann had been clinging desperately to the seat with her eyes shut tight. But in spite of her grip, the stop was so abrupt that the violence threw her clear of the carriage. She landed some two yards away in the swift icy water. She emitted one frightened yelp, and then began struggling with the multitude of petticoats which engulfed her from head to foot.

Fortunately the water was not deep at that particular spot, but it was more blind blundering than concentrated effort that brought her to the bank, where she sprawled ungracefully on dry ground. As soon as she could claw her bedraggled bonnet and hair from her eyes, she looked to see if she had an audience worth fainting for. Because the wagons were traveling some distance apart, no one but her own husband and her servants had viewed the spectacle, so she decided that hysterics were more in order. In that way she could vent her anger on Charles, and still retain her role as a pitiful female.

She was getting her show into full-swing when the Simons' wagon arrived at the crossing. Bub hopped up on the front of the wagon to urge the patient animals across the river, past the stranded carriage, and on up the opposite bank. He would have driven on had not Gale leaned forward and tapped him on the shoulder.

"Stop, Bub."

"What for, ma'am? She ain't got no use for you. What do you want to go fixin' to be nice to her for?"

"Never mind. Stop. She's half-drowned."

Charles Fairbanks was patting his wife's soggy back gingerly, trying in vain to stem the flow of hysterical screams, wild weeping, and angry words. He turned distressed eyes to Gale.

"Sister Simon, we've just had a most unhappy accident." He came close to the wagon. "Most unhappy, although I've been expecting it since we left the Missouri. Could I prevail upon your kindness in asking you to take Julia Ann with you for the rest of the journey? She's . . . she's frightfully upset. She might not act too grateful right now, but . . ." He took his handkerchief from his pocket and mopped his glistening brow. "You will take her . . . won't you?"

"Of course," Gale said laughingly. "We'll get her in here right away. Are her dry clothes in the carriage?"

"No. No, I regret to say that they have gone ahead with our baggage wagon. Could you spare . . . I mean . . . do you have perhaps . . ." He floundered, and pulled out the handkerchief which he had just put back in his pocket.

"Don't worry, Brother Fairbanks," Gale said, laughing again. "I'll have her in dry clothes in no time."

He let out a whistling sigh of relief.

"Oh, thank you!" He lowered his voice, so that the wailing girl on the creek bank could not hear. "Sometimes I . . . I wish Julia Ann were a little more like you . . . calm and . . . well, you know. Don't misunderstand me. Julia Ann is an estimable girl . . . I was not criticizing her, but . . ."

"Yes, I understand," Gale interrupted. "Bub will help you get her into the wagon. She must be freezing."

And so Julia Ann finished the remainder of the journey as a most ungracious and unwilling guest in the Simons' wagon.

A week later the company arrived in the valley of the Great Salt Lake. They looked around at the vast sea of dry desolation, with the handful of cabins and adobe huts huddled in a desert where the only vegetation seemed to be sagebrush and cactus. So this was the "land of milk and honey" where they were to spend the rest of their lives! Down here in the valley, the afternoon sun was hot on their backs in spite of October, and their eyes were still red and smarting from the dust that had been swirling about their wagon wheels. So this was home!

The drawing of lots took place immediately, and the Saints drove their wagons eagerly to their allotted land. Their own land! Each family looked over

289

the possibilities of their acreage, and began planning how their houses and gardens would be laid out.

Gale walked into the dark little fort where the drawing was taking place. There were few people in the room, and she took no notice of them, going straight to the desk where a stoop-shouldered man sat, writing in a ledger. He looked up, but said nothing.

"I'm Sister Simon. I want to draw a number for my lot."

Gloomily he went back to his writing. "Women don't draw for lots," he said. "Where's your husband?"

"He's still in California. May I draw now, please?"

He moved the ledger about on the desk, attempting to find a more becoming spot for it. "Well, they didn't tell me nothin' about givin' out numbers to womenfolk. I don't think it'd be legal."

She glanced around for advice. Eldridge and the Fairbankses were there. Eldridge spoke, "Gale, you don't want land. What would a girl like you do with a farm?"

She looked at him with cool eyes. "What will I do without one?"

"Don't be foolish, girl! You'll remarry again. Forget this idea about getting land. You'll be better off without it."

"I'm not marrying again, Isaac, as long as I have a husband," she said crisply.

"A husband!" He snorted. "So you're still parading under that banner, eh?"

She turned back to the man behind the desk. "I'll take my number now, if you don't mind." It was more a command than a request.

With uneasiness in his face, but alacrity in his

movements, he pushed a tattered hat toward her, containing folded slips of paper. She took one and looked at it.

"Remember, ma'am, I said I didn't think it was legal. If the elders decide I'm right, you'll have to turn the land back, you know."

"Number one thirty-nine. Where do I find my land?"

He looked in his book and coughed a little before he spoke.

"You'll find it down in the south end of town. Straight down this street here in front of the fort and then two blocks over west. Olaf Pederson's lot is next to yours. Know him?"

"Yes. Thank you. I think I can find it without any trouble."

She walked from the dark room into the afternoon sun with her head up. Outside, Julia Ann ran from the fort and caught her arm.

"Oh, Gale darling, I want to thank you for bringing me with you after that horrible accident! I don't want you to think ill of me for not being grateful. But you know how I abhor riding in a filthy jolting wagon like a common country woman, and especially behind those smelly oxen. Forgive me?"

Gale moved away so that the other's hand slipped from her arm. She did not like the feel of that warm silken little hand. "There's nothing to forgive. I brought you here because you were in trouble and needed help. I'd have done the same for anyone."

"All the same, I'm so grateful to you, honey." Then she dropped her voice. "I know you'll pardon my curiosity, Gale dear . . . It really couldn't be called curiosity, could it, since I've known you for so long? It's really only an interest in a friend's welfare. But what did you mean in there when you said . . .

291

that you'd not get married . . . as long as you have a husband. You told me that you were a widow."

A chill hardened Gale's eyes. There was hardness, too, around the mouth that kept smiling. "I'm afraid I've told you all I know."

"But . . . you told me that first day that he had died in the war!"

"No. I'm sorry you misunderstood. I merely said that he did not come back from the war."

"But . . . about the widow's weeds . . . you said . . ."

"Only that they are unbecoming. And aren't they?"

"Gale Simon, you deceitful creature!" Her face reddened with anger. "It's true then . . . what they're saying! I refused to believe them at first. That handsome missionary . . . he was so noble!"

Eldridge came out of the fort with a slip of paper in his fingers, but Julia Ann was too intent upon her hysterical reproaches to notice.

"I have refused to believe that he would run off with a barmaid!" she continued. "He seemed so wonderful that day at Lockwood. But it must be true. I've thought you were behaving mighty strange for a widow whose husband was killed!" Her voice had risen to an accusing shriek.

Fairbanks came out the door with his lottery number, but she ignored him, her voice rising in pitch and volume.

"Gale Simon, you're just trying to capture another husband!"

"Now, Julia Ann . . ." Fairbanks put a restraining hand on her arm.

"You're after one of ours!" she shrieked. "So that's why you took me into your wagon . . . so you could work on poor Charles' sympathy!"

"Now, now, now . . . Julia . . ." he was distressed.

"You want to be his second wife!"

Suddenly Gale remembered Julia Ann's hysterics at Lockwood. She smiled, thinking how little she had changed.

"Please . . . darling girl . . ." Brother Fairbanks implored.

"But I've been watching you!" she continued, accusingly.

Eldridge was watching the scene, and several others joined the group.

"I've watched you laughing and looking pretty and showing off for all the men! I know all your tricks!" She seemed to have run out of breath, for she stopped.

"You have an audience now," Gale's smile did not reach her eyes. "Is that what you wanted?"

Gale turned and left the group. Bub was still waiting for her at the wagon. Julia Ann's blue eyes narrowed to slits, Eldridge noticed. For a moment he saw malevolence working in the new girl's pretty face. Then she cast him a dazzling smile.

Thirty-Six

Gale settled herself for the winter in her wagon on her own lot. It was so late in the season that all the men were working frantically to complete their cabins before winter set in, and so she had no hope of obtaining help to build a home for herself before spring, at the earliest. Even Bub Leary, on whom she always depended, was elated over owning his own land and was busily engaged in building himself an adobe hut.

She set to work to make her wagon as weatherproof as possible. She borrowed a heavy canvas from Ad Jenkins and stretched it over the wagon top to make it more waterproof and windproof. She blocked off the rear opening and piled all her furniture and baggage in front of it, leaving the front portion free as a living room. The floors and walls she lined with deer skins, bear skin, and a buffalo hide for which she had traded at the fort when friendly Indians came in. After she had hung another skin over the opening for a door, she felt she was prepared to survive the winter. The greatest drawback was the fact that she would have to do her cooking outside over an open camp fire. She wondered how much snow fell in this mountain valley. But anything, she decided, would be preferable to the lot of Sister Nickols-Muldoon.

The Muldoons lived not far away, and so the Nickols girls were frequent visitors at Gale's "home." They were as charmed by it as though it were a dollhouse, and declared that they preferred it to a real house like everyone else had.

One day as Gale stood over her fire, stirring a batch of soap, Isaac Eldridge rode up, looking especially debonair and cheerful. He pulled his black mare to a halt and sat looking down at Gale with amusement. She nodded at him coolly and went on with her work, peering into the pot to see if the soap was ready. This was the first time she had seen him since the day at the fort.

"Tell me," he inquired, "do you have any Indian blood in your veins?"

A year ago she would have flushed and asked uneasily, "No, why?" Today she looked at him with steady eyes and asked, "What concern is it of yours?"

He laughed, and a little of the mockery left his face. "I like you, Gale. I like the way you're taking this thing with your chin up. I like your spirit. Moreover . . . I love you. Just because you're so damned easy to look at, I guess. Will you marry me?" He said it lightly, but there was a deeper undertone in his voice.

"No thank you, Isaac." Her reply was matter-of-fact. "Fortunately plural marriage is not yet the accepted custom for females, even among the Saints. And I'm still married, you know."

"Oh, that?" He laughed again, and the tender intensity was gone. "Never mind about that now. As I was saying, are you doing this camping out because it's in your blood? I would have thought you'd had enough the last two years. The rest of us are looking forward to living in real houses this winter."

296

"Yes, so I've heard. But I'm not much of a carpenter. So I've fixed up my wagon for winter quarters. It's quite comfortable, really."

"Gale! You're not planning to live in that thing all winter!"

"And why not? It's the only home I have." She stirred the soap with concentration.

"Have you heard? We're building a schoolhouse, every man of us putting in a day's labor. We'll have it finished next week, ready for the children to start school. We had a meeting of the elders last night and voted to hire you."

His quiet words burst like a bomb over her camp fire. She looked up in amazement.

"Hire . . . me?"

"Yes . . . to teach."

"But . . . I don't know how to teach!"

"You're the only one in the settlement who is qualified for the job. What shall I tell them?"

"But, Isaac . . . I wouldn't know how to start. There must be someone else."

"We understand that you've attended a young ladies' seminary, or something of the sort. True? Well then, you surely learned something more than the rest of us ignorant heathens."

She met the look of amused mockery in his eyes. "Tell them I'll take the job."

She stooped and lifted the kettle from the fire and carefully began to pour the contents into the wooden frame she had waiting for the soap.

Eldridge chuckled.

"Very well, queen of the soap pot! Be on hand to ring the bell for school a week from Monday morning."

Gale completed her first day's teaching with a

297

strange kind of excited contentment. She loved teaching! Before school was dismissed, little Sybil Nickols raised her hand. Gale nodded, and the child came to the front of the room to whisper with modest eagerness.

"Please, ma'am, who are you going to stay with this week?"

Puzzled, Gale looked down into the grave little face. "Why . . . I'm at my own wagon. Isn't Susannah coming? She always does."

"Oh, no! Didn't you know? When you're a teacher, you're supposed to take turns living around at everyone's house. Please, will you stay with us this week? Mother said I might ask you."

Gale looked out over the room full of faces, bewildered. She met the grinning gaze of Louisa Nickols. She was nodding eagerly. Sybil stood waiting, her eyes hopeful, her lips parted over the space where her teeth had been not long ago. Gale smiled.

"All right, dear. Tell your mother I'll be over tonight. But I don't know about the rest of the week. I must see first what I'm supposed to do."

Sybil skipped with delight back to the long bench which she shared with the other smaller children. Gale gazed at the room of heads, big heads and little, towheads and dark. She knew that the Saints had large families, but she hadn't realized how many there were until she saw all the children of the valley crowded into this one room. It was crowded to capacity, with the girls sitting on benches, and the boys squatting on their heels or leaning against the walls. She must ask the elders to provide more benches immediately.

"Let's everyone stand now, please."

There was a great rustling and shuffling as the children rose to attention, and the air was suddenly

298

hazy with the dust stirred up on the earthern floor. Several coughed, and one or two sneezed. When the noise quieted, Gale bowed her head and offered a brief prayer for the closing of the day's session. When it was over she looked up and met several dozen pairs of friendly eyes. A warmth surged up in her. She smiled back at them.

And then they were gone, and the room was empty, except for the rows of benches, and the thin cloud of dust which hung in the air. Before she had her books straightened on her desk and the coals in the fireplace banked for the night, she heard a step at the door and looked up to see Isaac Eldridge. He had to stoop a little as he came in the low door. He doffed his hat gaily.

"Greetings, fair lady! How did your education hold out today? Did they humiliate you, or were you able to conceal your ignorance? Come on, Gale, tell your old uncle everything. I'm waiting to know the worst." He sat down on a front bench.

Gale said, laughing, "So far, I hope, they haven't discovered my inadequacies. I like it, though. Children are great. You don't have to pretend with them. And they wouldn't believe you if you did."

"Fine! They're probably madly in love with you. A passion that I share with the poor little devils."

She gathered her books together and banged them on the desk. Why couldn't she and Isaac just be friends? Why must she always keep up her guard?

"We need more benches immediately," her words were curt. "Enough for twenty-three children."

"Twenty-three?" He raised one dark brow. "Alright, redhead. Anything your little heart desires. Hurry now and get your coat on. I'm taking you home with me. You'll not be spending the winter in that breezy wagon."

"No?" She sat down again and began rearranging her books. "Why am I honored by this overwhelming invitation?"

"Oh, didn't I tell you the other day?" A slow grin crossed his face, and Gale knew that this had been his plan from the first. The teaching position, her being boarded out, all so that he could take her home with him. "You're staying with us this week. You know, the teacher is to take turns boarding with different families in the community. And you're scheduled for the Eldridges' this week. Come, get your things on. Grace will be waiting supper."

She went to the fireplace and covered the coals with ashes. Then she took her coat from a peg and turned to face him.

"You're *very* thoughtful, Isaac. In fact, you seem to have thought of everything, haven't you? But I promised to stay with Sister Nickols and her girls . . . Muldoon, I should say. I must be going now. Tell Grace I'm sorry about the supper."

He grinned, a humorous quirky grin. "Oh, is Pat Muldoon so much better looking than I?"

"Oh, by all means!'" She laughed, her bright brittle laugh.

Before she quite realized it, he caught her in his strong arms, pulling her against him in a fierce embrace. One hand held the back of her head, tipping it back until his lips found hers. She struggled for a furious moment, and then without warning, the anger went out of her. In its place was a warm sense of peace. Against her closed lids was printed the image of Edouard, his dark head bent over hers, his arms tight around her. Edouard was back, and with him a beautiful, singing happiness. Involuntarily her lips responded to the caress with a hunger that she had almost forgotten. Then she felt Edouard's hands on her throat, hot, soft.

Slowly their lips parted, and she was staring up at Isaac Eldridge. Fiercely she pulled away, but her eyes still shone with the warmth of her passion.

"No . . . no . . . I want Edouard!" She spoke as one in a trance.

He reached out tenderly and touched the brightness of her hair.

"My God . . . you're beautiful!" he whispered. He continued with smothered violence. "Gale, darling . . . marry me, tonight! I can get Brother Pratt, or one of the others to perform the ceremony! Come my darling, there is no sense in waiting."

"No, Isaac! No!" Her face went white after the radiant flush that had suffused it. She backed away. "You won't understand, but . . . it wasn't you I kissed just then. It was Edouard! It sounds crazy . . . I don't know what happened to me, but . . . but I thought you were Edouard."

"Edouard!" he almost shouted. "Edouard didn't have a thing to do with it! It was *me* you kissed, and you know it! You let that prudish armor of yours slip for a moment . . . and you loved it!"

"No . . . oh, no . . ." She covered her face with her hands.

"Forget him, Gale, forget him! It's common talk that he's left you for a barmaid who isn't worth a hair on your head. What are you waiting for? Come, darling, give me a chance to show you what real love is. That kiss . . . Lord, what a woman!" He pulled her hands away from her face and took her in his arms again.

"Oh, no . . . no, Isaac!" She looked at him as though she were a wild animal caught in a trap.

301

"Please forgive me. I shouldn't have kissed you. But
. . . it was Edouard. That's all I can tell you."

"For God's sake . . . if you mention that stuffed
shirt again, I'll choke you! Now tell me the truth.
You *liked* that kiss, didn't you?" His eyes bored into
hers.

"No . . . no . . ."

"You're lying! You loved it!"

"Yes . . ." very faintly. "Oh, Isaac, it wasn't you!
Believe me, it was . . ."

"Not again!" he warned sharply.

"I . . . I must go now . . . please." She pulled
away and walked around her desk. "And forgive
me. Can you forget it?"

"Forget that magnificent moment? What are you
asking, Gale? I'll remember that kiss until I die . . .
and so will you!"

She put on her coat which had slipped to the
floor, and turned to the door. Her shoulders
drooped.

"I'm sorry . . . I almost wish I didn't love
Edouard so much."

She walked out the door alone and turned toward
the Muldoons, her head down. Once she glanced up,
more than half-expecting to see Edouard at her side.
He had been back, for that one bright moment.

Thirty-Seven

The following week was a nightmare for Gale. She went about, haunted by the memory of Isaac Eldridge's lips warm on hers, and hating herself for it. She should be hating Isaac, she told herself, but she couldn't, not with her own shame. Again and again she relived that moment, in an attempt to destroy the memory. He had been so like Edouard! The way his lips found hers, irresistibly, the way his hand cupped the back of her head, and the passionate strength of his strong hard body. It had been only because he was like Edouard . . . She would brush her hand across her eyes, trying to brush away the memory.

Gale found Sister Nickols infinitely older, with lines deep around her mouth. In spite of her own misery, she found deep pity for the second Sister Muldoon. Living in the same house with Mary Muldoon was not easy under the best of situations, but this was impossible.

Gale shared a bed on the floor with Susannah and Louisa. She tossed and turned on her hard bed, praying that sleep would come soon to blot out the memories. But the longer she lay there, the more wakeful she became. In addition to her mental discomfort, she was tormented by the creeping of bedbugs over her body. The cabin was infested with

303

these horrid little varmints which had come back with the Muldoons from Pueblo, in spite of the scrupulous war which Mary Muldoon waged.

For a time, Susannah too had been restless, but now she and Louisa were breathing with soft regularity. Nearby, Sister Nickols and her little girls slept quietly. From the other room came Pat's heavy breathing, the sound of his great bulk turning over in bed, and the dry rasping of his wife clearing her throat. But now even these sounds were silenced, and there were only the coyotes and the quiet breathing of many sleepers.

Unable to remain long on the hard pallet, she slipped out from the covers and went to the water bucket which sat on a bench beneath the window. After a long drink, unpleasant with the taste of alkali and her own dissatisfaction, she stood for a while, looking out at the brightness of the moonlight. At regular intervals over the desert, she could see the squat shadows of log cabins and adobe huts, the dark framework of empty wagons, and the ghostly shadows of tumbleweeds rolling before the night wind.

If Edouard had only come back! It would all be so different, the loneliness, the wide empty valley, even the Saints. With Edouard's reassuring arms around her . . .

She was startled by a movement behind her and turned quickly to find Pat at her shoulder, appallingly huge in a nightshirt. She was frightened by the silence with which he had gotten his great bulk out of bed and through the house to her side. He was grinning, with her coat in his hand. Evidently he had taken it from the peg as he passed. He motioned with a great thumb toward the door, and held her coat out to her.

"Come on outside, and let's talk," he hissed in her ear.

She shrank back in alarm, but his heavy hand was on her shoulder, and she could feel the heat of it through the thin muslin of her gown. Wrenching herself free, she slid past him and fled into the sanctuary of her bed with Susannah and Louisa.

Muldoon followed and stood looking down at her, an evil grin on his face. A long time he stood there, looking down upon her. She shut her eyes and crowded close to Susannah, but she could still feel him standing over her, watching. Panic assailed her, a wild, unreasoning fear which sent her heart drumming in her ears and strangled the breath in her throat. Common sense told that that a single cry from her would arouse the whole household. But it was no use. Pat Muldoon stood over her, panting.

Then came Mary Muldoon's voice, sharp, from the other room.

"Pat! *Pat!*" she called. "What in the devil are ye doin' out there, traipsin' around in yer shirttail? Come back to bed where ye belong!"

He went, and she could hear him settling into his bed beside Mary. It was almost three o'clock, and a rooster crowed at the far end of the town before the girl's tense body relaxed, and she drifted off into a troubled sleep.

The next morning at breakfast, she could feel his eyes on her pale face, and she knew he was grinning even though she didn't raise her eyes. The next day and the next he held his peace. On Friday morning he overtook her as she walked to school with the four Nickols girls. They heard him coming and clung close to her.

"Here comes Mr. Muldoon," Louisa looked over her shoulder. "What does he want?"

Pat caught up with them. "Run along, you kids," he said. "I gotta talk to your teacher."

Gale held tighter to the two little hands that were in her own. "We're going to school together. Anything you have to say, you can say in front of the girls."

Pat's face darkened. "I got business I got to talk to ye about. Now you kids, get outa here, before I lambaste a couple of ye!"

The two hands pulled away from Gale and the girls raced up the road. Muldoon laughed mirthlessly.

"Nice kids, them. They'll grow up into some likely lookin' wenches some day. An' I still won't be so old but what I can take on a few more handsome wives."

Gale shivered and walked as fast as she could, far to her side of the road. She knew that terror of physical attack was groundless, but she was grateful that it was daylight and that the street was lined with houses.

"Talk about stand-offish!" He gave her a sideways look as he wheezed, trying to keep up with her. "Where in the devil is the fire?"

"I have to go to school. I haven't time to talk."

"Say, about the other night . . ." His voice lost its surliness, and he went on amiably, "I want ye to know I didn't mean nothin'. I heard ye prowlin' around and knew ye couldn't sleep, so I jest thought we might go outside and talk a while. I didn't mean nothin' wrong. I knew we couldn't talk in there where we'd wake ever'body up."

She hurried on. Pat waited for her answer, breathing hard with her fast pace. When it became evident there would be none, he broke out in anger.

"Well, what did ye think I was goin' to do, ruin yer purity? If you women ain't all alike! Run yer legs clean off fer fear a man is goin' to touch ye! If ye want to know the truth, I was goin' to ask ye to marry me!"

Gale moved mechanically in her flight down the road. Thank heaven she would be staying at the Tavenners' next week!

"Well, what's yer answer?" he puffed her heels.

They had almost reached the schoolhouse now, and the yard was ringing with the shouts of children at play. She stopped and turned to face him, her eyes meeting his with contempt. With the children so near, she need not be afraid.

"I am sure, Brother Muldoon, that you know my answer."

"What do ye mean . . . no?"

His neck bulged over the top of his shirt collar, and his face turned a deeper shade of red. But with the children singing "London Bridge" close by, she could stand straight and eye him steadily.

"I mean no!"

He stared at her with bloodshot eyes. Then he spoke slowly.

"Ye stiff-necked little bitch! Think yer too good fer a common man, huh? More 'n likely settin' yer cap for a Church leader. Might even be layin' for Brigham Young to come back in the spring." He laughed in a way that sent the blood into her cheeks. "Don't worry, sister. There's ways of makin' a girl come down off her high horse." He stepped a little closer and lowered his voice. "Ye know, school-marms ain't very popular with folks when they get a bad reputation. And . . . it ain't very hard to get a bad name started, if a feller sets his mind to it."

His eyes lingered a moment on her lips. Then he turned and swaggered off across the sagebrush flats. It was some time before she could control the trembling of her body. She mustn't let the children see her like this.

Late one afternoon before Christmas, Gale heard a man's step outside the schoolhouse door. She caught her breath with dread and shrank in her chair behind the desk, for during the winter she had come to dread men, all men. She knew now why Edouard had said that he was marrying Cassie for her own protection, that an unmarried girl would have no place. He must have known, even then . . .

The children had gone home, and she was quite alone, with the fire burned low on the hearth. The door opened, and Olaf Pederson came in slowly. He stood just inside the door a long moment before he spoke. Gale's dread departed with infinite relief, and she smiled. She liked Olaf.

"I shouldn't be coming here like this," he said shyly. "But it's the only place I can talk with you."

"Sit down . . . over there by the fire. It must be cold outside."

He sat, uneasily. "It's pretty cold, all right."

Gale stacked the children's slates on a corner of her desk and waited.

"I guess I don't rightly know just how to begin . . ." He moved his big feet about, and a thin cloud of dust arose in the firelight. "It's about the children . . ."

"Oh? You mean their school work?"

"No, no. Not that at all. They're doing fine. It's . . . well, with Christmas coming on and all . . . Well, it's mighty hard on the little tykes without their mother. I'm afraid there's not going to be much Christmas for them this year. She always made a lot of Christmas . . . even when we didn't have much."

308

The picture came back to her of Sister Pederson in the dugout in Winter Quarters, touching each little hand and telling her children good-bye. Quick tears came to her eyes.

"Oh, Olaf . . . it will be hard! I'm sorry . . . I should have thought. I could have been making something for each of them. I haven't been thinking very well this winter . . . Please forgive me. I can still do something for them . . . if I hurry."

"It's very kind of you, ma'am." He flushed. "It's because you're so kind, I guess, that I'm coming to you like this. But . . . I don't think you understand. What I meant to say was . . . the children haven't got a mother . . . and you are all alone . . . I was wondering . . . would you want to try to be a mother to them?"

It was Gale's turn to flush. "Olaf . . . I'm sorry!" Poor Olaf! Life had not been good to him. She was remembering the night two years ago in Nauvoo when Hulda had died. Gale sighed and tried to rub some charcoal from the tips of her fingers. "Didn't you know . . . I'm still married?"

"Well, I know folks say . . . Brother Simon . . ."

She answered him gently. "He's still alive, Olaf. Or at least none of the battalion who returned know any differently."

"I know . . . but folks say . . ."

"Yes, folks say lots of things. But . . . he's still my husband."

"To tell you the truth," he cleared his throat uneasily and ran his fingers through his thick yellow hair, "it isn't just about the children I was thinking. It's about . . . you."

"About . . . me?"

"Yes. I've heard the things . . . the lies folks have been telling about you. It makes me mad the way folks turn against a person just because some-body starts some dirty stories going. I know how hard it's been for you lately . . . with everyone act-ing like they have. You can't go on fighting against this forever . . . so I just thought I'd let you know how I feel about it. You can marry me and tell them all to go and eat grass, if you want to."

Gale laughed. Then she stopped short, her eyes stinging with sudden tears. It had been so long since anyone had offered her any unselfish sympathy.

"Thanks, Olaf. I'll remember it. But . . . I just can't marry anyone, that's all."

Thirty-Eight

Despite Gale's elusiveness, Eldridge managed to see her often during that long dreadful winter, at the schoolhouse, on the way home at night, or as she walked to school in the mornings. And always she met him with fresh shame burning in her face, and the memory of that night last fall warm on her lips. He had been so like Edouard ...

But not again did he offer to kiss her. Sometimes she almost wished he would, so that she could strike out at him physically and thus erase some of their guilt. He was a strangely different Isaac, often quiet and morose, with none of the old gay cynicism which had been so much a part of him. Always when they were together she could feel his eyes on her, hungrily, like the eyes of a child on a coveted toy, but when she would look at him he would suddenly stare at the toe of his boot, or out across the valley floor toward the jagged range of mountains.

Often he made an effort at the old stinging banter ... but it was a futile effort. It had lost its sting, and Gale began to realize with shame that his superficial attraction had grown into something deeper. It is my fault, she told herself. My fault because for one moment I gave him a part of myself, and I can never take it back.

Only once that winter did he again speak of marriage, although she felt the consciousness of it in everything he said. They were walking home from school through the early winter dusk, and the sky was icy green porcelain over the alabaster of the mountains. They walked in silence.

"Well, Gale," he said at last, "have you changed your mind about liking this widow role of yours? It isn't exactly becoming to you, you know."

It was harder than usual for her to keep her voice light and careless.

"I never said I liked it. We can't like all the parts we have to play."

She caught a note of eagerness in his voice. "You mean . . . you've changed your mind about waiting?"

"No, Isaac. I haven't changed my mind." She sighed, and then hoped he had not heard. "And I never will. I'll wait for him . . . as long as there is any possibility of his coming back. Whatever he's done, Isaac, I can't help loving him."

His voice was again in control, but she could see the hard lines around his mouth. "Leaving you for that Voak woman! He doesn't deserve you, even if he does return!"

"Don't say that. I'm sure he thinks he is doing right, or he wouldn't be doing it."

"You really think he's coming back?"

"Oh, Isaac, I don't know what to think! Everything is so confused . . . and horrible! The only thing I know for sure is . . . I can't marry you, or anyone, ever!" She was weeping, and she did not try to conceal it.

"That fool! He was always so noble!"

"Don't ask me any more, please. I've been driven mad this winter, telling . . . telling people I can't marry them. Oh, why has Edouard made me bear

312

all this!" It was the first time she had said it aloud. Instantly she regretted it.

"Miss Voak was probably lonesome!" His voice was harsh. "And California is a long way off."

"Please . . . don't say that. I'm sorry if I hurt you that evening in the schoolhouse. But don't let that one time keep you hoping. I told you then, and I tell you now . . . I didn't intend that love for you."

"Alright! Alright!" he almost shouted. "Love your noble hypocrite!"

"Please, Isaac . . . Someone will hear you!"

"Go on putting up a silly show for the rest of your life . . . making yourself the common talk of the valley. This is a community where women don't go their way alone and get away with it. But if that's the way you want it . . . go ahead! Make a miserable fool of yourself if you want to! Go ahead!"

He turned back and let her walk on alone.

After that evening he didn't bring up the subject of marriage again. He managed to see her often, but he was always quietly impersonal.

The last week of March was her turn to stay with the Fairbankses, a week which was not anticipated with pleasure by either the hostess or the guest. It started off well enough, with both women assuming an attitude of bright friendliness. The role suited Julia Ann as well as any of the numerous roles which she assumed at will, and during this winter, Gale's brittle shell of gaiety had become a part of her. It was her only defense against the attacks of both men and women, and she wore it constantly except at school, where she could be herself.

One evening Gale sat in the charming living room of the Fairbankses' home, watching the fire on the wide hearth. The house was quiet, for the blacks had finished the evening's work, and Jules had retired to the little cabin behind the house with Fanny and his new wife, Oleander. The only sound in the room was the soft clicking of Gale's knitting needles, the snapping of the flames, and the occasional rattle of Charles Fairbanks' year-old newspaper, which he was apparently perusing with intense interest. Gale was too preoccupied with her own vagrant thoughts to notice that more than once his solemn round eyes crept over the edge of his paper to dwell on the clear strong lines of her face, the high bones of her cheeks, her straight brows, her lips, now softened in this moment of repose.

Julia Ann sat directly before the fire in her wing-backed chair, her white hands busy over a piece of petitpoint. The chair had come from Philadelphia in the baggage wagon, as a complement to her own beauty, for she knew that nothing quite set off her china doll prettiness as did that flaring chair. In fact everything in the room was designed as a background for herself, and she had done well in her choices. Gale had to admit, in spite of her personal dislike for Julia Ann, that the girl was a genius at creating a lovely home in the wilderness. The room was graciousness personified, from the whitewashed adobe walls and heavy blue velvet curtains, to the silver candelabra on the mahogany highboy.

Suddenly Julia Ann sprang to her feet with a soft little cry.

"Oh dear! How tiresome! Here I've forgotten to give Fanny her orders about breakfast, and now I have to traipse clear out to the cabin to talk to her about it! Isn't that silly of me?"

"Why not wait and talk to her in the morning?" Charles offered absently.

314

"Gracious no! You know I don't like to be disturbed early, and we mustn't have Gale late for school. No, I suppose I must get my wraps on and go out there tonight. Oh, dear, and it's so terribly disagreeable! It was snowing before dinner was served, and I'm sure it isn't any better now. Well, it won't be any easier, waiting. Will you excuse me, Gale dear?"

"Of course."

Charles put down his paper and got to his feet unwillingly. "Tell me what to tell her, and I'll go for you."

"No, no, no! I'd rather be frozen to the bone than to send you on such an errand. You wouldn't remember what I said by the time you got to the back door. No, I'll go myself. Perhaps it will teach me not to be so forgetful next time. If I don't come back right away, it will be because I've stopped to get warm at Fanny's fire."

She waved a hand at the two of them and went out through the door to the kitchen, wafting an odor of violets through the room as she left.

Gale sat as she had all evening, gazing into the fire or at her knitting, and thinking her own unhappy thoughts. She had entirely forgotten where she was until she was startled by Charles Fairbanks' voice, breathlessly abrupt, and low.

"Sister Simon . . . I hope you'll pardon my rushing into the subject like this, but I must speak to you before Julia Ann comes back! Sister Simon . . . will you be my wife?"

Gale turned to look at him with dismay. Her mind had been so far away that it was a full minute before she could collect her faculties enough to understand what he had said. She stared at him. He was rosy pink and perspiring, from the dome of his

315

bald head to his double chins. He took out his handkerchief and wiped his face, waiting for her reply, glancing uneasily toward the kitchen door.

"Er . . . if you'll pardon my discourtesy, may I ask you to answer at once?" He cleared his throat and mopped the palms of his hands. "Julia Ann might not understand . . . should she overhear us. And she might be . . . well, even unpleasant. Will you accept my offer?"

Before Gale could reply, there was a high shrill laugh behind them, and they turned to find Julia Ann standing in the kitchen doorway, just as she had left them, wearing no wraps, and with no sign of snow on her garments. Then the laugh was gone.

"That's all I wanted to hear! That's enough! I knew I had only to trick you into thinking you were alone with my husband for five minutes, and you'd have him making a fool of himself!" Her face was distorted with jealousy. "I've known you were nothing but a common harlot for months. Maybe you think I haven't watched you, with all the men in the valley running after you. You strolling by here morning and night with Isaac Eldridge . . . and the others! But tonight, I've proved it to my own satisfaction! And now you can go! Get out!"

Her attack had taken them both so by surprise that they sat staring at her speechless. Charles was the first to find words.

"Get out? But where will she go?"

"I'll not have a strumpet staying in my house another night! Get out, I say!"

"Now, my dear . . . come here and sit down in your chair, and relax a moment." He mopped his face and his neck beneath the collar of his shirt.

"Charles Fairbanks, shut up!" she screamed.

316

"You're in no position to tell me to do anything . . .
let alone relax! She has wound you around her little
finger so that you wouldn't know milk from ink!"

She approached Gale, her nails like claws, her
whole body shaking with the violence of her anger.

"Get out of this house."

Gale got slowly to her feet and went to get her
wraps and the carpetbag which carried her belongings. It would do no good to try to argue.

"But Julia Ann, my love," Charles interposed
with more courage than he was wont to display,
"must you be so severe? It would be difficult, as well
as embarrassing, to seek shelter this time of night. I
assure you, I shall not see or speak to Sister Simon
again this evening. I'll retire immediately."

"You'll assure me nothing, you fat old fool! That
woman is leaving, tonight!" She came so close to
Gale that she could see Julia Ann's pulse pounding
furiously in her white throat. "Leave quickly, before
I say something unworthy of myself! So far I have
been generous with you . . . too generous! But if
you stay a moment longer, with your insulting su-
perior airs . . . I'll . . . I'll lose control of myself
. . . and tell you what I really think of you!"

Gale tried not to listen as she gathered her few
belongings together and put them in her bag. Julia
Ann went on without pause.

"I'm *glad* it's snowing tonight! And I'm glad it's
cold! It's just the kind of night you deserve to be
thrown out into! It couldn't have been better if I had
planned the weather, too! And I hope there isn't a
family in town who will take you in! You'll be humiliated . . . humiliated just as I've been humiliated
in my own home tonight! And tonight won't be
the end of it . . . it's just the beginning! I'll see to

317

it that the entire valley knows what you are . . .
the entire valley, do you hear? Some already know.
Oh, yes, I've heard the gossip about you this winter
. . . but it's nothing compared to what there's going
to be! By summer there'll not be a decent home in
Salt Lake City where you can enter! You'll be
branded for what you are . . . branded . . . and
thrown out!"

She stopped, only because she had run out of
breath. Gale was at the door, with Julia Ann still
following at her heels like a spiteful yapping little
dog. Gale turned, her head high, and faced the
outraged wife.

"Julia Ann, you can ruin my name with lies and
insinuations. That isn't hard to do, because people
often believe what they've been hoping to believe."
She spoke with quiet dignity which made the other's
hysteria seem ridiculous. "But God will continue to
give me the strength to be honorable. You cannot
frighten me."

She went out, closing the door quietly behind her.
It was snowing harder now, and she took a deep
breath of the cold air. Even with the snow against
her face and the snow soft around her feet, it somehow seemed better than the warm scented air of the
Fairbankses' living room.

For a moment after she reached the blackness
that she knew to be the street, she stopped, irreso-
lute. She hadn't thought just where she was going or
what she would do. She stared into the thickness of
the night. She saw but two lights in the whole town,
glimmering faintly yellow in the snow. Where was
she to go to arouse a family to give her shelter at
this time of night? Saints retired early.

She hadn't realized until this moment what it was

318

to be totally alone. Wearily she turned her steps down the snowy road that led to Cliff Sutler's cabin. Perhaps they were still her friends . . . she hadn't seen them for so long.

Thirty-Nine

During the next two weeks Gale lived in the tiny
one-room cabin with the Sutlers. They had taken her
in without a question, Cliff briskly cheerful, and
Deborah properly reserved, as always. She told them
quietly and unemotionally what had happened. Cliff
snorted.

"Fah! That doll-faced vixen! I ain't liked her
from the minute I first set eyes on her . . . the day
she keeled over on Eldridge 'cause she liked his
looks. Don't worry, Gale lass. Folks won't pay no
heed to the tales she has to peddle. Other folks
don't like her no better 'n I do. I've heered more'n
one say they pitied that husband o' hers. She can't
do ye no harm."

Gale had the feeling old Cliff was talking more to
comfort her than from the truth of his own convic-
tions. But it helped to feel that not quite everyone in
the settlement was against her. The next two weeks
passed quietly enough, but she was haunted by the
dreadful premonition that it was not for long . . .
that it was only the calm before the storm. Surely
Julia Ann would not let her jealousy go unappeased.

But she could detect no change in the behavior of
those she saw on her way to and from school. The
women still nodded with the cold recognition that
they had shown her all winter. Some of the men
smirked as she passed and eyed her slender form

with insulting familiarity; others, those whom she had offended by fending off their matrimonial advances, scowled and ignored her presence entirely. Only the children were friendly, with the warm unaffected admiration that children show for someone they love.

Although Gale realized that her presence in the crowded cabin inconvenienced them, she felt at peace sitting beside the Sutlers' smoky little fireplace, with Deborah singing softly to the baby, and old Cliff sprawled on his homemade chair, his one leg stretched toward the blaze. She was at peace because here she could drop her mask of pretense. Cliff's twinkling blue eyes, when he looked her, looked on her as a friend and not a female, eligible for marriage. There was no need to be on guard.

Since the baby had come, Deborah had lost the old fears which had been a part of her for so long. Now she went about her work with a quiet singing confidence, and there was a happiness in her face that made its plainness almost beautiful. Gale, looking at the baby, could understand. The little boy lay in the cradle that Cliff had made him, kicking his chubby legs and laughing as he tried to capture his bouncing toes. Gale bent over him, hoping his parents would not notice the tears on her lashes.

Spring came early in the valley. The farmers had begun plowing in February, and now that April was here, sowing was in full swing. The entire colony was humming with activity; the creeks coming down from the mountains seemed to be imbued with this same feverish activity, which sent them churning between their banks.

Gale tried to tell herself that spring was here. All her senses told her that it was. Her eyes saw the buds bursting green along the creeks; her ears heard the chorus of red-wing blackbirds in the cottonwood trees; her nose caught the richness of fresh-turned earth; and her face felt the gentle warmth of the wind across the valley.

But for the first time in her life, there was no answering lilt in her heart. Spring had come, but there was no joy in it.

One Saturday afternoon she set off up the nearest canyon with a spade and a sack on her arm to get some young cottonwoods and vines to set out around the schoolhouse. Perhaps, she told herself, if she could get away from the Saints a while, away where there were just the sky and the birds and the trees . . . Perhaps she could find a little of the old lilt . . .

She walked and climbed swiftly, far up into the canyon, as though haste alone could take her away from the tormenting thoughts that pursued her. She hurried and stumbled along, forgetting the cottonwoods and vines. She could think only of Edouard . . . and of the past winter.

Then so suddenly that she did not realize what was happening, a rock turned beneath her, and she sprawled on the rough trail, a vast pain exploding in her ankle. She lay where she fell, stunned by the pain. Finally she sat up and began rubbing the throbbing leg.

A long time she sat there, trying to rub the pain away. Was it broken, or was it just sprained? At last she got to her feet and tried her weight on it. Instantly she sank down on the rocks again, moaning, a hard knot of nausea at the pit of her stomach. It must be broken.

She shivered. The canyon was getting quite dark, for the afternoon sun had long since slipped behind

323

the rim rock. She tried to clear her mind and remember how far she had come. It must have been a long distance, for it had been early afternoon when she left the Sutlers. The rocks under her were icy cold, and the air was rapidly growing chill.

The settlement which she had been so eager to leave behind now seemed the most desirable place she could imagine. If she had her choice between unfriendly Saints and a night alone in the wild black canyon without a wrap, the Saints seemed suddenly preferable.

She must get back some way! She couldn't sit here forever. She heard the lone wail of a coyote far down the canyon, and then the answering cry of another, much nearer. She struggled to her feet. She must get back! She must stand the pain, somehow.

As she began hobbling down the trail, she heard the dry hollow rattle of a horse's hoofs coming down the canyon behind her. Someone was coming! A fresh terror gripped her. It might be Pat Muldoon, or any one of several Saints she did not wish to encounter in this lonely spot. It might even be Indians. They had been causing some disturbance in the valley to the south. By the sheer determination of panic, she began running down the trail, with the excruciating pain pounding in her ankle.

She stumbled and felt herself swinging out in a wide arc over nothingness. She was drifting . . . drifting . . .

Gale was aroused by a rough rhythmic jarring beneath her. She realized that she was on a horse with someone behind her, holding her up. The long awkward arms about her were those of Bub Leary. Turning her head a little, she could see his homely worried face.

"Oh, Bub," she murmured, "I'm glad it's you! I was frightened . . ."

He looked down at her quickly. "How are you feelin' now?"

"I . . . I don't know. All right, I guess."

"What was the matter? Did you get hurt or somethin'? You still look mighty peaked, Miss Gale."

"I turned my ankle on a rock. It hurt so, I didn't know if it was broken or sprained. And then when I heard someone riding down the canyon . . . I began running. I know it sounds silly, but I didn't know who it might be."

"What was you doin' away up there, anyway? That must have been five or six miles from town."

"I was going after plants for the school . . . and I just kept walking. I'd lost track of how far I'd gone. Is it late?"

"Around six o'clock, I reckon. We're almost home now."

"Bub . . ." Her head was still swimming. "When we get into town, you must let me down. I can hobble the rest of the way somehow."

"I'm not doin' nothin' of the kind, Miz' Gale. You go tryin' to walk on that laig and you'll do yourself up for good. They ain't no sense in makin' a cripple of yourself for life, jest to keep up your dignity."

Gale laughed a little, but there was a somberness in her eyes.

"It isn't about myself that I'm thinking, Bub. It's you. No one can say anything more now that will hurt me . . . But it's you, Bub. You have a good name among the Saints, and I don't want it ruined on my account. They'll believe anything about me now . . ."

325

Bub looked straight ahead and urged the little horse to a faster gait.

"It don't make no difference to me what *folks* think. The only one that makes any difference is . . . is Susannah, and she'll understand. She likes you."

Gale turned quickly to look over her shoulder at him. "Susannah. You mean . . . ?"

"Susannah and I are goin' to be married as soon as the crops are in. But we ain't tellin' nobody, for fear old Muldoon might find out and raise a ruckus."

"Oh, Bub . . . I'm glad! Glad for you . . . and glad for Susannah! You both deserve all the happiness you'll get."

Bub swallowed hard. After a moment he spoke.

"It . . . it ain't the same as it was with . . . with Cassie. It couldn't never be like that again . . . not with nobody. But Susannah is mighty fine . . . and I'm goin' to be as good to her as ever I kin. She ain't happy . . . I've knowed it since last summer . . . when she used to come see you. But I hope she will be, after we're married."

They had ridden out into the late afternoon sunshine and were soon among the houses of the settlement. The wide streets were deserted, and the two rode swiftly along, with Gale holding her ankle away from the horse to protect it from the jarring trot.

Two blocks from the Sutler cabin Gale heard the brisk jingle of harness approaching from a cross street. She turned in time to see the Fairbankses' grays pass the intersection, with Jules driving. Julia Ann was only a flash of apple-green, sitting in the carriage in plumed bonnet and mitts, evidently returning from an afternoon call. But before the carriage disappeared down the street, Gale caught a glimpse of the woman's fair face, staring after them. She had seen them, then!

Gale shrugged wearily, wishing Bub had let her hobble home alone, wishing Julia Ann were still in Philadelphia, and wondering if life would always be such a struggle.

The public square was humming with the great crowd. People were jostling one another, trying to get in a position to get a better view of the proceedings. The usual shouting and laughing of a crowd was lacking, and although the occasion seemed to be an exciting one, the Saints talked to each other in undertones, frequently breaking off in the middle of a sentence to crane their necks toward the center of the square. Nothing like this had happened in as long as they could remember, and they didn't want to miss it.

Brigham Young didn't approve of public whippings . . . but Brigham Young wasn't in Salt Lake City. He was in Winter Quarters, and the elders had to put a stop to these immoral goings-on, somehow. They couldn't just let this wickedness go on, unpunished. No telling what it might lead to. If young men were allowed to ride around town with women riding before them on the horse, and no one to put a stop to it, no telling what kind of a den of iniquity the valley would become. In their opinion, a whipping post was a good thing once in a while, to set an example to the rest of the community.

The only thing wrong, some of them opined under their breath, was that it should have been that red-haired schoolteacher to take the whipping, instead of the Leary boy. No doubt she had led him into it.

Gale stood near the whipping post, where the

327

elders had ordered her to stand to watch the whipping. She stood tall and very straight, staring at the ropes that were to bind Bub's hands, but her face was like a death mask. Some of those watching her wondered, a little hopefully, if she might faint during the event.

There was a slight commotion at the southern end of the square as Bub appeared, stripped to the waist, walking between two elders. His tall thin body gleamed as white as marble against the dark clothing of the crowd. He walked with his head bent, his big hands dangling awkwardly. The shock of hair covered his eyes, and only Gale knew the shame that was burning in them.

A little behind came Isaac Eldridge, handsome in his black broadcloth coat and fawn-colored trousers. The crowd parted respectfully before his stern assured tread and stared at the black whip coiled in his hand.

Gale saw them coming, saw the clear whiteness of Bub's skin, and saw the whip in Isaac's tense hand, but not a muscle of her face moved. She might have been a Rocky Mountain stone for all the life that showed in her face.

Someone in the crowd broke away and ran to catch Isaac's arm. It was Julia Ann. She spoke to him in low swift words, her face up-turned, intent with her message. Apparently she had forgotten that her hand still lingered on his sleeve. As she talked, he watched her full red lips. When she had finished, his eyes met hers coldly. He shrugged her hand roughly from his arm and strode to the center of the square. The elders tied Bub's hands to the post before him and then stepped back. Eldridge uncoiled the whip.

"Ten lashes, gentlemen?" he asked the elders curtly.

They nodded in agreement.

He raised the whip and brought it down in a cruel cutting blow across Bub's white back. The lad winced, but his face was hidden between his arms. The whip dropped away, leaving a white furrow which instantly began to fill with blood. It ran over, and began to trickle in little streaks down his back. With the whip raised for the next lash, Isaac hesitated at the sight of the blood. He hadn't expected that. After a long moment he again raised the whip and swiftly laid on the remaining strokes without a pause.

Each blow sounded with a crack that ended with a soft thud. The boy was silent, but each stroke showed the muscles knotted along his shoulders in agony. The crowd watched in hypnotized silence.

Gale raised her eyes from Bub's tortured body to meet the eyes of someone staring at her from across the square. It was a look such as she had never met before, a look of suffering, and disillusionment, but most of all, a look of bitter accusation. It was Susannah Nickols, her pale face streaked with tears. Something in that look stabbed Gale deeper than all ten of the lashes across Bub's quivering flesh. It meant that she had lost a friend . . . another friend.

When Isaac finished there was a thin white line around his lips, and he was breathing hard. He handed the whip to one of the elders and turned swiftly to Gale.

"Come to the meetinghouse immediately. I want to talk to you."

The crowd began to disperse, taking long horrified looks at the crimson-corded flesh that was Bub Leary's back. The elders were untying his hands and

329

leading him away. The settlement had learned its lesson, with a pleasant chill of horror running through it. They could go home now and finish putting in their crops.

Gale walked unsteadily into the meetinghouse. Isaac was waiting for her, looking haggard and almost old. Gale stopped just inside the door, all her hauteur gone. Her head was bent. He watched her, wordlessly.

"Here I am," she said at last. "What do you want?"

"Oh, Gale darling . . . You can't go on like this, fighting . . . fighting against life! You're killing yourself . . . and killing that proud spirit within you! You're too beautiful to live the rest of your life alone. Men won't let you! You'll be hounded to your grave! It can't go on like this!'

Gale was silent for a long time. At last she spoke, woodenly.

"Perhaps you're right." She put her hand against the door frame to keep from falling. "If it were just me . . . it wouldn't make any difference. But I seem to be hurting everybody." Her chin dropped to her breast. "It can't . . . it can't go on."

His voice was gentle when he spoke again. "Gale, for your own peace . . . and because I love you . . . marry me!"

She raised miserable eyes to his. "You'll never know . . . what it means to be a Saint," she murmured.

He stared at her, puzzled.

"Why . . . what do you mean?"

"Only the women, Isaac, know what it means to be a Saint."

There was no answer to her strange words. He could only look at her and wonder.

"You mean, then, that you . . . ?"

She sighed wearily.

"Yes, Isaac . . . I'll marry you. I'm tired of fighting . . . alone."

Forty

The following week, the last in April, marked the end of school. Isaac was able, due to his position in the church, to see to it that Gale was allowed to finish the school term in spite of public condemnation. After that they would be married. Only the two of them knew and, to keep the Saints from suspecting and allowing their spirit of righteousness to become enflamed beyond control, Isaac agreed that he would not see her again until school was dismissed for the year. It would be best that way.

Gale found no pleasure in the prospect of becoming Isaac Eldridge's wife, or of sharing his home with Grace and Sophie and the Meier children. A heavy dread hung over her.

But, she agreed wearily, it couldn't continue this way. There was no place for a young unmarried woman alone. Such a creature would be forever sought by men and distrusted by women. Marriage was the only solution. Oh dear God, if Edouard had only come back with the battalion . . .

These last days she stayed as late as she could at the schoolhouse, dawdling over the children's books and slates, or just sitting, staring into the empty fireplace. She dreaded even the pity she met in the eyes of Deborah and Cliff, almost as much as she dreaded the scorn she met in other faces. She stayed late to be alone, stayed until the sun sank behind the horizon and she knew that Deborah would be waiting with supper.

One evening as she sat she heard the swift clatter of a horse's hoofs. They came up from the road and stopped at the schoolhouse. It couldn't be Isaac. He had promised not to see her again. And anyone else would mean . . . Her soul shriveled up within her and she sat rigid, waiting.

A stranger appeared in the open door, a shaggy man in travel-worn garments, shaggy hair, and a heavy black beard. He stood there a moment, uncertain, peering into the darkness of the room. At last he called softly.

"Gale!"

"Edouard!" He had come back! She sat motionless, stunned with disbelief. She had imagined it thus so many times. She had dreamed it, and prayed for it . . . and now it had come true! Only a moment was she frozen. Then she found her feet and ran, half laughing, half crying, into his arms.

"Oh, Edouard . . . my darling, you've come back!"

His lips sought hers and for a long time they were bound together in a union of overwhelming ecstasy. During that interval she forgot everything except that Edouard had come back . . . Edouard had come back! Then their lips parted and they stood back, looking at each other. The ecstasy was gone and they were strangers, staring wonderingly at each other. It had been so long . . . and so much had happened.

"Gale, dearest . . ." His gaze followed the lines of her face in bewilderment. "You are not the same at all . . . There is something in your eyes . . . something that was not there when I left. And you look so tired . . ."

334

He took her into his arms again, kissing her forehead, her cheeks, the lids of her eyes. "Oh, my darling . . . my poor darling. What has happened to you?" There was a frightened break in his voice. He held her very tight.

She rested quietly in his arms for a long time with a wonderful enveloping peace. It had been so long, so terribly long since she had known peace like this. Strange that just his arms around her could bring such an infinite beauty to the April dusk.

At last she straightened and pulled herself free, her eyes roving hungrily over his face. He had changed, too. Perhaps it was the beard, or perhaps it was the deep lines around his eyes.

"Tell me, dear . . ." he repeated, "what has happened?"

She shook her head. "No, Edouard . . . not now. There is too much . . ." Her eyes met his, wonderingly. At last she spoke it, the question that had seared its way across her heart all these past months. "Oh, Edouard . . . *why* didn't you come back?" It was a hollow tortured cry.

He caught her close to him. "My poor dear! I knew you would worry. Since November, when I discovered that the Mormon Battalion had left and that the passes were snowed in, I have been cursing myself for being such a fool! But darling, I came through as soon as the snow broke up in the mountains . . . came when the old timers and trappers said I was mad to even try it! I couldn't wait another day. I knew how it would be for you."

But he didn't know. He couldn't know. No one would ever know how it had been.

"But . . ." she had to have an answer, "*why* did you stay?"

"It sounds absurd . . . now that I'm here and

have seen your face. It seemed a great stroke of fortune at the time. The whole battalion had spread out through California last spring waiting for our enlistment to expire. There hadn't been any fighting, and there was nothing for us to do but wait. I met a fellow named Sutter who was looking for a carpenter to help in putting up a new mill at his place, a place they called Sutter's Fort. He was paying good wages so I took the job. I hadn't been there long until we uncovered gold . . . thousands of dollars worth of it, along the creek where we were putting up the mill. So I staked out a claim. I knew the battalion would be leaving, but I didn't realize they would leave so early. I thought I could still find someone . . . and send word to you.

"Then I found out that they had all left . . . and it was too late for me to get through the mountains. So I stayed on at the mill through the winter, panning the stream. And Gale darling, I've brought back gold . . . gold! Wait! I'll show you!"

He hurried out to the horse and took the bedroll from behind the saddle. Tearing it open, he took out two heavy sacks, in spite of the fact that they were small, and opened them for her to see. One contained dust, a dull yellow dust, and the other, odd looking little lumps of metal. His eyes were bright with pride.

"See, Gale, it's gold!"

Tears were in her eyes. He hadn't stayed in California to be with Addie Voak. She smiled a crooked smile and shook her head. It was hard to keep the sobs from breaking through her voice.

"Yes, it's gold . . ." She tried not to let him hear the bitterness. "What a terrible substitute for love!"

He looked up, shocked, from where he knelt on

336

the step. "Darling . . . if I had known . . . I didn't *plan* to spend the winter, you know."

"I'm glad of that!" There seemed to be more in her voice than her words were saying.

"Where is . . ." he looked slightly embarrassed, "where is Cassie?"

Gale looked toward the mountains, and a remoteness was in her face. "Cassie is dead."

"Dead!" He stared at her, and the bags were suddenly too heavy for his hands. He let them slide to the step. "Cassie . . . dead." He shook his head, like a man who has just received a blow from a fist. "Dead. I hadn't thought of that." After a very long while he asked, "And . . . her baby?"

"Baby Edouard is . . . dead, too. He looked very much like you. He is buried at Winter Quarters."

He pushed the bags of gold aside and sat on the step. Gale sank down beside him. She broke the silence, with an odd softness in her voice.

"Edouard . . . I have a baby buried at Winter Quarters, too."

He didn't look at her, for his eyes were on the ragged rim of the mountains, but his strong hand closed over hers with a grip that hurt.

"And all this to bear alone," he said. "So much for your slim shoulders . . . while I stayed out there . . . panning gold. You must hate me!"

Her fingers caressed the back of his brown hand.

"No, dear . . . I've only hated . . . being without you." She shivered. Darkness was settling down over the valley, and lights began to twinkle through the twilight. A chill breeze was coming from the lake, but it wasn't the breeze that made her shiver. "Edouard . . . I have so many things to tell you . . . so many terrible things . . . that may make you doubt me . . ."

337

He raised her hand to his lips and kissed it. "It can't be very terrible . . . if it's about yourself. I know you too well to believe anything very bad about you."

"Oh, Edouard . . . I wish I had had your faith!" Remorse cried out in her words. "I wasn't like you are . . . faithful and trusting. I believed what they said about you. Last fall when the battalion came back . . . and you weren't with them . . . they began telling me that you . . . you stayed in California . . . with Addie Voak. And after a while I came to believe them." Shame burned her face and she bent her head to her knees.

"The liars!" Rare anger flared in his voice. "Who told you that? They lied and they knew it! Every last man in the battalion knew that Addie Voak died . . . on the desert between Santa Fe and San Diego . . . died, trying to take care of the rest of us who were no worse off than she was! The damned, ungrateful cowards . . . after what she did for us! Who told you that?"

Gale was frightened by the fury in his voice. "It . . . it wasn't anyone who went to California," she hastened to explain. "It was just . . . just gossip, those who didn't know, and I believed them. Oh, Edouard . . ." she buried her face in her arms, "how could I have been so stupid, knowing you as I do? I should have known. But I was so bitterly disappointed . . . and so unhappy. I guess I would have believed anything."

He took her tenderly in his arms.

"Gale darling, let's forget it now, the whole miserable past. Let's start out fresh, from tonight onward. And there will never be distrust or suspicion between the two of us again, ever!"

They were too intent with their joy to hear footsteps coming down the road or to see the tall form hurrying up the path. They were startled when Isaac Eldridge stopped before the schoolhouse steps and glared with angry disbelief at Gale encircled by a man's arms. His hands knotted into fists.

"What is this?" His voice was furious.

"Isaac!" Gale cried.

"Yes . . ." and then he stopped, before his fury gave him away. His hands dropped slowly open. He was staring at Edouard, who was getting to his feet. "Edouard! It's Edouard Simon!"

And as Gale watched him, she saw the anger leave his face, and in its place came a tired resignation, and a look of sudden age. He held out his hand to Edouard and spoke with a quiet sincerity wholly unlike his old extravagant heartiness.

"I'm glad you're back, Edouard . . . for Gale's sake. She has needed you."

He then turned to Gale, with a gentleness in his voice. "Tonight has been worth waiting for, hasn't it?"

"Yes." She read in his eyes a tacit understanding, and she rejoiced in the generosity of Isaac Eldridge. She smiled her gratitude to him.

"The Sutlers were worried about you," he said. "Cliff has been hunting all over town. I happened to meet him down the road a way and told him I'd come up to see if you were still here. Shall I stop by their place and tell them to expect two for supper, instead of one?"

"If you will please, Isaac. I'd forgotten about supper . . . and Deborah. We'll be down soon." She wondered that her voice was so calm.

Eldridge turned and walked away into the twilight. Edouard looked after him.

"He's grown older . . . so much older," he said thoughtfully.

"Yes." Gale's voice was low. "We all have."

Gale stood at the end of the field, watching Edouard as he walked behind the plow. Her eyes drank in the picture . . . the oxen, the plow, and the strong, broad shoulders of the plowman against the vivid blue backdrop of the mountains. Behind Edouard the gleaming dark furrow was dotted with white gulls from the lake, their snowy wings making slow patterns as they arose from their feeding. The plowing was almost finished. Tomorrow they would begin sowing the seed.

Spring had come . . . and Gale's heart felt the old answering lilt. Looking out across the valley with its straggling ragged little houses, she suddenly saw the vision of a great city, with broad streets, and green parks, and gardens of flowers . . . and in the center, a Temple, more beautiful, even, than the one in Nauvoo. This would be where her children . . . and her grandchildren would live.

For the first time she realized that she herself was a Saint. No longer was she an outsider, looking at them with critical, distrustful eyes. She was one of them, and her heart soared. She had endured a baptism by fire and had come through badly burned. But the old scars were healing and she felt the stronger for the agonies she had endured. After the events of the past, she felt that life no longer had the power to hurt her. Reassured by the security of Edouard's love, she could face anything, even the possibility of another wife in her home. She hoped that it would never happen, but if it did she knew her house would endure. The courage of the Saints was a magnificent thing . . . and she was proud to be one of them. She would help build their empire!

Edouard was coming toward her, his head bent behind the oxen. She felt the jug of buttermilk to see if it was still cool from the creek.

She raised her face to the warmth of the sun. It had come again, the old magic that she thought she had lost . . . a springtime from the sky.